PERILS OF THE HEART

VESTAVIA HILLS
PUBLIC LIBRARY

1112 Montgomery Highway
Vestavia Hills, Alabama 35216

PERILS OF THE HEART

Faith, Love, Trust, and Forgiveness

By K. Patrick Abrams

iUniverse, Inc.
New York Lincoln Shanghai

Abrak

Perils of The Heart
Faith, Love, Trust, and Forgiveness

iUniverse, Inc.

For information address:
iUniverse, Inc.
2021 Pine Lake Road, Suite 100
Lincoln, NE 68512
www.iuniverse.com

ISBN: 0-595-31417-1

Printed in the United States of America

FALL 1993

Miles

I smiled as she cleared the table taking all the dishes to the sink. It was exciting watching her sashay across the kitchen floor. She wore khaki shorts that fit like a glove and a red sleeveless blouse that perfectly accented her narrow shoulders. The blouse was tied across the front exposing her navel and an abdominal area that was flat and firm. The slight bow of her hairless legs was a gracious compliment to her backside. She was an absolute delight to my eyes.

As I looked towards her in adulation, she turned her head to the right. Boasting honey brown skin complimented by dark brown eyes and thick eyelashes, she was picturesque. She had a natural smile that surfaced even as she spoke. It was that hypnotic smile which caused me to walk across a room and introduce myself a little more than two months ago…

I was in my first semester of graduate studies exercising my rights to a recent reward for exceptional work at Prudential. My work had been so impressive during the internship that I was quickly added to the payroll following completion of my bachelor's degree. After two consecutive successful quarters, I was granted permission to enter a company funded graduate program.

Between work, separation and night school my mind was stressed beyond belief. Seeking some relaxation, I visited Club 87 where a few friends and I would routinely jam. Often when I played, I would survey the audience to determine if they were feeling me. Amid the crowd, the smoke and music she stood out accented by a cranberry dress that appeared cut just above the knees. She sat…her back slightly arched…elbows on the table…hands beneath her chin, smiling and bobbing her head to each beat. The lady called me without uttering a word.

After the set, I introduced myself and commented on her smile. She told me that the secret in knowing if you've warmed her heart and truly made her smile is to observe the appearance of a dimple in her right cheek. Her response and that smile remained with me following the first meeting…

"Miles…earth to Miles!" "Oh I'm sorry, I was daydreaming." She smiled and as the small indentation formed on the right side of her face I was certain she knew what I had been thinking.

The day had been especially wonderful. When I arrived around 2pm, it was sunny but not too hot so we decided to drive downtown and spend the afternoon on the beach. Once there, we both took off our shoes and walked along the shore. As usual it was crowded. There were surfers riding the waves, groups yelling and screaming as they enjoyed a game of volleyball and others were riding flotation devices relaxing in the sun. Naturally there were also people lying around absorbing the heat in hopes of capturing the perfect tan.

Walking along the shore's edge, I began to muse over the joy I always felt as water rushed in then slowly withdrew from the sand. It was incredibly soothing when the water flooded across your feet and equally as exciting as it ebbed. You could feel the sand slowly being washed from beneath you.

I was in heaven and could sense that many eyes were upon us…most of which I knew were male. Desiree Bonet' was fine! A native of St Thomas with one of the most wonderful British accents I had ever heard. Her hair was shoulder length with a rich black color. Her figure reminded me of the character *Thelma Evans* from the sitcom *Good Times.* She was perfectly endowed in all the right places and every man on the beach that day took notice. The astonishing part was that she was with me. I began smiling with a never before experienced feeling of confidence.

After a few minutes of walking, I offered to buy some ice cream. "That's a wonderful idea Miles." Pointing towards an ice cream cart on the boardwalk we turned and made our slow approach towards the vendor. As we walked she began softly singing and swaying our arms back and forth. I couldn't determine the melody initially but as she continued it became clearer. *Patti Labelle's, You Are My Friend.* Reciting the song in my head took me back to a live concert where *Patti* was headlining. The lady could put on a show especially when *Girlfriend* breaks it down offering a sample of her range. Our swaying rhythm was in perfect stride with my recollection of *Patti's* bringing down the roof improvisational lyrics…

So, I sat there grinning from ear to ear, daydreaming about our wonderful afternoon on the beach. We had just finished a wonderful dinner she prepared to validate the boasting about her cooking the last few weeks. Being the adventurous person I am it seemed logical to try some. She steamed two large Maine lobsters and prepared drawn lemon flavored butter. There was rice pilaf and broccoli with cheese sauce. And if that wasn't enough, she prepared cloverleaf dinner rolls and a rich chocolate mousse as dessert. I was far from disappointed-marveling over every bite knowing that her hands had touched each piece I swallowed.

After rinsing all the dishes placing them in the dishwasher, she turned and walked towards the table acknowledging my stare with a smile. "Why are you staring Miles?" "No particular reason, I was just in deep thought." "Anything you wish to share?" She sat across from me smiling like a kid who had just discovered a secret and harbored no reservations about taunting me. "I enjoyed our afternoon at the beach." Nearly choking to swallow the last of my Chardonnay I paused a moment. "Thanks, so did I." My body began to warm from embarrassment sensing that she knew my private thoughts. I adjusted in my seat massaging the stem of the wineglass.

"Have you ever seen the ocean at night? There is a beautiful light that's seen as the waves move inland." She crossed her legs then placed her elbows on the table. Focusing her eyes intently on mine, she smiled folding her hands placing them beneath her chin. "No, I haven't." "Well, I would love to show you tonight." "Sure, that would be lovely. What time?" "It's about 8pm, now is a perfect time." "Okay, give me a moment while I visit the ladies room." "All right."

As she slipped into the bathroom, I began looking around the room. There was a mirror mounted next to the door so I took the opportunity to look myself over. My hair was neat, mustache perfect and my clothes were fresh even though we had been out all day. I still looked good.

"Okay, Miles, I'm ready." We did a little chitchat as we walked towards my car. I opened her door, waited until she was comfortably seated then gently closed it. Anticipating that she might be looking at my rear, I made a quick calculated tour towards the back of the car. Always the thoughtful gentleman, my intent was for her to save face while taking a sneak peek. When I got into the car, I smiled as she adjusted the mirror. "Desiree, was there a problem with the mirror?" "No Miles, I was checking my make-up." I gloated from affirmation of my original thought. "Desiree, you're not wearing make-up." She flipped down the passenger side visor to check if I was mistaking. "Oops...I guess you're right...silly me!"

We left her condo and drove to the on-ramp of Hwy 44 east. As we cruised down 44 the radio station *102 Jams* was playing some smooth R&B rhythms.

Desiree began singing and bobbing her head. I chimed in as we pretended to be *Dennis Edward* and *Siedah Garrett* singing *Don't Look Any Further…*

Once downtown I parked on Atlantic Blvd. near *Peabody's* Dance Club. People were lined up for an entire block waiting to enter. We exited the car slowly navigating our way past them towards the beach. Since the wind had picked up, I anticipated increased wave activity and plenty of that romantic light. Stopping at the edge of the boardwalk, I reached for and grabbed her hand. "Let's keep our shoes on this time-we can walk along the shoreline." "That sounds splendid, Miles." We then began our slow romantic walk along the Virginia Beach coast.

The sky had bright stars and a crescent moon, seagulls were gracefully float-ing with the wind and you could hear live bands playing at the local pubs. Holding hands, we began talking and laughing as music faded and the crowds thinned the further we walked. The evening seemed like magic, a beautiful woman…beautiful beach…cool breeze and plenty laughter. "Wow! I didn't think life could be any better." "I'm sorry Miles did you say something?" I stopped along a fence that trimmed the boardwalk where just beneath there were evenly spaced benches. "No just talking to myself out loud." Placing my foot on the bench, I leaned forward to rest my forearm. "You should be careful; someone might think you need professional help." We shared a brief laugh.

"There!" I said pointing in the distance. "It illuminates with each wave." Desiree leaned against the fence gazing as though she were a newborn infant who's finally attached a face to the voice it's heard for the last several months. She watched perplexed by the beauty I had moments ago mentioned. As each wave of light emerged she moved closer to me. Her movement was both sen-sual and methodical as she moved back, then forth, up and down until her body signaled her brain that it had found the perfect fit. Then she nestled in like a child who's found a safe place to rest. All space between us was erased.

"Oh that's beautiful Miles." Resting my hand atop hers, I smiled with the satisfaction having shared with her a portion of nature's beauty. Her skin was so soft and enticing to the touch that I began massaging it with the tips of my fingers. She started humming, swaying her hips from side to side as though dancing. Each movement was like some unspoken language that was quickly translated by my lower body. I felt embarrassed because my mind was appar-ently so slow on the uptake that I was surprised when my pants began to tighten. I'm certain she knew exactly what I had just moments ago discovered. My manhood was screaming for freedom but I was determined to keep it on lock-down.

We didn't speak a word because they had already run their course and were no longer required. Our bodies were communicating in a language of their own. We just stood there watching the waves and cuddling under the crescent moon with ocean light. She continued that intoxicating sway making the moment so sensual that when our faces touched my body trembled as her unimpeded energy circulated through me. I felt as though I was a kettle about to whistle as it reaches its boiling point.

"Miles are you cold darling?" "No actually I'm fine…Desiree." "Yes Miles." "It's getting late and I should be getting you home. I hope you're not disappointed." "Not at all, the light is everything you said and more. If you're ready to go, that's fine with me." I liked that she never attempted to overburden a moment. To my surprise that tiny gesture was a slight turn-on.

Once I stopped massaging her hand she stepped out and away from me. As the night breeze entered the void between us, my body and mind were once again speaking the same language as evidenced by the looseness of my pants…

The car was silent on our way to her home. It seemed like there was nothing left to say. I pushed the power button to the stereo tuning in*102 Jams*. They were still playing some nice grooves but neither of us seemed to be in the mood to sing during the return trip. We acted as though hypnotized by the experience on the beach and if I didn't know any better, I would swear we feared talking would somehow break the spell.

Exiting off Hwy 44 I got on VA. Beach Blvd and begin smacking my lips hoping to go unnoticed. My mouth felt sticky and dry so I stopped at the 7-Eleven for gum and a soft drink. The silence was broken when I asked Desiree if she wanted anything. "No thank you."

When I entered the store there was a young couple standing near the beverage cooler kissing. They hadn't noticed me as I approached. "Excuse me I'd like to get a Pepsi please." They took a reprieve from their pleasure and started towards the counter. As they walked away the young woman looked back at me then whispered in the young man's ear and snickered. "Take it to a hotel." I muttered while reaching for a 16 oz. Pepsi. On my way to the counter, I looked around recalling how the layout of convenience stores is just a huge set-up. The register always seemed to be surrounded by things you don't need. So I fought the set-up by ignoring the shelves filled with impulse products.

After placing the Pepsi on the counter I happen to rub my tongue across my teeth almost gagging. Hmph, oh well…they got me…a complete set-up. I grabbed a pack of Juicy Fruit from the shelf placing it next to the Pepsi. "Is that all?" The clerk asked. "Yes, thank you."

When I returned to the car, I opened the Pepsi and began gulping as if I had gone seven days without a drink. Before I could finish Desiree grabbed my arm. "Miles may I have a sip?" "I thought you didn't want anything?" "I didn't want anything but I would love to taste what you're gulping so quickly." "Sure." I handed her the remainder of the Pepsi. "Was I that loud?" "Yes darling, I'm sad to say that you really were loud." We both shared a laugh as I opened the pack of Juicy Fruit offering her a stick and placing one in my mouth. After starting the engine, I placed the car in gear and headed for her condo.

Once we arrived, I walked her to the door and we stood there talking like teenagers after a date waiting for the climatic ending. "Miles, can I offer you some wine, coke or something to drink?" I didn't hesitate. Before I could utter a word my feet were inside her door. "I'll have a little wine please." "I have some chardonnay or white zinfandel-is that okay?" "Chardonnay sounds nice…with no ice please?" "Great, why don't you have a seat and make yourself comfortable. I'll get the wine." Nervously rubbing my hands I walked into the den. "By the way Miles, no one drinks wine with ice." "Ha! Ha! Ha! You're quite the comedian."

Nodding my head in submission from ignorance, I pushed a throw pillow to the side and sat comfortably on the sofa. "Miles darling, start some music." "Do you have a preference?" "No, whatever you choose will be fine." "All right I can handle that." Pondering a few ideas, I looked at my watch. "Hmm.11pm the quiet storm should be starting." I tuned in *102 Jams* and smiled as the ballads began to fill the room. Desiree had begun snapping her fingers in the background so I knew that my selection was perfect. "Oh yes! That's perfect Miles." They were playing an *Ole Skool* tune by the *Bar-Kays* called *Anticipation*. The song accurately reflected the mood I was experiencing.

When she returned with two long stem glasses of wine I took my glass as she sat down then seated myself next to her. "Should we have a toast?" "That would be splendid. To what should we toast?" "Let's have a toast to friendship." "That's a wonderful idea." We raised our glasses staring intently into each other's eyes. When the glasses touched we both smiled then began drinking. I surprised myself by finishing my entire glass. "Would you like a refill?" "No thank you, I have to drive home." She smiled and muttered, "The jury is still out."

Uncertain of what to make of that remark, I pretended she didn't say it and sat my empty glass on the table. When she placed hers next to mine, I noticed she hardly drank any at all. Desiree looked at me and smiled while The *Bar-Kays* were still crooning in the background. "Miles, I've had such a wonderful time today. I can't recall the last time I've enjoyed myself this much. You're such a wonderful man." "Thank you."

She extended her hand towards my face. "You have such a handsome smile." Embarrassingly, I made a futile attempt to restrain as she began circling my mouth with her fingertip. My body was responding and there seemed little I could do about it. "And I just love that dimple in your chin". I felt like a kid when she put her finger in my dimple pushing my head backward. We shared brief laughter while I repositioned myself. "Now, I usually open up a can of whip-ass when someone does that to me but for you, I'll make an exception."

The laughter became silence as I nervously reached out my hand to touch hers. As strange as it seemed we both had sweaty palms that cooled and became dry upon contact. I started caressing her hands enjoying the softness of each palm. "Yeah, I've enjoyed sharing the day with you too." She looked down then slowly raised her head gazing her eyes upon me. As though drawn by a magnet, I raised my right hand to touch her face and began caressing her smooth skin. She closed her eyes and began kissing my hands. Watching the gentle touching and kissing, I extended my finger brushing her upper lip. Just as her lips began to separate, I slowly immersed my finger into the warmth of her mouth experiencing a slow methodical massage from her tongue. I was stunned by my immediate excitement from this oral experience. Looking into my eyes she slowly withdrew kissing my fingertip. "Now you know how I felt the first time you kissed me."

Succumbed by the moment, I pulled her towards me pressing my lips against hers. She inhaled deeply as her lips parted. Our breathing shifted from normal to sporadic as the kissing became more intense. My hands began to massage and explore her lower back then her hips. I gently squeezed her hips continuing my journey onto her thighs. She moaned in pleasure as I began exploring her inner thigh slipping my fingers along the leg of her shorts then underneath her silk panty. Her soft folds had moistened in anticipation of my exploration. I slowly traced a trail of nectar leading to the depths of her sweetness. As I pierced the seam with a slow push she began the swaying rhythm I had experienced on the beach. "Oh Miles...Miles please stop!" I immediately pulled my hand away. "Did I hurt you?" "No baby, you're doing everything perfectly."

She raised her hips and began removing her lower garments. I just watched in anticipation as she unveiled. After pulling off her blouse and bra she lay back exposing the soft treasure I had moments ago only touched and imagined. "Don't you think this is better baby?" I smiled as she pulled my head towards her sweetness. "Take me to a special place Miles." With a subtle nod, I leaned in exploring every inch sampling her sweet nectar. Her breathing was heavy and swaying intense as she opened wider to accommodate me. Massaging my head she began whispering. "Oh yes Miles…just like that baby." I knew she was pleased when her back arched and she clinched my head with her legs screaming and attempting to push my entire mouth inside. I raised my head kissing her tender nipples one-by-one and with each kiss her body twitched while she whispered something I couldn't understand.

"Desiree?" Her eyes opened with an intense stare as she began opening the door to my caged manhood. It popped out throbbing and staring directly at her sweetness. I pulled her hips towards me shoving deep inside her warmth…

"Miles! What's wrong?" Just as quickly as I had entered, I withdrew from her sweetness. "What the hell am I doing? This is a mistake." "What do you mean darling?" she said franticly. "We both wanted it…this feels right." I shook my head in disagreement and returned my throbbing manhood to its cage. "Do you want to talk about it Miles? Just talk to me. Let me help?" I straightened my pants and began rummaging for the car keys. "I need to get out of here." As I raced towards the door, I could hear Desiree struggling to clothe her body. I opened the door and was gone before she could stop me.

When I inserted the keys to open the door, I noticed my vision blurring. Tears had begun to flow down my face as I unlocked the door. Once seated, I started the engine and put the car in gear driving off muttering an oral prayer as the car cruised down VA. Beach Blvd. "Lord Forgive Me! Please GOD…Help Me! Forgive me Lord!"

I took VA. Beach Blvd directly to Bird Neck Road arriving home 30 minutes after my sudden departure from Desiree's condo. Being careful not to waken my roommate, I quietly entered my apartment removed my clothes then entered the bathroom. A condemning stranger watched as I stood in front of the sink. I looked away and turned on the hot shower. Returning to the sink, I noticed the stranger with his teary red eyes begin to fade. Relieved that I had escaped judgment, I jumped into the shower and began scrubbing. I scrubbed and scrubbed then scrubbed even more. My efforts were fruitless. No matter how much I scrubbed, I couldn't wash away or erase what happened.

The next morning, I awaken to a phone call. "Hello," I said. "Mr. Stewart please," replied the voice. "Speaking," I said. "How are you this morning sweetheart?" "Fine, thank you." "You seem distant and don't blame it on the miles between us either." "Oh! I'm sorry sweetheart I'm just a little out of it this morning." Damn! I hadn't recognized her voice. Hopefully she won't grill me about my weekend because I haven't sorted it for myself. "How was your weekend?" A small knot developed in my throat preventing me from speaking. "What did you do?" Damn!

Desiree

Outside my window, my neighbor and his wife were holding hands walking their little dog around the park. I smiled rinsing the remainder of the dishes reflecting on my afternoon with Miles. Actually, I had surprised myself being with him given the circumstances. For starters he's 10 years my junior and...Well, I won't even go there. I can't think about it.

Miles was a welcomed freshness to my otherwise stale life. He offered a perfect dose of therapy since I was still feeling the dizziness of my most recent roller coaster. I had just stopped seeing Anthony. He was a sexy man with dark skin, broad shoulders and bowed legs. Not that it concerned me much, but he also managed his father's luxury car dealership. So it was no surprise that we often toured the city in whatever car enticed his appetite. Everything from Benz to Jaguar, all of which should have signaled that if he was a water puddle and I happened to step into him, the only part of my anatomy in danger of getting wet would be the soles of my feet.

Maybe that is too much of a generalization. I actually enjoyed spending time with him. We went to plays, musicals and I especially loved the jazz clubs we frequented. He was wonderful up until the sixth month of our relationship. That marked a sudden change or perhaps my eyes had been defogged.

I guess the caution lights had flashed and I rushed right through them. Looking back, the first sign was when he began ignoring my feelings. He would be missing in action an entire day until he wanted to get into my bedroom. No explanation and no discussion. Then during the times we discussed his career and our future my opinion was either ignored or dismissed. He may even have made subtle remarks that I ignored. I don't know or don't recall but one thing's for sure, the red light did come on and I could no longer ignore the signals.

It was a Friday evening he arrived complaining about some problems at the dealership. I attempted to comfort him as we talked. Our conversation graduated into where our relationship was heading. We had, what I considered, a disagreement at which point he had the nerve to tell me a man is in charge of the relationship and the woman should be submissive. The man even held up the palm of his hand for effect. I remember chuckling and the next thing I recall is a throbbing on the left side of my face. My stomach ached, my ribs hurt and my lips had swollen. I don't remember how it happened but when I awaken in the hospital the next day Regina was by my side. Regina was my soro from college. She informed me that my neighbors had phoned the police when they heard a scuffle and that Anthony had been arrested for assault and battery.

Well that was the end of that ride. My mother didn't raise a fool and certainly no male punching bag. After one courtroom visit, a little expert testimony followed by deliberation-his ass went straight to bloody jail. It's been a year since that happened but I still feel the dizziness.

Miles was different, he listened intently to every word I uttered and had a unique way of making me feel as though everything I said was priceless. He was a complete gentleman, having an innate ability for making me feel special and it can be so bloody hard to find a male friend that truly listens. When you do, well it's difficult to ignore much less allow it to pass by.

With that thought, I turned my head looking right into his eyes smiling and whispering his name. "Miles…Miles…Earth to Miles!" I finally screamed. "Oh I'm sorry, I was daydreaming," "Oh really?" He was staring so I pretended not to notice his obvious evaluation. As I turned and continued rinsing the dishes, I began thinking about my hectic day at the Omni Hotel…

There was a doctor's convention and every hotel on the Waterside was booked to capacity. I was standing in for Regina at the receptionist desk while she was away for lunch. This old gray haired gentleman approached the desk with a very bad attitude.

"Excuse me gal," I'm Mr. Eubanks and I'm here to check in." *Gal*…That really irked me to the core but I remained pleasant. "Sir, do you have a reservation?" "I beg your pardon?" He raised his right eyebrow and sucked his teeth…God that irritated me. "Did you understand who I said I am?" I smiled, struggling to remain professional. "Sir I understood you perfectly." There went that teeth sucking sound again. I was cringing inside and smiling on the outside. "Well then you know I've been coming here for more than twenty years and I take my usual accommodations. My loyalty is without question and I demand and expect to be treated accordingly."

I informed him that all guest are treated special. He sucked his teeth again but this time on both sides as though trying to remove something. "Listen here gal." I shook my head in disbelief…Oh no he didn't call me gal again! Adjusting my stance, I flexed my right hand in preparation to introduce it to the side of his face if he continued. "Let's get this perfectly clear. I'm the customer and if I feel the hospitality is below standards it's your obligation to correct it! Do we understand each other?" The man actually pointed his crooked finger for emphasis.

I was steaming inside after that remark and ready to strike. The other manager, hearing all the fuss, slipped up behind to grab my arm before there was a formal introduction of old fart's face and my hand. "I'll take over from here Ms. Bonet'. Is there a problem sir?" Steven had perfect timing. I began coughing pretending something was in my throat then excused myself before I slapped that old fart. It's hard to believe that it happened yesterday because when I awakened this morning, I was still upset.

All that quickly changed the moment Miles arrived wearing white denim slacks and a gold crew neck T-shirt. The fit of those pants on his butt, complimented by that T-shirt revealing his shapely torso made him appear delectable. I loved the way he looked as he walked his 6'1" 200lb frame through my door and past me. He had a conservative yet confident sunder. Not to be confused with *Mr. America* or anything like that rather he was slender with broad shoulders and perfectly toned. So when he arrived my afternoon brightened.

After loading the dishwasher with everything from the sink, I turned and began walking towards the table. "Why are you staring Miles?" "I was in deep thought." "Anything you want to share?" Even though his thoughts were written all over his face, I decided to make him squirm a little. I sat in front of him staring directly into his eyes. "I enjoyed our day at the beach." "Thanks, so did I." He cleared his throat and asked if I had seen the ocean at night. "No, I don't believe so." "I would love share that experience with you." It seemed like a silly suggestion but I hadn't seen it and since our day had been wonderful, I reluctantly agreed.

"Okay, give me a moment while I visit the little girls' room." "Great, you won't regret it." "Okay, I believe you. I'll be back in a moment." I excused myself and entered the bathroom. After taking care of a few personal issues I washed my hands, took a quick glance at my face then freshened up my lipstick. "Perfect." I clicked off the light then exited. "Okay Miles, I'm ready."

As we exited my front door, I began summarizing my previous day at the Omni Hotel. He didn't interrupt or judge me. I was his focus and what I had to say was important, even if I knew in my heart it was trivial. When we approached his car he opened my door. The naughty side of me hoped he would walk around the rear of the car so I could take a glimpse at his butt. I smiled when he did but had to play it off when he caught me adjusting the mirror.

On our way to the beach we sang. It was an absolute pleasure being with him and the last few weeks had revealed that fact. Miles knew how to enjoy himself. We would go dancing, bowling and putt-putt golfing. The man enjoyed himself like there was no tomorrow. He wasn't wild or irresponsible rather he was focused and knew where he was going. Equally admirable is that he took the time to enjoy the journey while holding fast to his vision. I recall having gone against his wishes and called him early during the day. He was quick to correct me and explain his philosophy. "Desiree, I'm in college. If I can complete all my assignments and study early then enjoying myself and your company will never be a problem."

He often talked about his graduate studies and how he planned to take full advantage of his employer's education program. During that conversation, I also made a new revelation. He was in an aggressive pursuit of a Florida assignment, having aspirations of growing within the company and becoming one of its future leaders. I liked that about him and found it unusual for such a young man. So as we continued singing and enjoying the ride down Hwy 44, I found myself drawn even closer to him.

Once we arrived downtown he parked in front of a nightclub where lines of people were waiting to enter. Miles exited first then walked around to assist me. I didn't need help but I truly enjoyed the way he instinctively opened and closed doors for me. We bumped into people as we slowly inched our way past the crowd. When we got to the boardwalk, Miles led me to this secluded area. I can't even begin to articulate the kind of intoxication I felt watching those waves and mysterious light. What I do know is that I was in heaven and a woman needs to hold some special moments, even if indescribable, in her own secret place…

The next morning I telephoned Miles. As the phone rang, I aimlessly walked through my home, stopping in the den where only hours ago passion filled the air. My eyes surveyed the room when I noticed a glimmer beneath the sofa. I walked over to inspect and to my surprise there it was partially covered by my panties. "What is this?"

I was a complete wreck after Miles' abrupt departure last evening. I had struggled to get dressed and chase him down but he was out the door before I knew it. The last thing I saw was the taillight of his car as he sped away. The remainder of the night was restless. Though I tried to sleep, each hour I awaken. Answers...Yes, that's what I needed more than anything but they were not surfacing. I considered phoning him once I thought he arrived home but didn't want to awaken his roommate. Afterall, it was 2am.

What in the world went wrong? Our day had been wonderful and so had our night. I was into him and I felt certain he was into me or at least it seemed that way. I desperately needed to uncover what made him walk away so mysteriously...

When Miles answered the phone, he was cold and distant. "Miles what happened?" "I can't see you anymore." "What's that supposed to mean? Do you need time to consider last night?" "No! I just can't see you anymore. Forgive me Desiree but last night was a terrible mistake." The gravity of his words stung. "Please don't call me again." Goodbye was the last thing he said to me before the phoned clicked.

I was stunned by his insensitive attitude. This had to be a dream. How the bloody.... This man must think.... I was so angry I couldn't finish a thought. I called him again but the phone just rang. "Shit!" I slammed the receiver down in disbelief that this was happening to me. Why did I even acknowledge his 24-year-old ass? "He is so bloody immature." I cursed him but in my heart I knew he was not to blame. Miles had been open and honest with me from our first introduction. I entered this fantasy unabated. My eyes were completely open...I just decided somewhere along the line to ignore everything standing before me.

I could feel moisture flowing down my face and across my upper lip. As the seam between my lips overflowed, I opened my mouth tasting the bitter tears from my broken heart. My day and my body had become a complete mess; I hadn't bathed or brushed my teeth. As the hours past, I just sat on the bed next to my telephone, staring at the wall and feeling stupid for ignoring reality...

When the telephone rang, my heart began racing anticipating that Miles would be on the other end. What would I say? What would he say? Will he apologize? In my nervousness I allowed the phone to ring five times. I didn't want to seem anxious so I waited to answer on the sixth ring. Slowly lifting the receiver and bringing it to my ear, I listened for any background noise that might indicate the identity of the caller...Not a clue...After adjusting the phone against my ear I said a nervous hello.

"Girl what's up with you? I was about to hang up." The voice barked. "You act like you can't answer the dang phone." I sniffled clearing my throat. "Hello

Regina." "So, how are things with you girl? You sound terrible. Do you have a cold or something?" "No, I'm just a little tired." "Oh really? Is that because of a long night with Miles? Did my sista get her freak on?" "Yes, but not in the way you think. Let's just say I should have known better than to be with him." "What happened? Did he hit you? If that bastard did, I'll kick his ass!" "No Regina, nothing like that he's too much of a gentleman. Besides, I thought you liked him?" "Hmph, only if he's treating my girl right." "Well it's nothing like that; I just made some poor decisions where he's concerned." "So what has you in such a sour mood?" "Regina, I appreciate your concern but its okay, I can handle it. Can I phone you later? I don't feel much like talking right now." "Sure Desiree, if that's what you want." "That's what I want." "Okay then, call me when you want to talk." "Thanks Regina, I will as soon as I'm up to it."

After I hung up the phone, I began thinking of the first time Miles kissed me. He didn't just kiss me he was in tune with my body…

It began with the way he talked to me. I loved the way he talked. His ideas were so clear and his voice inflexion so harmonious that he dialed directly inside my being. I found myself captivated by his voice, his vision and his gentlemanly nature. This mixture in a young man made him attractive.

He also loved to touch me. When I listened to him speak he would sometimes begin massaging my hands. My God! His touch was so soft, so gentle and so right. Many times before he had massaged my body and held me close. His hugs always conveyed two messages: I miss you and don't worry you're safe. My God! He could hug. Miles would touch or hug me, never assuming or attempting anything more. It was as though he knew what my body needed and provided me with it.

So it was a pleasant revelation on this particular occasion as we progressed. He massaged my hands then kissed them one at a time. No rush just a slow journey covering my entire hand and wrist. I remember feeling his passion and instinctively rotating my wrist slowly spreading my fingers. The man pressed his lips against my fingertip for effect then swallowed my narrow finger into his mouth. He methodically massaged my fingers one by one with his tongue. All I could do was close my eyes and exhale as he shifted to kissing me gently along the neck and ear lobe. Patient kisses that seem to anticipate my body's reaction. He then gently kissed my lips…

Before I knew it his tongue was sliding into my mouth circling and massaging my tongue with pleasure. I responded by reciprocating with a little circling and massaging as well. He permitted me and I liked that he allowed me to take control. In fact, that small gesture on his part intensified my already burning fire. I was able to massage and groove in a way that satisfied me. Not that he couldn't, it's just that a woman knows how she wants something to feel. I was more excited because Miles was comfortable enough to allow me. The memory of that first kiss caused more tears to fall.

Gosh! He was so young but very attentive to my physical needs, so attentive to my emotional and social needs and now he was gone. I stacked two pillows and lay on my side, drawing my knees towards my chest; I closed my eyes to remember and to forget. Miles should never have been but he was and now I had to let him go.

As I lay there crying, I noticed my panties on the floor and remembered. I raised myself wiping away the tears then picked up the gold watch. Rotating it in my hands, I noticed the inscription on the back. *To Miles w/Love T.S.*

Summer 1998

Miles

It was blistering hot. I had the day off and intended on catching up on all those chores I had promised to complete. My list was extending beyond belief. Everything from wash the car, cut the lawn, change the oil and painting the kitchen. Damn! That was more than enough to keep me busy.

As sweat rolled down my face, I stood in the garage contemplating where to begin. My skin felt sticky and to make matters more unpleasant, simply walking through the garage I could feel my boxers sticking to my butt with each step. I hadn't been outside 10 minutes and already my butt was sweaty.

Anticipating the heat, I wore loose cotton shorts for relief. Relief on the other hand was a stranger in this heat. So I reached back grabbing a hand full of my shorts and boxers. With one quick tug, I hoped to separate them from my skin without anyone noticing.

The heat left little room to contemplate which chore to begin. Definitely whichever required the least time and offered relief some from this heat. I turned on the garage stereo tuning in *101.5*, then picked up a bucket, grabbed a sponge, and detergent. The big decision was now reached. I walked into the heat turned on the water and began spraying down the car.

"Miles, would you like something to drink?" I looked back and there standing in the doorway was Tyler. "Sure baby, make it lemonade please." Tyler was an expert when it came to making fresh lemonade. She would allow the lemons to soak overnight in a pitcher of warm water. The next day she would combine sugar, ice and some other ingredient I can't convince her to disclose. Whatever it was, the lemonade was perfect.

Tyler, I thought to myself. God knows I'm fortunate to have her in my life. She was about 5'8" with caramel skin and dark brown eyes. Her smile was especially captivating, reminding me of *Regina King* in her role from *Enemy of the State*. Of course that wasn't her only attribute that resembled Ms. King.

Tyler's profile was like an inverted question mark, I occasionally found myself marveling over her endowments in the way that *Martin Lawrence* would describe *Gina* in his show. (*My girl has the body like, Bang, Boom, and Pow!*)

We met during an Independence Day Celebration. I was home for summer break visiting family and friends. Tyler just happened to stop by with my cousin Veronica. We were introduced and things grew from that moment.

"Miles, here's your lemonade." "Thanks baby, are you coming out here to help a *brotha?*" "Please, it's too dang hot out here." I began smiling. "Well, I was hoping that a little osmosis would occur between the heat and your nature." "Oh, so you think sweating out here will somehow stimulate my libido?" I winked at her. "Please, the only thing this heat makes me think of is a cold shower and maybe you should too." I took aim with the water hose soaking her after that comment.

"Miles! I'll get you!" I burst out laughing. "There's your cold shower." It was cute watching her because she still wore her silk pajamas. They were sticking to her body in much the same way as my shorts had been sticking to my butt. She took off and ran inside pouting, "Payback is hell Miles." I continued washing the car and laughing as she went inside.

Once the last of the filth from my car's bright shell rinsed away, I began to admire its luster. Damn! It looks sharp after a bath. I could see my reflection as I paced around. While drying the car, I noticed some familiar music in the background-*Dennis Edwards and Siedah Garrett.* Talk about flashback, I hadn't heard that tune in more than five years. I remembered being in total bliss listening to that tune experiencing an intoxication that transcended into fantasy. A fantasy, I had no right to explore. Scrubbing more than 1700 times since that day but the memory never faded, nor had I forgiven myself.

Thoughts of how terrible Desiree must have felt and how she might be doing cruised through my mind. I had disappeared and never returned somehow convincing myself that distance would bestow upon me some feeling of absolution. Pondering my pending appointment, I hoped for just a little understanding. After years of denial, I accepted the obvious fact that no amount of scrubbing would remove what happened.

"Oh Shit! What the…? Where did that come from?" As water began to glide down my face I turned to catch a glimpse of the culprit.

Tyler

I entered the bathroom laughing and dripping wet. When I looked in the mirror, my hair was soaked and flat. He got me good I thought. I opened the closet door grabbing my favorite fluffy pink towel. After padding my face dry, I wrapped my hair. "Damn that water was cold," I said out loud. The worst part is that we had the air conditioning on 70 degrees. So when I took off my wet pajamas my already hardened nipples remained just that, hard and erect. I grabbed another towel from the closet and began drying my body. "Oh my…" I giggled feeling embarrassed by the tingling sensation from the towel brushing across my breasts. Since Miles was still outside, I narrowly escaped that intimate desire.

After dressing in an exercise bra and short set, I slipped outside hoping to go unnoticed. Miles was preoccupied with detailing so I quickly conjured up a retaliatory strike. Walking out the side door of the garage, I picked up the hose and slowly turned on the water hydrant. After the hose fully charged I aimed at the back of his head, released a mischievous *girly* smile and squeezed the trigger.

"Gotcha! I told you payback was hell baby." Miles screamed and took off like a rock from a slingshot shaking his head and arms from the drenching. Even though his head and face were covered, I continued spraying him as water started flowing down his back. He shrugged his shoulders arching his back as he ran to escape my wrath. "Okay baby, you got me. I didn't think you would come at me so soon."

His shorts began to sag and stick to his body and since he never wore a shirt while washing the car his torso appeared freshly chiseled…glistening from sweat and water. Actually he looked quite sexy. "Miles, are you finished?" "Well, I guess I am now…. I just need to shower." "That sounds nice. Can I scrub your back?" "Will I be allowed to reciprocate?" "Oh Miles…I wouldn't have it any other way."

I walked into our bedroom smiling. As visions of Miles' carved body embracing my flesh entered my head, I started thinking about the night before. I had worked late and my body was dog tired. Miles had surprised me by covering the bedroom with rose petals. The room had the fragrance of a garden with rose petals covering the bed, the floor and leading up to our 10-foot marble tub. The tub was filled with a strawberry bubble bath and scented candles lined each corner. If that wasn't enough he had also placed a dozen roses on the vanity. I was so elated, my eyes began to water.

He rubbed my shoulders and slowly slipped the dress from my body. I felt like a ripen banana being peeled for eating. My breast breathed for relief after he removed my bra, cupping my breast in each palm. As he peeled away my panties, I watched in excitement sensing the moistness of my sex. He took his time and it was exciting watching him unveil me. He didn't touch me sensually rather he made certain I knew he could, leaving the act to my imagination.

Miles bathed me slow and methodical washing away every hint of my tiresome day. Following that wonderful bath, he dried my body then carried me to the bed of roses. I lay there with my eyes closed listening to the squeezing sound of a bottle. Then I felt a cold wet film being rubbed onto my legs. He massaged my entire body, relaxing me completely. I opened my eyes and asked him how his day had been but he chose not to respond, keeping to his work. Like a professional masseuse, he worked every tired muscle in my body until it was relaxed. He then topped it off by giving me a pedicure. Next thing I knew, the alarm clock was ringing…

Upon entering the bathroom, I smiled looking down at the petals regretting I had been too tired to make love to him. In fact, he may have tried only to be averted by my snoring. I started the water adjusting the nozzle to slow pulse. After undressing, I stepped into the shower allowing the stimulating streams of water to take charge of my body. I lowered my head as the water flowed through my hair and onto my face. Slowly tilting my head backward, I welcomed the pulsating streams to my breast. I hadn't bothered to grab the soap or a sponge anticipating that Miles would soon join me.

After hearing music echoing outside the shower, I knew Miles must have entered the house. When the clear sensual saxophone increased in volume, I knew he had entered the room. Anxiously, I glimpsed at the shower curtain anticipating its movement when he opened the bathroom door but the glimpse became a stare that seemed to last for hours.

I'm no jazz connoisseur but *Kirk Whalum's* rendition of *Anytime* was moving things inside me. I remembered that particular selection because Miles had talked about buying it after the jazz concert a month ago. Damn! It sounded good and for the record the entire album was sensual. So when the shower curtain finally moved, I leaned forward against the wall, closed my eyes and exhaled allowing the water to slide down my face and chest anticipating Miles' touch.

The music was louder and clearer so even though my eyes were closed, I knew he was near. Then suddenly his hands gently touched my shoulders. "Do I ever cross your mind?" I smiled and turned towards him. "You're always on my mind." He then kissed my cheek and whispered in my ear. "I love you Tyler." Before I could utter a response he was kissing me. Our bodies slowly drifted under the showerhead. As water ran down our faces, my thoughts were charged with excitement imagining how we must have glistened as the water flowed with its erotic power…

Our pleasure was halted when I pushed him away. "So Mr. Stewart, are you going to wash my back?" He smiled and picked up the sponge. "Whatever makes you happy baby." I started laughing because Miles could do many things but he seemed to be inept when it came to making lather…

I loved lots of suds on my body but he was on the border of disappointing me. "Sweetie, would you like me to show you how to make the suds?" He laughed handing me the soap and sponge. "You know I normally use the soap only baby." "We'll keep working on your skills." We both continued laughing as I vigorously rubbed the sponge with the soap. As suds began to develop, Miles embraced and turned me around. He was attempting to pull me closer when I felt a nudge in the small of my back. Reaching behind to give it a slight push downward, I shifted my legs to accommodate him. "Now hold me tighter baby."

Resting my head on his left shoulder, I slowly rubbed my neck and chest with the soapy sponge. Suds began to travel my entire body as I started to sway. "Mmm…Wash my back Miles." Handing him the soapy sponge, I leaned forward while he bathed me gently. Raising my legs one by one so that he could cleanse my lower body, I trembled as the sponge cruised over the pearl of my sex. I raised my arms over my head leaning against his chest as the sponge traveled upward crossing my hardened nipples.

We must have been in the shower more than 45 minutes because *Kirk Whalum's* saxophone no longer filled the room. Miles slipped out of the shower grabbing a towel. I turned off the water and waited for his return. He walked towards me and began the slow sensual process of drying my body. Turning me around the towel cruised down my back, across my butt and down my legs. "Tyler, turn around." I complied then he dried my face and arms. I'm not sure if I was just hungry for him to touch my breast, but he seemed to be taking an awful long time to find them. I almost ordered him to touch them but decided against doing so, remaining silent.

He then dried my hips and thighs, ignoring my sex. I was becoming increasingly aroused when finally he dried my breast. I moaned in pleasure and tried to convey my delight by kissing him only he wouldn't allow it. "Miles is something wrong?" "Good things come to those who wait." "Well you had better not make me wait too long."

He then slowly dabbed my sex with the towel. It was a feathery touch that teased causing my body to tremble. "Stop it Miles! It's sensitive." He just smiled. "I'm finished. Why don't you go into the bedroom and wait for me? I need to dry myself and use the little boy's room." I started laughing. "What's wrong Tyler?" "It's just that I have to go to the ladies room." We both shared a brief laugh as I exited to the spare bath leaving him to handle his business.

After sitting, I mused over the intense passion that filled the house. I assumed Miles must have been finished since music began to fill the house again. He had changed the CD and now *Paul Taylor* filled the room. I was proud of myself for learning the artists but then again the way Miles plays the life out of a new CD anyone could do it.

Once I finished washing up, I sprayed on some Vanilla Fields and took off in a sprint to our bedroom. "Miles...where are you?" There was no answer. I laid on my bed of roses inhaling, to allow the sweet scent to circulate inside as my eyes closed. I then rolled onto my back, stretching my arms over my head. My body jerked when I felt him unexpectedly kissing my feet. Raising my legs, I rested them on his shoulders as he kissed my ankles and massaged my heels with his tongue. It was so sensual...so soothing that I began pointing my toes.

One-by-one he kissed and sucked them as though they were ripe succulent strawberries. I moaned to convey my delight then whispered. "Miles...baby what are you doing to me?" I wanted to open my eyes but couldn't nor did he speak a word. He started massaging my legs, my hips and buttocks. I began swaying arching my back as he continued sucking my toes. I could feel the warmth of his mouth with each gentle...

"Shit! Miles make love to me baby." Releasing my toes from the oral pleasure, he slowly rolled me to my side. As he kissed my calves, I rolled onto my stomach enjoying the subsequent stroking and caressing of the back of my legs that transitioned to tender kisses at the back of my knee. "That tickles." He squeezed my cheeks as my legs instinctively separated. I don't know exactly what he did back there but I raised my butt, grabbed two hands full of the comforter and exhaled passionately. It felt damn good and by now my body was screaming for him.

I could feel his strong hands gliding across my hips. He then began kissing my lower back. My body began a slow grind in anticipation of him entering me. I loved the way he kissed my back. It seemed like a symbolic and sacred gesture where he conveyed to my body that I am his queen. When he rolled me over, I finally found the strength to open my eyes.

"Miles please make love to me." He smiled grabbing both my breasts and squeezing them the way I like. No longer could my eyes remain open as he laid his warm body atop me gently kissing and plucking my nipples with his tongue. I responded by wrapping my legs around his waist. As I attempted to pull him towards me, I felt a familiar nudge on my butt so I reached down and guided him into the door of my goodness.

"Ah, Can you feel how much I want you baby?" My body began a slow swerve as we enjoyed each other's warmth. I then wrapped my hands around his head caressing and kissing him as our movements shifted from slow to intense. My insides were trembling and I wanted him to know my pleasure and felt certain he knew when my body went into convulsions.

"I love you Tyler." "I love you too Miles." He then rolled to his side pulling me close. The way he held me afterwards made me feel safe, protected, beautiful and more importantly loved. Inhaling the sweet scent from the rose petals, I closed my eyes as the fragrance circulated my body. Peacefully, I nestled in the comfort of his arms. We then entered into a well-deserved sleep.

Miles

(5pm) Damn, I must have been tired. Tyler was still sleeping so I quietly slipped out of bed contemplating the chores I still had remaining. The lawn, painting and oil change. Thank God today is Friday so I at least have the remainder of the weekend to recover. My baby is hard to resist when she's in one of those moods.

Tyler had mentioned that my brother would be visiting. Lamar and I hadn't seen each other in 6 months and I wanted to have everything complete prior to his arrival. Shoot! I promised Tyler we would attend her office party tonight. I'll be pushing it close just to finish all these chores before Lamar arrives. She knows I like having things in order before we have guest. If push comes to shove we won't be going to any office party since she hasn't bothered to help. I can't be expected to do everything. Besides she's off today also.

I decided to take the car to *Texaco Quick Lube*. The plan was to drop off the car and return home to do the painting. Lamar wouldn't arrive until tomorrow afternoon so the paint would have plenty time to dry.

My home being conveniently located near the area businesses was a priceless commodity. It always seemed to nullify any loss of time associated with my poor planning. So I smiled realizing nothing would prevent getting everything done.

After putting on a pair of blue shorts, a tee shirt and sneakers, I grabbed my wallet. Tyler was snoring heavily, which indicated she must have really been tired. I walked quietly towards the bed so as not to awaken her, planting a gentle kiss on her cheek. She rolled over but continued her peaceful sleep.

When the phone rang, I was about to walk out the door. "Shit! No need to wake Tyler." I ran to the phone picking up the receiver before its second ring. "Hello." "What's up partner?" "Braxton?" "Oh! So you don't recognize a *brothas* voice?" "No, I was about to take the car to *Texaco Quick Lube*. What's up with you?" "I'm cool. Hey, do you remember that club downtown called *Natilies?*" "Yeah, that's the one on the waterfront…we went there a week ago." "That's the one…Guess what's happening there tonight?" "I haven't heard anything." "Amateur night my brother…So pack up that soprano saxophone and bring your ass down here. The amateur show begins at 9pm and goes to midnight. After that the usual party kicks off."

"Damn partner, I have to do some painting and I promised Tyler we would go to her office party." "Come on partner. We can't do it without you. Shoot! We might even win this thing." "Hey frat, I like playing but it's not about all that…you know what I mean? It's not like this is our livelihood." "Don't give me that modesty crap. I know you like to get your groove on and compete. Come on frat, do it for us if nothing else." "All right, let me think about it. I've got some things to finish up right now. I'll get back to you." "All right, Peace."

I walked out the door and into the car thinking how nice it would be playing at *Natilies*. Women loved to watch a man work his horn. I could even try out some of the improv I had been practicing. Although my promise to Tyler is important, she knows how much I enjoy working an audience. Besides she doesn't really want to go to an office party anyway.

It had only taken 5 five minutes to arrive at *Texaco Quick Lube*. The attendant waved his hand directing me into the stall. I slowly entered until he signaled me to stop. "Sir, what can I do for you today?" "I would like an oil change and the fuel and air filters replaced. I live around the corner, so I'll be leaving the car and returning for it later." "That will be fine; we're open until 7pm." "That's perfect." After completing the required paperwork, I walked out the door and was about to stretch when the attendant called out to me. "Sir, I'll phone you if we find any problems." "Thank you." I quickly stretched my calves then began my sprint towards home.

Running is an activity I didn't enjoy but did it because my body felt good afterwards. Extending my stride my breathing shifted from moderate to heavy, inhaling and exhaling as my pace quickened. I held my head up and back straight determined not to surrender to pain. "This was a walk in the park." I began singing a cadence I once heard from the movie *Renaissance Man with Gregory Hines* as the drill sergeant. "Tiny Bubbles…In my wine…Makes Me Happy…Makes Me Feel Fine." Before I knew it, I was approaching my driveway. Circling near the mailbox, I began my cool-down and walked another hundred yards before stretching followed by push-ups and sit-ups. After my cool-down, I started back home.

Upon reaching the driveway, I checked the mailbox. A few magazines and bills were the only contents. I walked inside the house directly to the refrigerator. "Ah! Gatorade." Tossing the mail on the kitchen table, I grabbed the bottle and opened the top. After a long gulp, I released a 15-second burp. "Urrrr—up! Damn! That was loud." "Disgusting too, I might add." "Oops!" I started laughing. "Excuse me Tye; I didn't think you would be awake."

After wiping my mouth with the back of my hand, I threw the empty bottle in the trash. "Tye I dropped the car off for an oil change. The guy said it should be ready within the hour so I'm going to finish my project in the kitchen." "Okay, I'm going to the market for a few things I should be back in about 45 minutes." She walked over and kissed me on the lips. "Hmm, is that all I'm getting?" She looked into my eyes while massaging my face then smiled and kissed me on the nose. "Satisfied?" "Very funny, hey this painting shouldn't take long since I've already prepped the walls." "All right baby, would you like me to bring you something?" "I'm okay." "See you shortly." She turned and floated towards the door while I concentrated my attention on her every move until the door closed.

Before beginning the painting, I turned on some music for a little energy to coincide with my labor. After a few disc changes, I settled on the perfect mix; *Zapp's Greatest Hits.* The beat was perfect for what I had planned. My idea was to paint up to eight feet along the wall. Since I had cathedral ceilings in the kitchen, I envisioned highlighting with a multi-print border to bring the upper wall together with the lower section…

The phone rang as I applied the final coat of paint. "Hello." "May I speak with Mr. Stewart please?" "This is he." "Sir your car is ready." "Thank you, I'll be there around 6:50pm." "That will be fine sir just keep in mind that we close at 7pm." "Okay, thank you." After hanging up the phone, I looked at the clock realizing Tyler hadn't returned.

Since it was 6:30pm, I figured on getting the car and still having time to apply the borders. I put the paint away and placed the roller and brushes in a bucket of warm water. Just outside the door, I placed the bucket in the garage then sprinted towards *Texaco Quick Lube.*

Once I arrived, the attendant presented my bill. After a brief inspection, I paid for the services and was out of there before 7pm. On my way home I noticed Tyler's car in front of me. "Damn! I still haven't talked to her about Braxton's call." When I turned the last corner to the house, she had already parked and gone inside. I parked next to her car then went inside.

"Tyler, can you come into the kitchen please?" "Sure baby, I just have to use the little girl's room first." "Okay." I started applying the borders, which didn't take much time at all. I smiled thinking how smart I had been to buy pre-pasted borders. The kitchen began to shape into the warm friendly space I had envisioned.

"Oh baby! The kitchen looks nice," she said as she entered. "Just wait until I'm finished." "So, what's up?" I continued applying the borders as she put away the groceries. "Well, I was wondering if you still wanted to go to the office party." "What do you mean? We have already discussed it and decided on going." "I know but I talked with Braxton earlier and he invited me to join him and the *fellas* for an amateur show at *Natilies*." "And…What is that suppose to mean?" She opened a cabinet door staring directly at me.

"I want you to be with me." "I want to be with you too…It's just…I would just love to play at *Natilies* tonight. Braxton thinks we can win. The amateur show begins at 9pm and ends at midnight." I snapped my finger as though an ingenious idea had entered mind. "We can do both." There was a smile on my face believing I had the perfect solution but Tyler just rolled her eyes. "We'll go after I play the set."

"Miles the office party starts at 9pm. You know as well as I do that it will be over by midnight." She then turned and walked away as the room suddenly filled with silence. No *Zapp* and no Tyler just a deafening silence. I walked into the living room kneeling down next to her. "Baby you know how much I love to play the sax." She sighed without even looking into my eyes. "Miles baby I know."

I was surprised by her comment. Sounding almost sympathetic to my wishes, I took her hand in mine but she just sighed staring out the window. "You go ahead baby. Play something for me and tell Braxton I said hello." "Are you sure Tyler?" "I've had a slight headache all day." "Are you sure?" "Yes, I'm sure. We can do something tomorrow." "Can I get you an aspirin?" "No, I'll just go and lay down." "Thanks sweetheart, you're so very understanding."

When she left for the bedroom, I walked into the kitchen noticing the ice cream on the table. After placing the soft box in the freezer, I started applying the remainder of the borders.

My mind began wandering into *Natilies*. Which song would I play? I loved playing with the guys although Tyler didn't care for it much. We were not professional and we certainly couldn't boast that our few and far between gigs paid any bills. It was a hobby and nothing more but I enjoyed playing songs by other artist as well as our own. We could throw down some serious grooves given the right song.

As I began to apply the last border the phone rang. I knew Braxton would call since I hadn't so I ran to answer it. "What's up partner? Are you hanging with us or what?" "I talked with Tyler and she's okay with me playing tonight." "Cool, I'll pick you up at 8:15. We'll get there around 8:45. By the way I took the liberty of pre-registering us." *(Click)* "What's that sound? Is someone trying to reach you on the second line?" "No, it must be your phone." "Hold a minute while I check." All right…"Okay, I'm back. They must have hung up. I'll see you at 8:15." "All right, peace!"

After the phone call, I walked to the bedroom where Tyler was lying across the bed reading an *Essence* magazine. Contemplating appropriate attire, I entered the closet perusing and zeroed in on a white silk crewneck shirt. It was one of those shirts that fit as though I wore nothing at all. Tyler always said I looked sensual wearing it. In fact the first time I wore it she said it curved my chiseled torso in such a way that she was eager to examine underneath.

I decided on black double pleated slacks to maintain a conservative look. They were a little baggy but didn't hang off my butt. So I was in style but not too flamboyant.

Once I decided what to wear, I undressed and jumped in the shower. The warm water was soothing to my body. I stuck my head under and washed my scalp. Now usually Tyler would have joined me but the shower curtain never moved. I must admit a part of me felt disappointed however, the other part of me knew that Braxton would be here on time. He was not a brother that operated on *CP* time. Knowing that, I was well aware that if the curtain moved Tyler wouldn't be far behind and I would certainly be late if making it at all.

I got out of the shower and dried off in front of the mirror. While examining myself, I noticed Tyler's reflection. Her eyes were closed so I assumed she must have just dosed off because the magazine lay on the carpet next to the bed. I rubbed on some deodorant, splashed on a little *Joop* then dressed myself. After that, I walked into the study and packed my instruments contemplating the evening and my determination to make the most of it.

Once I finished packing my equipment, I went to the bar and prepared myself a scotch and ice. Picking up the remote, I powered the CD player and after several disc changes settled on *Kim Waters.* The brother was smooth.

Closing my eyes, I intended to enjoy my scotch and meditate on finding the perfect groove. Before I could make the connection the doorbell rang. I looked at my watch (8:15) that had to be Braxton, on time as usual. I walked to the door and unlocked the deadbolt slipping him the brotherhood grip. "What's up partner?" "Not much, just getting my mind in the flow. What about you?" "I'm ready to do this partner."

Braxton played the guitar and swore he was always ready for the big time. He was smooth when he found his groove and tonight would be our opportunity. "The guys will meet us at *Natilies.*" "That sounds good."

We were a band of four. Tony Jones played keyboard, piano and bass. Winston Marshal played percussion and the bass. We all had our individual histories in music but the thing that united us was college.

We met during *Rush Week* on the campus. I remember one evening after we finished our task the dean of pledges asked us to play something for him and his girl. I spoke and told the girl this tune's for you. From that night on we were dubbed *FOUR You.*

After a few months of challenging moments with the brothers, a few step shows and some service projects we were wearing black and gold. We also stumbled upon a musical sound and when we all ended up working in Jacksonville we continued playing together.

After Braxton and I finished our greetings, I offered him a drink. "Hey man, do you want a scotch?" "Yeah partner." "You know where to find it." I excused myself to kiss Tyler goodbye. She was still sleeping so I kissed her on the forehead and stepped quietly out of the room. "Let's roll partner." "What the hell? So, you're not gonna let a *brotha* finish his drink?" "I'm sorry, I thought you were ready." Braxton threw back his head finishing his drink then placed the glass in the sink. "Is Tyler not going?" "You know she's not really into this, besides she's asleep." "Okay partner, let's do it."

Tyler

(*Phone ring*) Hell—Hello. "Dang Tye, you sound terrible." "Oh, Clarissa...what's up girl?" "I just called to find out what time you and Miles are planning to arrive at the party?" "We're not going." "Why not? I thought you were looking forward to it. If my memory serves me correct, you were bragging about doing the electric slide." I began laughing when she made that remark. "I know but Miles has apparently decided that something else is more important." "What could possibly be more important?" "Take a guess." "Does it have something to do with that saxophone?" "Yes among other things, I told him he could go but hoped he would make the sacrifice for me." "So why didn't you tell him? The brotha can't read your mind." "I know but he should know my heart and put me first sometimes." "Please, I've told you about playing those teenaged games. You know he's young and still growing."

Here we go again, another freaking lecture by my local mom. "Girl you better stop playing these silly games. Communicate with your man so he knows what you want." "Screw you Clarissa, you wouldn't understand. That's why you don't have a man." "Oh! Hold up! I know you didn't go there. I do have a man thank you." "Besides we're talking about you." "I'm sorry...I just don't feel like being judged." "Its okay but you really should stop shielding him from your feelings under the assumption that he should guess what you want. It's a silly game. And don't you even start that 'you don't have a man shenanigans' okay?"

A little smirk surfaced on my face as the tension subsided. "All right, can we discuss this later?" "I'm not in the mood right now." "Hey, I'll be over in 20 minutes. Then we'll have a little girl chat." "You don't have to do that Clarissa." "Listen, I'm grown and I know what I do or don't have to do. I'm out the door, Bye!" (*Click*)

Dang! I'll definitely have to get up now. My God, I don't feel up to being grilled by Clarissa. I'm not being irrational. I just want Miles to put me before all this other shit. I shouldn't have to tell him what I want…he's my man and he should know. I just want the same consideration he gives others. In fact I should get more…I'm the woman in his life.

Rolling out of bed, I rushed to the bathroom grabbing my stomach. Anxiety always caused my stomach to boil. I hated that about myself because my body seemed to always react to my mood. Here I am pretending to be okay with Miles making other plans but my body knew better.

Sitting on the porcelain throne, I began pondering the letters I had read.

Miles

It was 8:45pm when we stepped into a crowded *Natilies*. I began to feel a touch of nervousness as tables of people gathered engaging in conversation and drinks. My belly warmed signaling I might need to excuse myself and release the butterflies from captivity. Winston and Tony approached with drinks and after I took my first sip the feeling subsided. We greeted each other then began talking. "The crowd is huge tonight." Winston said, "Indeed my brother. Take a look at all these *honeys*." Tony gave Winston a high five and said, "Oh yeah my *brotha!* They are out in full effect tonight."

Since we had arrived early and Braxton pre-registered the group we had a chance to feel out the audience. Tony said, "Yo fellas! Let's check out this joint. We'll meet backstage afterwards." We all nodded in agreement then split up going different directions. It seemed as though we were casing the club, which I guess we were to a degree.

Walking down an aisle near the bar all the fellas gave me a *'what's up brother'* type nod. I responded in kind, recalling how everywhere you go brothers understood that gesture. It somehow conveyed an unspoken declaration of comraderie or welcome. The women, on the other hand, were unpredictable. I could never figure out if a smile, a stare or a look the other direction meant anything. So I continued my sunder only making brief eye contact. From initial observation everyone looked good so after satisfying my curiosity I started towards the dressing room.

I assumed the others must have been detoured since I was first to arrive in the dressing room. Braxton had mentioned that a lottery was conducted to determine the order of the six acts on schedule. We would be last. I'm not sure if that matters to the judges but it at least gave the fellas an opportunity to mingle. I began mentally rehearsing some rhythms to make certain in my mind things would be perfect. With a crowd this size you had to come correct or not at all. And since I played most of the leads, I usually found myself doing most of the worry.

As the music faded, I heard the D.J. introduce the M.C. whom later introduced the judges then began offering details of the nights events…

"What's up people? We have a bomb of a show for you tonight. There are six local acts here tonight, offering at your mercy, their own unique talents. You know the rules: no boos and no trash on the stage. So act like you've got some home training. *(Laughter)* The judges will make the final decision. So, are you ready for the first act?" I could hear a resounding yes from the crowd that increased in volume when the fellas opened the door and entered. "These ladies have the look of *EnVogue* and call themselves *Spice*. They're singing…*Don't Ask My Neighbor*…Lets give it up for, *Spice*". I assumed the curtains must have opened because the guys began barking. Admittedly, the ladies sounded very sensual and they even spiced up the song with improvs to highlight their individual ranges. After they finished, the crowd screamed and shouted with acceptance…

"Yeah…Come to me when you want to know something! Let's give it up one more time for *Spice* everybody. Okay, Okay we're gonna keep it going. Coming up, we have five brothers with a message to the ladies. They're performing an interpretation of a classic from the Elements of the Universe; *Can't Hide Love*. Give it up for *Imagination*." I remained in the back listening because we had this belief that watching the competition created a distraction. *Imagination* sounded nice and surprisingly thus far the acts had an *ole skool* emphasis. I felt challenged by the saxman after hearing a few solos and that would certainly work to our favor. No way would someone come to *Natilies* and show me up tonight.

As I listened more my confidence was slowly giving way to an unbearable anxiety. After having sat listening to the first four acts, I decided to witness our immediate predecessor. Slipping quietly outside, I stood next to the bar as the M.C. stepped out to center stage…

"Let's put them together one more time for *Deuce*. The brother plays a nice piano…All right, all right are you ready for the next act? Is everyone having a good time?" A resounding yes echoed. "The next act features a guitarist. Rumor has it he's a mean fiddler too. Are you ready for it?" *(Yes!!!)* "All right then…give it up for, *Diamond* with their interpretation of…*For the Love of You*." I hated when the M.C. added too much commentary. Sometimes the comments, or lack there of would tend to influence the crowd's reaction. Even though there are judges, if the truth is told they consider crowd response in their decision. My conscious was telling me to go back stage but I decided to witness the guitarist that our M.C. felt compelled to endorse.

The lights were dimmed and the spotlight beamed on a well-dressed man with his back to the crowd. The band began playing and moments later, I heard subtle guitar strings. It was as though he was toying with the crowd. Not to low, not too loud but enough to give the feeling that he was about to go off. I had to give the brother his *props*, he worked the audience. That guitar talked to the crowd and looking around heads were bobbing with feet tapping as proof the music was on point. In fact, one of the judges began a subtle finger snapping motion. "Oh well, so much for impartiality."

I didn't watch the remainder of the show but could somehow sense they were the ones to out perform. So I conjured up an idea and walked quickly backstage. "Hey fellas, that group Diamond seems to be the real deal. I watched the crowd's reaction to their music." "Miles, what the hell are you talking about? You of all people should know that you never watch the competition. The shit will get you flustered." "I know but I was getting anxious hanging out here." "I have an idea." "Partner you should have talked with us if you felt anxiety." "I know just hear me out fellas. Do you remember that *Kirk Whalum* tune we practiced?" "Yeah partner, but we only practiced it a few times. We certainly never intended to play it tonight." "I know but do you remember the vibe we felt while playing it?" Tony began pacing franticly. "Aw shit! *Brotha* wants to change things." "Come on fellas, I think we can generate that same vibe. I really feel good about this. Just follow my lead." Winston was my first supporter. "It's cool with me, let's just get it right." Braxton and Tony chimed in, "Alright, let's do it." "Thanks guys, you won't be disappointed." Tony grabbed my shoulder to get my attention. "I hope this move is right, I'd like to walk away a winner."

(Knock at the door) "Excuse me, you're up next." "Thanks," I said. We all gathered ourselves and began walking to the stage. I picked up my horn and walked out last observing the stage-master loitering near the entrance. "Hey brother, would you kill the lights and place the spotlight on me when you hear the saxophone?" "Sure man, whatever you need." As I approached the stage, I noticed the lights fading. The M.C. began his introduction...

"How's everybody doing? The talent has been tight tonight." The crowd screamed and applauded. "We're going to close with this last group. These gentlemen call themselves *FOUR You*. They're going to play...." I rushed over and interrupted the M.C. realizing we had forgotten to make him privy to our last minute change. "Oh, it seems there was a small change. *FOUR You*, will be performing, *MY ALL*. Let's give it up for the group, *FOUR You*."

I jogged over to the fellas for some last minute *dap* then took center stage. Facing the crowd with my head bowed, perspiration began to cover my palms but I was ready. Tony began with the keyboard and I followed his cue as the spotlight beamed on me. I played a few heart-searching lines to create the mood which culminated into Tony's subtle stroke of the wind chime. Braxton plucked his guitar as its smooth stirring rhythms captured the minds of listeners taking them to the next level. Winston then plucked his bass to create the foundation for our romantic mood. As the synergistic sounds began flirting with the crowd, I took a brief glimpse and noticed that heads slowly bobbed to our beat. With each line I played, my body swayed in slow motion. My efforts were elevated as I began thinking of Tyler. With each note, I imagined kissing, caressing and making passionate love to her. The imagery was so vivid, so arousing, I could feel it transcending into each note I played. We were in sync with the crowd and I had definitely found my groove.

After the final note the only things I heard were cheers. The M.C. took stage and began his commentary. As the stage lights brightened, we all looked at each other smiled then in a single motion bowed and exited the stage. "Damn! Give it up for *FOUR You*. The brothas brought the funk didn't they?" *(Cheers)* "Well judges you know what to do. In the meantime lets P.A.R.T.Y."

I could still hear cheers after we entered the dressing room exchanging high fives. "Miles you were in the zone my brother." "Tru Dat, brotha was on." Tony nodded and said, "Your groove was tight." "Thanks fellas but we all created the mood." "That's some modesty crap! Did you see honeys?" "I saw the honeys." "No-did you really see the honeys? Man, the way they adjusted their seats as you played that horn was scandalous. They were *feelin* your vibes man. It was steaming up in here." We all started laughing and said in unison, "*True.*"

"Hey let's go out and mingle while the judges decide." "That's cool I just need to put my stuff in Braxton's car." "That's right we'll meet you guys in a few. Everyone doesn't have the luxury of using house equipment like you two."

When we returned from Braxton's car, the M.C. began requesting that all contestants return to the stage. Braxton and I received compliments as we walked past to join everyone. I smiled because it seemed as though the crowd had dubbed us winners. On stage everyone shook hands wishing each other good luck. Braxton and I assembled with Tony and Winston as the M.C. began his commentary…

"Tonight was a treat but before we announce the winner lets give it up for all tonight's contestants." The crowd cheered and I could swear some of them were even saying: *FOUR You, FOUR You!* Attempting to convince myself that winning or losing didn't matter, I was feeling nervous.

"Now, the moment you've been waiting for…the judges say they had a difficult decision. Everyone was superb but we can declare only one winner. The winner of the 5th annual amateur night at *Natilies* is…Ha, Ha, Ha; I bet you thought I was coming with it huh?" The crowd shouted superlatives and began laughing. "Okay, Okay, the winner of the amateur show is…*Diamond.*" My heart sank as I looked towards the others. Everyone had a straight face except Tony who was biting his lower lip and nodding his head. His words were silent but his gestures left no room for imagination. Tony was miffed.

You could sense the enthusiasm as everyone congratulated *Diamond.* One member nearly cried as they all bowed and thanked the judges. Tony made his way out of the club without even saying goodnight. We understood so the rest of us shook hands with the other contestants then exited the stage. Winston had captured the interest of a woman seated near the stage so I figured he would be okay. Braxton and I found a table that had been recently vacated. Even though it was a little messy we sat down then I signaled the waitress realizing our good fortune given the crowd. "What can I get for you?" "May I trouble you to clear the table?" "Oh I'm sorry, that's no problem at all." "Thank you and I'll have a double scotch on the rocks." Braxton raised his index finger. "Make that two." "Okay, I have two doubles of scotch on the rocks. I'll be right back."

"So partner, what the hell went wrong? I figured we had this wrapped up given the crowds reaction." I held up both my hands as though surrendering in defeat. "No clue…we both thought the same thing my brother. You can never be certain about the judges…but we did sound good." Braxton waved his hand to dismiss my comments. "Yeah, but we were not good enough. We shouldn't have changed the song." "Come on; let's not go there, the song was perfect. It just wasn't our time." "That's some bullshit partner and you know it. We should have won this shit." "All right Braxton lets agree to disagree and just enjoy the rest of the night." "What night? I'm *steppin* after I finish my drink." "That's cool with me." By that time the waitress had returned with our drinks. "Here we go gentlemen; two double scotch on the rocks. That will be 15 dollars." I handed her a twenty and signaled that she keeps the change.

After a couple of sips, Braxton had finally calmed himself. Moments later the D.J. played a *Maxwell* tune. The beat must have struck a cord in us both because we were bobbing our heads and chiming in; "*We can do a little somethin somethin*." Feeling the urge to dance, I looked around the room for a perspective partner. There was this woman dressed in gold standing near the entrance. The dress was cut above the knee and hugged every curve on her frame. I quickly looked away fearing that she noticed my gaze.

Braxton had started eyeing this woman seated next to us. They began talking so I was left to find something to do after foolishly gazing across the room. I thought to myself that if I smoked I could just light up. Instead, I tilted my head back and threw down the remainder of my drink. When I lowered my head and placed the glass on the table the gold dress was moving. It floated across the room covering a 5'6" frame, with honey brown skin and short black hair. If I hadn't known better, I would have thought I was *Tae Diggs cheesin* over *Nia long*. The woman walked and radiated with familiar confidence.

"May I join you?" Her eyes were dark and provocative. I stood and said, "Please do." Since Braxton had gotten comfortable at the next table, I didn't bother him for introductions. "You should have won. Your performance was moving." "Thanks, you're too kind." "How long have you been playing?" "Wow, I guess a little more than twelve years." "Oh really? You're quite talented." "Thanks again." "The music selection had a certain voice to it. I mean it actually spoke to me." "So, you're a jazz connoisseur?" "Oh yes, I find it an absolute joy to close my eyes allowing music to take me away from my surroundings. I liken it to a romantic escape, even if just for a moment." I nodded my head smiling in admiration of her descriptive response.

"Actually, I closed my eyes while you played." "Is that right?" "Yes." "So where did your journey take you?" She began laughing. Her laughter was so genuine she seemed more like a close friend than admirer and at the same time vaguely familiar. "Wouldn't you like to know?" "Sure, but only if you're willing to share it." "Okay, I'm willing to share." She adjusted in her seat as though her already perfect posture needed attention. "Your music...it touched me in a special way. It was as if each note tiptoed across my skin...teasing me. Not rough...but like a feather's gentle stroke. The music conveyed something deep or maybe personal from you to me. I felt intoxicated by the rhythm as your music seemingly cut away my heartstrings."

"Hypnotized by the sounds, I felt as though you were attempting to take my heart as your own. Each intimate sound from your horn cut a string making me weaker. You know...sort of like when you're enticed by something that you shouldn't have...each sample slowly erodes your inhibitions until they exist no longer. The only thing left to do is give in.

It was so provocative that my eyes closed to enter and experience the world you were creating. Sadly, I was left suspended as you reached your final note leaving my mind and body aching for more." "That was a beautiful description...So are you telling me you only reached the doorsteps to the world we created?" She laughed again. "I hope that I didn't offend you being so candid?" "Not at all, it's refreshing to hear such a genuine description.

I don't mean to sound coy nor do I wish to seem like a *Soap Opera* enthusiast but you have a striking resemblance to that beautiful sister on the *Guiding Light*. Her father was a saxman also; I believe the character's name is Hampton." She just smiled. "Well, I just wanted you to know that I enjoyed your performance. Please excuse me? I have a busy day tomorrow." I stood and said, "sure and thanks for your kind words." "Anytime you deserved that and a great deal more."

Opening her purse, she removed a business card. "Here, the number on the left is for you." I looked at her astonished. "I didn't ask for that." She stood and smiled. "I know." Then she walked away.

"Hey partner, who was the honey?" I was so preoccupied that Braxton's question never quite registered. He shoved my shoulder. "Miles! Who was the honey?" "I'm not sure...just an admirer." "You sat there talking for thirty minutes and you don't know her name?" "It never came up. She just wanted me to know how much she enjoyed our show." He pointed at the table. "So what's up with the business card?" "I don't know. I didn't ask for it." He laughed. "You didn't throw it away either." "Let's just get out of here man?" "All right, I just need to say goodnight to this honey." "Okay I'll meet you outside." "Here take the keys. I wouldn't want you standing around outside." Braxton tossed the keys my direction and I caught them just as they were about to strike the table. The business card still lay where the lady in gold had placed it. Without much thought or even a glimpse of the name, I grabbed the card stuffing it in my pocket.

After exiting *Natilies*, I walked directly to the car. As the gentle breeze surrounded me soothing my face, I took a moment to look to the heavens. The sky was starlit and a full moon brightened the streets. My moment was disturbed by a faint but familiar voice. "Hey frat, we were good tonight." I looked back to find Winston snuggled up with the woman from earlier. I waved the brotherhood sign then entered the car and waited for Braxton...

I jumped when the door opened. "Hey partner, did I have you waiting long?" "No I'm cool." "That honey wants to hook up later." "Yeah, Yeah, that's good for you." "Damn man, you're acting all tired and shit." "I am, wake me when we get to my driveway." "Partner, its just 2 o'clock, what's with the sleep monkey?" I turned to the side resting my head on the window. "Just get me home safely my brother." "All right partner. Sorry ass!"

Tyler

The doorbell rang just as I flushed the toilet. No doubt in my mind it would be Clarissa since I wasn't expecting anyone else. Clarissa and I met four years ago. My firm, *Bentley Group*, had been seeking an associate *CPA*. She mailed in an impressive resume that spoke volumes before she steeped in the door. A *sum cum laude* graduate of Howard University, previous employer was *Winthorpe and Associates* of New York and numerous meritorious citations. She moved to Jacksonville with her husband whom she met 19 years ago during a *Fleet Week* celebration in New York. He was a pilot aboard the Aircraft Carrier Kennedy.

Clarissa had confidence and savvy. I recall a *morning coffee* discussion about her interview. Our senior partner said that during her interview he asked, "What her career goals included?" She stated that she wanted his job and would work aggressively to make herself such an invaluable asset that merit alone would justify consideration. When I heard that all I could say was a silent "You Go Girl."

Clarissa was a strong and gorgeous woman that you would never believe is forty. She started her career late because she wanted children. She and Franklin had agreed that she would remain home with the kids during the impressionable years. When the two girls reached their teens, she began her career. After Franklin retired from service, she pursued her career more aggressively.

Clarissa was like a mother figure for me. She didn't judge, at least intentionally. She just offered a degree of wisdom and unconditional support. So even though I didn't want to be bothered I knew her company would be great. Besides, Clarissa was always candid and if I were overreacting she would tell me in an instant.

I quickened my pace towards the door as the bell rang a third time. When I opened the door Clarissa stepped in and hugged me. "How are you doing girl?" "Fine thanks, how are you?" "Much better than you look girlfriend."

"Thanks a lot *Miss Thang!* Can I offer you something to drink?" "Yes please, my throat is little dry." "What do you want?" "What are you offering?" "*JAW-WBS.*" "What in heaven's name is that?" "There's juice, alcohol, wine, water, beer and soda." She started laughing. "Did you spend the last year coming up with that?" We both laughed. "Just have a seat and I'll pour us some wine." "That sounds good."

Clarissa was seated on the love seat when I entered the living room. I handed her a glass then sat next to her. "The kitchen looks beautiful; when did you have that done?" "Thanks Miles painted it this afternoon." "So that's what I've smelled?" "Yeah, the paint isn't quite dry." "Well, it adds a nice touch." "Yeah, I think so too." "So, what has you in such a sour mood?" "Nothing really, I was just disappointed that Miles made other plans." "Did he make plans or did he ask what you wanted to do?" "Well, he asked me but we had already made plans so there was really nothing more to ask or discuss." "I see, so why didn't you go with him?" "He didn't ask me." "If it was that important to him you should have made it a point to let him know it was important to you as well, with or without an invitation?" "Please, I'm not running behind a man if he doesn't want my company." "That is so hypocritical of you Tyler." "What do you mean?" "Just think about when the two of you started dating you probably went out of your way to let him know that anything important to him was also important to you." "I guess you're right now that I think about it but I've got him now." "Girlfriend that's where the work begins a relationship doesn't strengthen on its own." "Actually, I probably don't have him anyway, maybe I never did." "What is that suppose to mean?"

"It doesn't matter. How are you and Franklin these days?" "Changing the subject I see." "No, it just occurred to me that I've been rude not asking about you. Do you mind?" "Its Okay, we've got time." "Thanks, so how are things? Are you two back together?" "We're taking our time. You know the best and worst thing that happened to us is the separation." "What do you mean?" "Well, we love each other but after he retired things became strange. You know we had spent a large portion of our marriage separated because of his assignments." "Yes, I remember you sharing that with me." "Anyway, he had some issues that surfaced late in our marriage and it changed everything because there was so much I couldn't understand. On top of all that, I started pursuing my work, which became my immediate focus.

Franklin wanted me to remain home while we resolved the issues but I needed to get my career moving forward." "Why was there such a big fuss over you working?" "I guess he had gotten used to my being home. Maybe he felt threatened by my quick growth in the company, who knows?" "I thought he wanted you to pursue your career?" "So did I, but he became too inflexible where working was concerned. It was like he wanted everything to be on his terms. He wasn't abusive or anything, I was growing and he was no longer growing with me. I know now that something more was going on but we haven't addressed the issue.

You know we still go out to dinner every Friday. In fact, we do everything together except live." "How do you manage to keep it together?" "I don't want anyone besides him in my life but he was suffocating my need to grow. Not to mention the other issue he has failed to handle." "What issue is that Clarissa? You've mentioned the word twice." She picked up her glass and drank the entire glass of wine. "Dang girl, Can I pour you some more?" "No thank you." She returned the glass to the table. "Let's just say, the separation has given us a chance to realize the importance of individuality and each other.

I regret not lying next to him the last year but had we not experienced this, I'm not sure what would have happened." "So will you remain married?" "Yes, we talk about living together all the time but I want to be sure his insecurities are under control." "Well, I don't think Miles and I could do that, he'd just find someone new." "What makes you arrive at such a dire conclusion?"

"Clarissa, I had always believed that I was the only woman for him." "So, what's changed?" "He and I visited his parents a month ago and I was just looking around and came across some letters from someone named Margo." "Looking around? So, these letters called you and asked to be picked up?" "Screw you!" "I'm just keeping it real Tyler but I know you didn't read them?" "Well, I couldn't resist." "Oh my, so you've given in to insecurities I see. And what dear lady did you find out?" "Clarissa please don't be condescending, he's been with her. God, I can only imagine in what ways. I was pissed at his ass. Everything he said to me was a lie! I was no more special to him than any other woman." "I'm sorry for sounding condescending you know that's not my intention. So tell me, where is Margo?" "I don't know." "Is he still seeing her?" "I don't know anymore." "What does that mean and when were these letters written?" "I think it was a little more than five years ago." "What, you've got to be kidding? You're *trippin* over some relationship that happened more than five years ago." She looked at me as though appalled I would be angry. "Evil heart brings evil thoughts and evil thoughts make a wedge." "Screw you Clarissa!" "I've got to tell how it is girlfriend. I bet Margo has forgotten both of you. You know if you didn't try to sneak and know everything you would still be glowing. Why didn't you just ask his parents to throw them away or do it yourself? Girl the man can't erase who he was, just because you enter his life." I began crying.

"There was supposed to be only me." "I think there is something with you that made you feel compelled to snoop. Call it whatever you want but unless he gave the letters to you to read you had no right." "I was and still am his girl, so I had every right." "I don't agree but it's done. Now what does that have to do with you being first?" "I just want him to consider me before he does things. Like tonight when Braxton called. The moment he asked if he was with them, I came second. I heard him say it on the phone." "Well I can't speak about all that but take a look around you; it seems he has put you first. You need to open up to him about the way you feel."

I looked around in agreement. "He is wonderful and makes me feel special. I can say with certainty he doesn't mistreat me and he plans and provides. I never felt like I wasn't his number one but when I read shit like this. It's all just lies Clarissa. He would do the same for anybody so I'm not special. I just don't know anymore." "Talk to him and let him know your insecurities. Don't let it fester."

"You're scaring me Tye, talk to him before you imagine yourself out a good relationship. Focus more on what's in front of you and release all this baggage. The only person weighted down by baggage is you and it will surely tear away at the person you are."

"I know, I know and I'll talk to him." "Please do, don't ruin something good over unresolved issues and more importantly don't allow it to destroy you."

Clarissa held me in her arms as I boohooed and sniffled. Just as I had expected she offered a little wisdom and support. The baggage was subtly affecting me. There wasn't always a conscious acknowledgement of the issues, I didn't have it in the forefront of my mind but certain things would trigger it causing the baggage to drop on my heart pushing everything I feel out of my body.

(Click) "Tyler someone's at the door." "It must be Miles." Since I had been crying I jumped up and ran to the bathroom. Clearly I needed to talk to Miles but not at a low point. The fact that I had been crying was something he definitely didn't need to know. "Clarissa you'll have to excuse me a moment while I freshen up," I yelled as the bathroom door closed behind me.

Miles

"Hey partner, wake your sleepy ass up!" "We're here already." "Yeah man. Hey, whose Volvo is that in your driveway?" "Do you remember Clarissa Green? She's Tyler's best friend." "Oh yeah, she split up with her man." "Right, she and Franklin have been separated for about a year I think." "So, is she *kickin it* with anyone?" "Tyler says she's not. In fact the lady has espoused celibacy since the separation." "She needs to let a brotha in on some action." Braxton pulled into the driveway and stopped next to Clarissa's car. "You're *trippin*. I'll get with you later frat." "All right partner. Hey what's up for tomorrow?" "I'll likely be making up to Tye for tonight. What about you?" "I haven't made plans yet but I may surprise the honey from the club." "Well if you should plan something that's appropriate for couples then give me a call." "All right partner, Peace out." "Later man." I gave him the brotherhood grip and exited the car.

Damn I'm tired. I assumed the ladies would be having a girl's talk session but after entering the house there was only silence. As I walked into the foyer, I noticed Clarissa seated in the living room. "Hey! What's up lady?" I walked over to her then leaned down to kiss her cheek. "So, are you keeping my baby up all night?" She kissed my cheek and smiled. "Hi Miles and no I'm not keeping her awake. I was about to leave just as you entered." We both gave each other that, *You're a Damn Lie Look* and started laughing then I walked into the kitchen.

"I'm getting something to drink, would you like something?" "No thank you, I'm fine. Tye told me you were performing tonight. How was the show?" "Yeah, Braxton heard that amateur night was happening at *Natilies* so we entered the contest. We played pretty good but lost." "Oh, I'm sorry to hear that Miles." "It's no big deal our competition was more than qualified and the group that won was exceptional." "Is that right?" I opened the refrigerator grabbing a *sunny delight*. "Oh yes! They had a smooth brotha on guitar. They played an old *Isley Brother's* jam." "Oh really? Which one are you talking about?" "It was *For the Love of You.*" "That's a nice one. Were they singing?" "No, apparently *Norman Brown* put together a rendition on his album and they modified it with their own spin." "He's pretty good isn't he?" "Oh yes." "So what song did you guys play?"

I began walking towards the living room sipping my juice. "We changed songs at the last minute because of this vibe I was feeling. So I convinced the guys to play *Kirk Whalum's My All.*" "No you didn't? That song is nice. One of my other girlfriends bought the CD a few weeks ago. There's something about the song that…Anyway, what happened?"

Tyler entered the living room and upon noticing her I walked directly over kissing her lips. The kiss was cold but I pretended I hadn't noticed. "I'm sorry you didn't win baby." I stood there and continued talking as Tyler sat down next to Clarissa. "The crowd seemed to be flowing with us but it just wasn't our night." "Dang that's terrible. Anyway, you can give me more details later I need to get home you two." Clarissa got up and started towards the door. Tyler followed. "Tye I'll call you later." "Okay, thanks for coming over." "Anytime girl, anytime."

"Clarissa, I'll walk you to your car." "Thanks Miles. Tye he's such a gentle-man." "Yes I know. Goodnight girlfriend." Tyler hugged Clarissa then walked into the bedroom and closed the door. Clarissa and I walked to her car. Once she entered, I waved goodnight and ran inside. After locking the door, I made a quick security-check of the house. When I secured all the lights, I looked towards the bedroom surprised that no light emanated from underneath the door. That meant Tyler had gone directly to bed.

Entering the bedroom, I could see she was under the comforter because the moonlight brightened the entire room. "Tyler, is there something wrong?" "No Miles. I'm just tired. Can we just go to sleep?" "Tye your kiss was very cold ear-lier. I just thought something was on your mind." "I didn't feel like kissing. Can we please just go to sleep?" "Okay, I just wanted to give you an opportu-nity to speak if something is troubling you." "We can discuss whatever you want in the morning. Let's just go to sleep, please?"

I pulled the covers back and lay down next to her. "Do you mind if I hold you?" "I don't mind." I hated when she distanced herself with all this empty talk. A whole lot of things said but no real feeling behind it. I sensed she was upset about the office party. Certainly if that's the case she could at least be honest…

Pulling her close and tight, I wasn't sure if my purpose was to take charge of the situation or just hold her really close. Whatever it was, I squeezed her as though she was my personal package of *Charmin* bathroom tissue.

If she really wanted to go to that office party she should have told me. She certainly has no reason to pretend nothing's bothering her. I've had many discussions with her about never going to bed with unresolved issues…

"Goodnight Tyler." "Goodnight Miles." I closed my eyes feeling a little hypocritical. I was actually relieved she didn't wish to discuss anything. I had cowardly elected not to outright ask her about the subject I suspected was troubling her. In that regard I'm no more correct than she is.

Tyler

The next morning I awakened before Miles so I decided to prepare breakfast. We usually enjoyed breakfast and coffee on Saturday mornings. It was a special moment we shared and looked forward to after a long week. We agreed that whoever awakened first would prepare the meal.

My body was in need of a *pick me up* so after entering the kitchen, I reached into the cabinet for some French Vanilla coffee. While filling the coffee pot with water, I happen to rub my tongue across my teeth noticing a familiar morning film. Since it would be a few moments before the coffee was ready, I used the time to wash up and brush my teeth. When I entered the bedroom Miles was still asleep. I took a peek at the clock (6am) recalling we planned a seminar with some of the community's teens at 10am.

Miles had volunteered to teach computer basics and since we both were familiar with information systems, I volunteered to assist. It was wonderful the way he offered of himself to help others. He was so genuine that a person wouldn't feel threatened by his help. Sometimes however, he was too generous and perhaps a bit naïve but always sincere.

When I removed my hair scarf, the mirror quickly conveyed that my hair was three steps from being ready. With a whip of my brush, a tease here and there, I was done. Afterwards, I opened a tube of ambi and began cleansing my skin. Once the application was complete, I brushed my teeth while looking around. The room was still covered in rose petals.

"Shoot! I've got to clean this up." "You sure do." "Oh good morning, I didn't realize you were awake." "Yes, I've been just laying here admiring you." I smiled. "I'll help you clean up the room after breakfast." "Well, I haven't pre-pared anything yet. I just started the coffee and came in here to brush my teeth. So you'll have to wait a few minutes." "Can we just have cereal and some milk? That would be very quick." "Sure, if you don't mind *Fruit Loops.*" He smiled.

"That sounds delicious to me. Just make sure you're there with a *brotha* to enjoy it." "I'll be there. Just make sure you are without the morning breath." He started laughing. "I thought you liked me that way." "I don't think so Miles." "Okay, I'll take care of the morning breath." "Thanks baby." I finished brushing then rinsed my face and returned to the kitchen.

After removing two large bowls from the dishwasher, I placed them on the table. Knowing that Miles would be shaving in preparation for our commitment, I had plenty time to pour and enjoy a cup of coffee. I paused for a moment of reflection after reaching into the cabinet…

'Share My World,' the day Miles gave me that mug I cried. It wasn't the gift rather, the way he presented it. We were walking in the park on the Fourth of July. An hour must have passed because I distinctly remember complaining that my feet hurt. I had worn sandals, not for comfort rather because he always complimented me on my feet among other things. I must admit, after his first compliment, I passed it off as a fetish but the way he made love to my feet and the rest of my body told me otherwise. My heart warmed recalling our history.

Anyway, we returned to his car and he said, "I have a person to person request for you," I smiled and nervously awaited his request. "Close your eyes, I have to get something from my trunk." He opened his trunk retrieving an object causing my heart to race in anticipation. "Open your hands." As I complied with his requests, my palms began to perspire. "Miles what are you giving me?" "Be patient baby." When the object touched my hand, I felt deflated because of its size. With no idea what I was holding, its mere size immediately eliminated one possibility. I wanted desperately to cry but held back. "Okay Tyler, you can open your eyes." When I opened my eyes, I saw a coffee mug. After I read the inscription, I cried.

Removing the mug from the cabinet, I reflected on the little hook just beneath the inscription. Since then I've been drinking coffee everyday. With a slight smile on my face, I began humming *Share My World*. After dropping a scoop of *French Vanilla* in the cup, I poured in the water then sat down to enjoy my coffee.

"Hey baby, I'm all cleaned up. Can a *brotha* get some love?" He walked over and kissed me. I touched his freshly shaven face and said; "now that's how I like my baby." He smiled then sat down. We both began eating our *Fruit Loops* and enjoying each other's company.

"Miles baby, how many kids do you think will show up today?" "I'm not certain but I'm hoping several. You know with the way everything is computer based its imperative that these kids become comfortable with computers." "I know what you mean." "It would be nice if every school system could fund computers in the classroom. It's a challenge but funding at least one grade level giving them access would be a move forward. If our young people don't have computer skills it will be a major step backward." "Well, that's more of a reason to make sure we arrive on time. So, before you get started remember where we should be at 10am." "Okay baby, you're right."

We finished our breakfast then entered the bedroom to tackle the remnants from our passion over the previous two nights. Miles emptied the rose petals in the trash. I made up the bed and gathered all the laundry. Once we finished, I looked around and folded my arms. "Now the room is clean!"

(Phone rings) "What's up Tyler? Where's my partner?" "Hi Braxton, he's taking out the trash." "Do you two have plans later this afternoon?" "Well, we're going to the community center for a few hours. After that nothing is planned as of now." "Cool, so why don't the two of you come over for some *Bar-BQ* and swimming." "That sounds nice but I need to discuss it with Miles first then he'll call you. What time should we arrive if we decide to come?" "How about 4pm? The grill should be right at that time." "Okay, do you want to hold on until he comes inside? "No, just make sure you two make it." "Okay, we'll let you know, take care."

Miles

Tyler and I had been involved in the community outreach program for about a year. The program itself had been ongoing in the city for about 10 years having survived mainly from gracious donations and volunteerism.

Once we arrived at the community center, Tyler and I peeked through the door to a surprising group of twenty-four teens. Until today there hadn't been more than five to ten kids at a time. "Tyler, why don't you take half the children and I'll take the remainder." "Sounds like a plan. What do you intend to review with them?" "Well I was thinking Microsoft office would be appropriate. Perhaps even touch on e-mail. You know set-up, sending and receiving." "That's a good idea. I can discuss e-mail while you discuss office. Then we can exchange groups so that each has a new facilitator for discussions." I looked at her and said; "how did you become so smart Tye?" She smiled tossing her head to the side responding confidently as though surprised by my query. "It's in my blood. Now go and work some magic." "Okay, let's plan on rotating in an hour." "Dang!" She held her hand in the air in annoyance by my comment. "Does every detail have to be planned to the minute?" I smiled. "I wouldn't have it any other way." "All right, one hour. Now go and split the group. I'll be waiting in the room next door."

After I entered the room, I accidentally bumped against a chair causing an annoying screech. All the kids turned their heads towards the noise to find me standing there. They were seated quietly wondering what I might do next. I placed my laptop on the desk then cleared my throat for introduction. "Good morning, I'm Mr. Stewart. I'll be one of your facilitators this morning. Before we get started I would like to split you into even groups for today's session. The left side of the room will remain here and the rest of you should proceed to the room next door. Once there your facilitator will assist you."

The right side of the room cleared in an orderly fashion while the others chattered softly and remained seated. "Now that we have that accomplished, why don't you all move towards the front and we'll introduce ourselves. Please don't be shy, just share your name at a minimum and if you're comfortable feel free to share more." Each child stood and shared their name. Quite honestly the whole process was more for my benefit, because they all seemed to know each other. I made that conclusion after remarks by others that followed every child's introduction.

As the introductions continued, I connected my laptop to the projector. The equipment that had been donated was the latest available. Each desk was equipped with a desktop allowing me to walk them through the process of using the various programs.

Once introductions were complete, I began coaching the kids through the programs. There was a great deal of positive interaction and I was feeling so good sharing the information that I ignored the time. Since the kids were very responsive and eager to learn, I just cruised right into a discussion of e-mail, Internet use and several other aspects of the information highway. Once the kids seemed comfortable, I suggested they play around to become more comfortable.

Two hours had passed and I was certain Tyler would be fuming about my apparent oversight. I excused myself then stepped out of the room and walked next door. To my surprise there was Tyler with all eyes glued on her. She had apparently ignored the time as well. I took a few minutes to observe her, admiring the way she seemed to connect with the kids. Her million-dollar smile and her friendly demeanor made people feel at ease. She could replicate the same results regardless of the setting.

Tyler was completely genuine and I must admit that at times I felt envious of her innate charismatic nature. We could go places and she would take 20 seconds to acclimate herself to the setting then instantly fit in. There was never a conversation that she couldn't make a contribution. She seemed to be knowledgeable about everything even though I knew that she wasn't. Tyler was also a huge flirt, which sometimes irked me but she would always bring me into the situation salvaging my feelings.

I tapped on the door to get her attention. She signaled in acknowledgment then suggested that the kids use the information they had discussed to browse through the programs. "What is it Miles? I'm a little busy." "Well, I had gotten so involved with my lecture that I overlooked the time and apparently, so have you." "Oops I lost track of the time. Looking at her watch she apologized revealing that she also reviewed office and the Internet?" I started laughing. "What's so funny?" "I did the same thing." We both shared a brief laugh. "Give me twenty minutes then we can wrap up for today." "Okay, don't lose track of time again." She waved and walked away smiling.

Tyler

We sat in the car feeling a huge sense of accomplishment. The kids were very receptive and seemed to be enjoying the new electronic world Miles and I had shared. "Miles this morning was wonderful." "Yes it was. I could sense that you were really into it." I pushed him on the shoulder. "Look whose talking, so were you." He shrugged his shoulder and smiled. "In fact, as I recall *MR time-keeper* you had lost track of time too." "That's true. Let's just say that we both were taken by the joy of giving?" I gently rubbed the side of his head with my finger. "Okay, I can accept that baby." "So, how would you like to spend the remainder of the day?" "I'm a little hungry, so we can start with lunch." "How about *California Dreaming?*" "That would be perfect Miles."

"Oh, I forgot to mention that Braxton phoned. He wants us to come over for swimming and some of his Bar-B-Que." "O really, what time?" "Well he said 4pm. I told him we didn't have plans and you would call him back to confirm." "Do you feel like swimming?" "That would be refreshing in this heat but it really doesn't matter with me so long as we're together." "Okay then, I'll call him to say we'll be there."

"Miles! You're going to miss the turn." I jerked the wheel nearly driving over the median. "Shit! Tye you startled the hell out of me." I started laughing. "Miles you were going to miss the turn." "Yeah, but you made me feel like I was about to hit something." "I'm sorry, but you need to pay attention to the road if you're going to try and talk as well." "Ha! Ha! Ha! That's very funny Tye."

"Miles, do you know what my taste buds are craving?" He looked at me with a mischievous grin. "My sweet kisses?" I adjusted myself in the seat and flipped my wrist holding up the back of my hand. "Please, I have that when I want it." "Is it like that Ms Tyler?" I shook my head from side to side. "Yes it's like that Mr. Miles." We both started laughing. "Seriously though baby, I want some apple pie." "I'm sure there's a piece with your name on it." As we made our approach to the parking lot I turned and looked towards Miles. "There had better be because I want it desperately." Miles stopped the car and placed it in park. I lowered my head and whispered like a child. "Miles baby?" "Yes Tye." "Can I have some ice cream too?" He started laughing. "My baby needs some ice cream and apple pie worse than a hog needs some slop!" I slapped him on the shoulders for comparing my craving to a hog. "That's so gross Miles." Hardly containing himself with his laughter, he stepped out of the car. People begin staring attempting to determine what was so freaking funny. He was still laughing as he walked around to receive me. "Sure baby, whatever you want let's just go inside." "Okay."

I had always heard people talk about this restaurant and had asked Miles several times to bring me. People were standing in line talking about everything from *Monica Lewinsky* to Sports and it didn't matter if the line happened to be the first time you've met. This elderly gentleman turned around and started talking to Miles about the new NFL team. I on the other hand began speaking with his wife and discovered they were clients of *Bentley Group*. I enjoyed the conversation but my mind was occupied by the fact that I would finally experience this place everyone had been talking about.

As we made our journey to the entrance I wanted to share my excitement with Miles but decided not to embarrass him. So I took his hand and squeezed. When he looked at me I said a silent *I Love You.* I knew he understood when his lips conveyed the same message.

It took twenty minutes for us to be seated. Once we arrived at our table the waitress handed us menus that were slightly overwhelming. There was a wide range of entrees from seafood, to Mexican, Italian and American Classics, which made it difficult to decide. "What are you having Miles?" "I think I'll begin with a small salad, then steak and shrimp." "I'll have the chicken and shrimp." We gave the waitress our orders then began talking over salad. Fifteen minutes later our food arrived. We hadn't eaten since early this morning so it came as no surprise that we both finished every bite. "That was delicious." "Yes it was and it hit the right spot."

"Do you know what I want right now?" "Yes baby." Miles signaled the waitress and ordered two slices of apple pie with ice cream. "Thanks baby, I've got something special for you." "Oh really, what is it?' I smiled. "Good things come to those who wait." He began laughing and nearly lost a piece of pie on the table but he managed to cover his mouth before embarrassing himself. "Well, don't make me wait too long."

Miles

Following lunch we drove along the freeway towards home. I decided against Atlantic Boulevard because I knew from experience that traffic would be horrendous. There was a certain constant about the city. Everything was within a half-hour drive but if you intended on getting some place within that time always take the freeway, especially on weekends because the entire car driving population seemed to be on the roads.

"Tyler, did Lamar call this morning?" "No. The only call we received was from Braxton." "Well, I suspect he should be arriving soon. It would be cool if he joined us at Braxton's this afternoon." "Yes that would be nice. Speaking of which, you should call Braxton so that he knows our intentions." "Thanks for reminding me baby."

I pulled up the antenna on the cell phone then punched the code for Braxton. "Hey what's up brother?" "Hey partner. How's it going? Are you and Tye coming?" "As a matter of fact we are and I wanted to phone and let you know. Also, my brother should be in town this afternoon. I'd like to bring him along if that's okay." "Partner, you don't have to ask. Bring him along. Does he swim?" I laughed. "I'm not certain but I know he can throw down some Bar-B-Q." "Tru dat, I'll see you guys later then?" "Yeah, I just need to stop by the house to change clothes. Tyler and I went to the Community Center this morning and just finished lunch." "Yeah, Tyler told me about the community center when I phoned earlier. So, where did you two have lunch?" "We stopped at *California Dreaming.*" "Is that right? How did you two like it?" "It was a nice experience not to mention good food." I happen to look in Tyler's direction and the expression on her face signaled that she thought I was rambling. "Anyway, I'll tell you about it later." "All right partner, I'll see you later, Peace Out."

"Miles, you two acted as though you haven't spoken in weeks." "Tyler, don't even go there. We're no different than you and your girlfriends when you're on the phone." "Yeah right. What time do you expect Lamar?" "I'm not certain. He didn't call to let me know when he planned to be on the road but it takes about 6 hours to get here from his home. So it should be anytime now."

"Hey you, are you going to wear that two-piece bathing suit I bought?" "Excuse me?" I smiled and rubbed her thigh. "Are you going to wear the tan two-piece bathing suit I bought you?" "If you want to be technical Mr. Stewart you've bought all my bathing suits. So, it's quite difficult to be certain as to which bathing suit you're referring." "Okay silly, now that you know which one are you going to wear it?" "Is that what you would like?" I smiled shifting my head and shoulders making a *Chris Tucker* imitation, "And you know this…MAN!" We both then enjoyed a brief laugh. "You're too silly baby." "Yeah but you love that about me." "True!"

"You know Miles, the tan bathing suit happens to match my toes. Was this all a part of your master plan the other night?" "Who me? No, not at all, the colors just tastefully compliment your flesh tone." She reached over and grabbed my hand. With her forefinger, she gently tickled my palm. Tyler had told me early in our relationship that a tickle of the palm was a subtle mating call. So when I felt that touch my body warmed in anticipation of loving my queen. We continued the remainder of the drive holding hands in silence…

When we arrived home Lamar was outside playing catch with the neighborhood kids. "That's just like Lamar to make himself at home." "Yes it is. I hope he hasn't been here long." I blew the horn and waved at my older brother. He was grinning from ear to ear while he tossed the ball. The kids were the same ones that I played with as well. Tyler found it humorous that they would often come by the house and ask her if I could play. We had a special connection with the neighborhood kids and I have to admit it was cute having them think of me as a pal. "Well it seems the neighborhood kids have found a new friend." "Miles are you pouting?" We both started laughing. "No sweetheart, I'm not pouting."

When I parked Lamar took a reprieve and ran over towards the car. Tyler exited first. "What's up sis?" He said, as he lifted her off her feet in a bear hug. "Put me down Lamar, you know I don't like being picked up." Tyler sounded miffed but she smiled the entire time. Lamar complied with her wishes and Tyler hit him on the shoulder. "I told you to never pick me up silly." "Okay sis, I'm just excited to see you." "So, how are you Lamar? You've lost some weight and sporting a bald head." He sighed then mustered up a smile. "I'm doing okay." "I'm sorry Lamar, did I embarrass you?" "Not at all it's my new look."

"Cool." Well I'm going inside to change I'll leave you two alone." Lamar nodded his head then walked over to me. Tyler waved goodbye and walked inside.

"So, what's up Lamar? I punched him playfully on the shoulder. "You know her observation is correct. You have lost some weight. Are you refining your body for Brittany?" "Nothing like that, I'm just trying to make it my brother. But I can't complain I'm feeling fine and doing well." "Well you know complaining does no good anyway." He began laughing as we hugged. "I know that's right." "Let's go inside." I placed my arm around his shoulder as we walked towards the door. "Tyler and I are invited to a cookout and so are you." "Is that right? I haven't had any good Bar-BQ all year." So, dad hasn't fired up the grill? "No, he visited Uncle Nathan for *Memorial Day*. He'll probably do a little grilling for the *Fourth*." "I should be able to come home for a visit during that time. So, how are mom and dad?" "They're doing well. Just spending quality time together since they both retired." "Well that's wonderful to hear. They definitely earned it after all those years of working."

"What can I get you to drink?" "I'll find something. You go ahead and change." "Why don't you go ahead and bring in your bags. The guestroom is all set for you." "Okay, I just have an overnight bag." While walking towards the bedroom, I remembered that we might be swimming. "Hey Lamar, do you swim?" "Yeah man, you ought to know." "I wasn't sure. Remember, I never learned until I left home." I could hear him laughing. "Look man! Just bring your swim trunks."

When I entered the bedroom Tyler was pulling her hair back to tie it. "Oh baby! You look so sexy with your hair tied back." She looked at me and rolled her eyes. "We don't have time for playing around." "I know." I walked over and kissed her deeply. "I just thought it would be nice to convey my delight after seeing you." She slapped me on the butt. "I love you." "Dido."

I quickly undressed then put on some shorts and a T-shirt. "Hey, why don't you take the black trunks that I like?" "You must have read my mind Miss?" "No. I just know what I like on your body." "Ahhh! *Sookie, Sookie* now. Are you going to be staring at a *brotha?*" She shook her head and shoulders showing some of her own *Chris Tucker* imitations. "And you know this! MAN!" I started laughing so hard that I nearly wet my pants. "Excuse me baby I need to use the bathroom." "Okay, I'll be waiting in the car. We need to get going." She then exited laughing at her *Chris Tucker* antics.

Tyler

As we drove along the freeway, Lamar and I talked while Miles concentrated on the road. Every once in a while Miles would chime in but mostly it was Lamar and I talking. Lamar had been a fireman for the last ten years and married his high school sweetheart Brittany. They were experiencing some turbulent times, which made it no surprise that he arrived alone.

"So Lamar how are Brittany and Jr. these days?" "They're fine. I spent yesterday with them. Brittany celebrated her 29th birthday." "Oh really, did the two of you do anything special?" "Yeah we spent the afternoon at *Shelly's* and the evening at the theatre. I bought tickets to *Phantom*." "That sounds nice did she enjoy it? I remember her telling me that she loved theatrics." "She had a wonderful time."

"So, how is *Shelly's*? Miles keeps telling me about it but we haven't dined there yet." "It's very nice with an exquisite ambience. They have a pianist that plays all kinds of instrumentals. The waiters are dressed in tuxedos and treat each customer like royalty. There's just too much class to mention. You'll have to experience it yourself." "Well the next time we're in the city I'll have Miles take me." "What was that sweetheart?" "You heard me Miles. I want to eat at *Shelly's* the next time we visit Birmingham."

I wanted to ask if he and Brittany had reconciled but didn't want to pry. Instead, I talked around the subject hoping he might satisfy my curiosity. "Lamar, why didn't Brittany and Jr. come with you?" "We're still giving each other some space." "Oh, I'm sorry I thought you two had worked things out." "It's okay. We're doing fine."

"Tyler sweetheart, let's not bother Lamar with those issues." "It's okay Miles. We're family. I don't mind. "Tyler, I left because I haven't got the courage to share a secret with her. Actually, she gave me an ultimatum. There was a few thousand dollars missing from our checking account and she wanted to know why but I couldn't tell her. I don't know what she assumed but she told me to either tell her what the money was used for or leave…" "I didn't mean to bring up a sore subject Lamar so maybe we shouldn't discuss this further?" "I agree Tyler. Besides, we're here."

When we pulled into Braxton's driveway you could hear music blaring from the back yard. "Sounds like Braxton got it going on." "Yeah he usually has nice socials." "I hope so. I could use a little excitement."

The front door was open so we all just marched in. Miles led the way through the house and into the backyard. There were about 30 people. Miles' crew of Winston and Tony the rest were people I had met but couldn't remember. Dang! Some of these women need to cover themselves and some need to change clothes altogether. This one sister had boobs too big for that small two-piece she wore. When she walked around her stuff almost popped out. That's Braxton for you, still trying to be a ladies man. All these floozies…I mean, who would I do any girl talk with?

I was relieved when I saw a familiar face. Shannon and Tony had visited us a few times. She was a pleasant personality and I really enjoyed her company. "Hello Shannon, how are you girlfriend?" "Hello Tyler, I'm fine how are you?" "I'm doing wonderful." As we began talking, I could hear Braxton yelling in the background. "What's up partner? I'm glad to see you guys have made it." He and Miles exchanged greetings then began talking. "So Shannon, did you bring a bathing suit?" "Yes. I just haven't gone in to change." "Girl lets go change so we can get wet." "Sounds good."

Miles

Braxton and I were laughing and talking when Tony approached. "What's up fellas?" I hugged him exchanging the brotherhood grip. "I'm sorry about last night but I just needed to get out of there." "No problem my brother, we gave it our best shot. Besides we still make some nice grooves together.

"Tony do you remember my brother Lamar?" "Oh yeah, we met some time ago, what's up?" "Not much, just visiting family." "Cool. Did you bring your family?" "No, they're home." I could sense that Lamar felt a little uneasy about that question so I conjured a way to excuse us. "Hey Braxton, I'm going to make myself a drink. Lamar come on I'll show you the bar." "That's cool partner-you know where to find everything."

When we arrived at the bar, I poured two glasses of scotch. Lamar was rubbing his temples so I knew whatever was on his mind must have been heavy. My suspicion was that it involved the conversation he and Tyler had earlier. I handed him a glass and took a long sip of my own drink. "So, what's up brother man?" Lamar circled his glass observing the swirling ice. "Miles I need to tell you something?" "Lamar you know that you can talk to me about anything." "I know but I haven't spoken to Brittany about it." "Whatever it is I'm sure she'll stand by you. You should trust in her understanding and be assured that she'll forgive you." He started laughing. "What's so funny?" He tilted his head and threw back the entire glass of scotch. "You and your damn assumptions, it seems as though you suspect I'm about to confess some sort of sexual exploit." My mouth dropped from embarrassment. "I didn't mean to imply…." He held up his hand to silence me.

"That's the type of thinking that always ruins relationships. It seems like people are more comfortable concluding infidelity among anything else." I tried unsuccessfully to defend my response but he wasn't hearing it. "Lamar, I'm sorry for my assumption." He motioned again with his hand. "The truth is that I have been visiting a woman; a doctor to be exact." "Lamar perhaps you should tell this to Brittany." "Will you shut your damn mouth? I'm trying to tell you I'm..." We were interrupted when Braxton came over to see if we found everything.

"Hey partners, did you two get lost or what? Everyone is asking for you two." "We were just having a brother-to-brother moment." "Yeah, that's right. I was just telling Miles that life has no guarantee. You never know if you will ever get a second chance to say I'm sorry or I love you." "Well, that is true but why don't you two change and come on out to the pool?" Lamar and I hadn't discussed what he told Braxton so I couldn't fathom why he would go through the effort to make up such a story. I do admit regrettably, Lamar and I hadn't been as close as I would like over the last few years but we are brothers and I love him. It just seemed that when we became adults we stopped making time for each other.

I needed to know where this conversation was going but Braxton's interruptions made it difficult. After Lamar went into the bathroom to change Braxton grabbed a beer and walked over to me. "So partner, why haven't you changed?" "We were getting into a heavy conversation." "Damn, I'm sorry partner. I didn't know." "It's okay; I didn't exactly expect to get into it myself." "I'll leave you two to chat then." Just as Braxton spoke Lamar came out of the bathroom. "Let's plunge fellas." "Lamar I'd like to finish our discussion." "Later for that shit man, let's get wet." He walked outside leaving Braxton and I standing in the den. My mouth dropped at this abrupt change. "Well partner, let's get wet?" "Let's do it."

Outside, everyone was in the pool. Following all the greetings and kind words about our performance, I looked at the pool and saw Tyler gliding under the water. She looked like a dolphin gracefully exploring beneath the surface. I walked towards the side where I expected her to pop up for air. When her face broke through the water I was waiting there smiling. "Hello handsome, how did you know that I longed to see your face?" "Well, I just happen to be in the neighborhood expecting the same thing." She gave me a huge sensual smile. "Miles baby, will you bring me a towel?" "Certainly, would you like anything else?" "I'll think of more while you're away." I walked over to our bag grabbing her pink towel. When I returned, she and Shannon were talking like hens. So I took to a moment to chat with Tony and Winston. We were hand slapping and laughing about the previous night and maybe having too much of a good time for Tyler's taste.

"Excuse me Shannon; I'm going to get out for a while." "Okay, I think I'll swim a bit longer. Hey Miles, I'm sorry about last night. Tony told me what happened." "Thanks but it just wasn't our time." Shannon submerged then glided away. "Okay sweetie, I'm ready." I turned from the guys finding Tyler standing near the bank of the pool. "All right baby." Excusing myself from Tony and Winston, I turned towards Tyler. She extended her hand then stepped out of the water. Her body glistened as the water ran down her smooth skin. I nearly got an erection until she pushed me in the pool. "Shit!" I went under then came back up gasping and shaking water from my face. "What is up with that Tye?" Everyone was laughing. Tyler held two fingers to her lips as she laughed. Her body shook as she made futile attempts to contain her laughter. "I thought I'd help you get over the shock of the cold water." "Well you succeeded. Luckily I'm a good swimmer." "Now you know I wouldn't have pushed you if that wasn't the case." "I know I'm just giving you a hard time." "Let me see your backstroke?" I then threw my arms back and began my slow groove atop the water feeling damn good…

Lamar was floating face down with his arms spread eagle. I swam towards him and spoke with a solemn tone; "if I didn't know better I would swear you appeared…" "Dead?" "Well, yes." He turned to his back and continued floating. "Sorry to alarm you." "So why did you walk away as though we weren't talking?" "I needed to change the subject." "I thought you wanted to tell me something." "We'll discuss it later alright?" "Okay, whatever you say."

Treading the water, I happened to notice Tyler with a plate. "It's feeding time my brother." "What do you mean?" "Well, my lady is over there eating and I'm about to join her." "I'll follow your lead." I began laughing. "Well don't fall too far behind there may be nothing left." "I know that's right."

"So Tye did you make a plate for me?" "No, you were swimming and I didn't want to make a plate that might get cold. I know how you can be once you start swimming." "Thanks baby, you know me well but I'm ready to jump on some of this food. Would you like anything more?" "No I'm fine for now." "Okay, I'll be right back." "Take your time."

As I filled my plate Lamar walked behind me. "Hey bruh, you've got some cool friends. A person needs good friends." Stacking ribs on my plate I responded to Lamar's observation. "You're right about it…and I can count on each of them." "Yeah, I was talking with Winston and he told me how you helped him a few weeks ago." "Yeah, he hit some hard luck and needed a jump-start to get going again. You know, he asked his father to recommend me for that internship during college. Thanks to him I not only got that internship but a job as well…"

"Hey bruh, I don't want to stop you from talking but I want to get my grub on." "Tru Dat, I'm right behind you."

"*EEE Electric Slide,*" Braxton had turned on some old dance tunes and everybody jumped to their feet dancing around the pool. "Go Tyler, Go Tyler, Go, Go, Go Tyler." Tyler was showing some moves she had been practicing. We had five lines, six deep doing the slide. Even Lamar jumped in the mix. Tony and Winston started stepping the way we used to back in the day. "I said Bur-rrrrr, its cold in Here…"

The whole setting suddenly seemed like college days. Though we had all grown up the memories seemed like yesterday. Everyone was having fun but we were definitely not in college anymore and after doing a group slide we began winding down. When the next song started Tyler and several other women began fanning themselves as they walked towards their chairs. Braxton and I joined the brothers for a step routine we performed in our last statewide Greek show. Everyone sat back watching as we stepped to our hearts content. After we finished we exchanged brotherhood greetings. Tyler and Shannon were screaming in unexpected unison "*Skeeeee Wee!*" They both looked at each other and hugged. "I didn't know you were a soro."

Following the step routine, Tyler jumped into my arms and kissed me. Shannon hugged and kissed Tony then Braxton and Winston locked lips with the girls from last night.

"I love you Miles," "I love you too." "Hey, Shannon is my soro." "I heard you two acting like you were on the yard." "Yeah it felt good." "So, are you about ready to go?" "Well, give me some time to go over and talk with her. Why don't you check with Lamar before we decide?" "Okay."

As I walked towards Lamar brothers were giving me high five and doing the Fraternity yell. "Hey Lamar, I'm about ready to step. What about you?" "I'm ready when you are, just say the word." "Word!" We both started laughing. "Hey Braxton, I appreciate the hospitality but we need to get home." "Alright partner, I'll walk you to your car." I signaled Tyler as we walked past everyone. "Goodnight y'all-Goodnight Miles, Tyler, pleased to meet you Lamar." As we approached the car Braxton gave me the brotherhood grip. "I see Tyler found a soro?" "Yes, I'm surprised they didn't discuss college life when she visited us." "Yeah that's true."

"All right partner, drive carefully. Lamar it was good to see you…be cool." "Yeah, you too Braxton." Tyler and Shannon walked towards the car and exchanged hugs. "I'll be in touch with you Shannon." "Okay Tye, I'll do the same."

"Well! That was a good time." "Yes it was-wake me when we get home sweetie." "Tyler you're kidding? We haven't started down the road yet." "I'm getting a head start baby." "Ha! Ha! Ha! Ha!" "What are you laughing at Lamar?" "You're on your own brotha, I'm going to sleep too," "You two are sorry. I need some company for this drive." "Please, it only takes 40 minutes."

Clarissa

"Come on girls. You need to eat some breakfast before your father arrives. He said he would be here at 10 am to pick you up. Tamara, Tia do you two have your dance clothes packed and ready to go?" They both responded in unison. "Yes mam." "Well hurry up your father will be here soon." "Tia is taking too long in the bathroom." "Tamara, the last time I checked we had two bathrooms. Permission granted to use the other one." "Yes mam."

Dang! 9:30. I still hadn't spoken with Tyler about what's troubling her. Surely she and Miles would be at the Youth Center by now. "Mommy, are you coming to our rehearsal?" "Yes dear but I have some errands to run. I'll stop by later." "Daddy promised that we would go skating tonight. Are you coming?" "Oh did he now?" "Yes mam." "Well he and I haven't discussed any such plans but I'll be sure to ask him when he arrives. Now hurry up before your food gets cold." "Okay." "I made your favorites, pancakes and bacon with orange juice." "Ooh! Thanks mommy." "You're quite welcome Tia." "Tamara! You better hurry up mommy made pancakes and bacon!" I started laughing. "Sweetheart you don't have to yell."

I loved the way they made me feel. My two children were the best gift GOD could have given Franklin and I. Tamara was now 14 and Tia 10. We decided when they were still crawling that we would enroll them in dance. They struggled in the beginning but we continued to offer encouragement. Tamara was afraid of flips but Tia on the other hand feared very little. They seemed to motivate each other and as the weeks and years passed there were significant changes in them both. Their confidence soared beyond our expectations.

(Ding Dong) "That must be your father." Tia jumped up from the table and ran to the door. Tamara fearing she would be out done followed her cue. They opened the door and yelled in unison. "Daddy!" Franklin embraced them both and kissed them on their cheeks. "Hello my beautiful little ladies, Good morn-

ing Clarissa how are you?" "Good morning Franklin, how are you?" "Just wonderful now that I'm surrounded by the women of my life." I ignored that
comment. He released the girls from his embrace and stood there as if waiting
for me to run into his arms. "Would you like some breakfast? The girls just
started and still need to finish." "Hey little ladies, would you like me to have
breakfast with you?" "YES!" "Okay then, I'll have coffee and pancakes please.
Will you be joining us?" Tia yelled, "Come on mommy sit down." "Okay but
you need to hurry up. It's about time for you to leave. Practice starts at 10:30."

I made two additional plates then poured two cups of coffee. When I sat
down Franklin offered a prayer. Afterwards the table was silent as we began
eating. It felt wonderful having him here reminding me of old times.

I took a reprieve from reminiscing to clear my throat. "Franklin, Tia mentioned that you promised to take them skating but we hadn't discussed it."
"Forgive me but I had hoped to persuade you to join us, if you don't have prior
plans?" "Come on mommy, say yes." My temperature was starting to rise. I
hated when Franklin made plans with the girls and didn't discuss it with me.
He assumed I would always accompany them. The presumptions seemed too
dang manipulative even though I knew in my heart that his intentions were
pure. He was simply being a husband that plans an evening with his family.
The reality however, is that we're separated. "Tia, your father and I will decide."
Wiping my mouth I got up from the table. "Excuse us for a moment…Franklin
dear may I have a word with you in the den?" "Oh, you sure can." I was determined to keep my cool. So when we entered the den, I vacated my streetwise
antics. "Franklin I love it when we're together as a family. I love spending time
with you too but we've not begun to deal with the issues between us. So please,
talk with me before you plan things with the girls? I don't want to be forced
into compliance. I know that's not your intention but I'm given very little
room for discussion when the subject is broached in the presence of the girls."
"Forgive me Clarissa. I truly never meant to come across that way. Should I tell
the girls you can't make it? I promise that I won't put you in a situation like this
again." "No, don't tell the girls I'm not coming. I would love to skate with you."
He smiled from ear to ear then we returned to the kitchen. The girls had finished breakfast and were outside with friends. "Well you had better get going."
"Okay, I'll see you later this evening." "Drive carefully Franklin." "I will…have
a wonderful afternoon." "Thanks."

When Franklin and the girls drove away, I began assessing our relationship.
Franklin had retired from the Navy and transitioned to city council. We had
also started a successful coffeehouse in the downtown area. Business had gone

so well that we employed full time management as Franklin began to feel comfortable stepping away from the day-to-day routine. By most standards we were doing well. At least on the surface...Franklin was meticulous about everything. He had planned our life from beginning to now. He said that we would have a comfortable bank account. He said that we would travel. He said that our children would be exposed to everything. He said I would never have to work. He said that no other woman would come between us. All that and more became true except that I want to work and that *trifling trick*. God, how I wish we could get past these issues.

I picked up the phone to call Tyler. Dang! The answering machine...they must have gone already. Her not being home gave me the perfect opportunity to do a little shopping. Tomorrow would be Franklin's 45th birthday and I wanted to buy him something special. So I quickly got myself together and left for the mall. When I arrived it took twenty minutes to find parking. Saturday was terrible for a last minute shopper. Every teenager in the city loitered in the mall. Everywhere I turned there was loud music and young boys with their pants below their butt. The young ladies-not to be out done-wore short skirts that were too revealing.

I was happy our children hadn't yet succumbed to this fad. Our girls were wearing khakis and button down collared shirts with penny loafers. That was their attempt at shunning dresses on a daily basis. I laughed to myself because it doesn't really matter anyway. It's all a part of kids finding themselves. But I sure as heck wish these kids could find themselves on a day when I didn't have to shop.

Finally parked, I began walking towards the entrance. There was a group of young men exiting as I approached the door. "Yo! Yo! Lady, allow me to hold the door for you." One of them barked as he swaggered out the door. I felt a little annoyed by his antics but it was a gentle stroke to my womanhood to know that at 40 I could still turn heads. After a brief moment of marveling in my own esteem, I walked directly to the jeweler. Franklin had been talking about a gold nugget ring for years. The man was too dang cheap to buy it himself so I thought it would be a nice surprise. After all I do love his fugal behind.

There were two young women behind the counters and several people were window-shopping. I couldn't help but overhear a young couple that was examining wedding sets. The young man seemed disinterested in looking but the girl had a glow in her eyes. She practically had to drag him over to view the rings. I was certain she felt embarrassed because I remember having that glow many years ago myself. Franklin behaved the same however I discovered later that he behaved that way because he didn't want me excited about something he wouldn't be able to provide. He said that he wanted me to have anything I wanted and that he felt inadequate if he couldn't give it. I smiled and continued looking.

"Good morning, may I show you something in particular?" "Yes, I would like to take a closer look at your gold nugget rings for men." "Certainly, we have a small selection because of the limited variations. Is there a particular weight you're interested in purchasing?" "I'd like a 24 carat piece." "Sure, we have this piece. It's truly magnificent." I didn't really care for sales people going overboard with descriptive jargon, especially when I had already decided to make a purchase but she seemed like a wonderful spirit so I indulged. "I'll take it." "What size do you require?" "Size 10 would be perfect." "Okay, I'll take care of that for you. Will it be cash or charge?" "Charge please. Also, I'd like to have the lifetime warranty please." "Certainly, that is no problem...That will be $1071.79."

I gave her my visa and began looking at platinum wedding rings recalling some discussion with a few friends about the latest fashion in bridal sets. I must admit they did have a certain appeal. "Miss, may I have your signature here please?" "Oh! Sure." "Here's your receipt and please come again." "Thank you." After leaving the jeweler, I perused a few windows finally stopping at the floral and card shop to purchase a card befitting the occasion.

Exited the mall, I looked at my watch (11:50) realizing the girls would be practicing until 12:30. Rushing to the car, I opened the door anticipating that with moderate traffic the drive to the studio would be no more than fifteen minutes. Thankfully it was much easier leaving the mall. No searching and waiting for parking...just exiting. I turned on the radio and cruised up the boulevard leading to the studio just a few blocks north of the mall.

"In concert tomorrow night only...An evening of jazz featuring Gerald Albright, the Braxton Brothers and Will Downing...Tickets on sale at your local ticket-master...Spend the evening with someone you love." As the DJ finished his advertisement, I thought to myself how complete Franklin's birthday celebration would be if we went to that show. Pondering the thought, I pulled out my cell phone and called ticketmaster for two tickets. After completing the call, I had entered the parking lot for the dance studio then looked at the clock realizing the time was 12:10.

"Hello everyone, how are you doing?" "Clarissa, I see you made it." "How are the girls doing?" "Wonderful. Why don't you peek in so that they know you're here?" "Okay." I walked towards the door and cracked it open. Monica

Simmons was sitting near the door with a grin that showed all her teeth. "Clarissa girl you've got it going on." "Pardon me?" "Chile, Tia's hair came loose and she started crying. All the women here thought we would have to bail out your husband but the *Brotha* fooled the hell out of us. The man actually braided the girl's hair...shocked the shit out of us." I smiled in annoyance because Franklin shared all the responsibilities where the girls were concerned. Added to that, I believed some women-Monica included-had outdated perceptions of fatherhood because he was just that kind of man. Not perfect because he certainly had his flaws, he just loved the kids. "Oh girl you should see him in the kitchen." She extended her hand giving me a high five. "You go girl!" Even though Monica had a shallow view of fatherhood nothing would be gained by making her uncomfortable so, I shared with her a brief laugh to keep the mood pleasant. "What are you two snickering about?" I cracked open the door and waved at the girls. When they smiled in acknowledgment, I closed the door directing my attention toward Franklin. "Just girl talk, nothing to concern yourself with."

"So Mr. Green, do you have plans tomorrow?" "No, I had planned to go to church and relax afterwards. Why do you ask?" "Well, I just happen to have two tickets to the jazz concert tomorrow night." "Okay...what does that mean?" "Don't play silly with me Franklin. I'd like to take you if you don't have plans." He began laughing. "That sounds wonderful...So tell me, should I pick you up or vice versa?" "Why don't you pick me up at 6pm?" "What time does the show start?" "It starts at 8pm but I thought that since it will be your birthday we could have dinner." He raised his right eyebrow..."I see you've planned a birthday celebration for a *brotha?*" "I guess you might say so. Will the guest of honor be joining me?" "Mrs. Green you can definitely count on my being there."

When the door to the studio opened all the little girls came running towards their parents. Tia came charging towards me. "Mommy, mommy did you see me?" Tamara walked over and wrapped her arm around my waist. I hugged them both with each arm. "Yes, I saw you Tia...You were wonderful. Tamara you seem to have your routine down cold." She smiled confidently. "I've been working hard to get it right." "I know baby and it's paying dividends too." Franklin had started talking with one of the other parents about the recital the girls were scheduled to perform in a week. "Franklin the girls and I are about to leave. What time are we going skating?" He excused himself from the parent whom he had been talking. "I'll pick you guys up at 6pm." "Okay that sounds good. We'll see you at 6pm." He nodded in agreement and returned to his conversation. "Tia and Tamara say goodbye to your father." The girls ran over to hug Franklin and said goodbye as I started walking towards the car.

After I approached my door, I looked back to locate the girls. They were 20 yards behind and walking towards the car with their father. Tia was skipping as she walked and Tamara walked along holding Franklin's hand. Watching them made me so happy I smiled. Franklin was their hero and his presence was a beacon that brought joy to their lives. Tia believed he could fix anything. I remember once when an electronic toy of hers stopped working. Franklin was on the ship…She brought me the toy saddened that it no longer worked. I told her we would buy a replacement but she looked at me and said, "Call my daddy I know he can fix it." The comment surprised me. Franklin was indeed a *jack-of-all-trades* but I would never have expected Tia to notice.

Opening the car door, I sat inside. Tamara sat in the front and Tia in the back. Franklin buckled Tia in and kissed her on the forehead. After he kissed Tamara on the cheek I found myself getting nervous. We had been separated a year and I still felt the jitters when he tucked the girls in their seats. Prior to his retirement, I used to drop him off before his ship deployed. He would perform the exact ritual with the girls followed by a passionate kiss of my lips. Inside my body ached to relive those moments but it was definitely the wrong time. So I sat nervously as I had on previous occasions during the last year. Franklin walked around to my door surveying the car and avoiding eye contact. "Hey lady it seems the Volvo needs a bath." We both started laughing. "I'm still waiting on the hired help to take care of the job." "Can't find good help these days huh?"

He always seemed to break the tension with some silly remark. It was as though we both experienced the same feelings and didn't wish the other to know. Nonetheless I was relieved. "I'll see you later Clarissa." "Okay." "Bye daddy." I started the car and drove off as he waved to the girls.

Tamara was staring out the window. "Mom I miss dad not being home." My heart skipped a beat. I had practiced my response to that comment a hundred times. Only Tamara never mentioned it. For an entire year she had been silent about the separation. In fact, I began to assume that she understood. I had attempted to explain what was going on but she always seemed nonchalant. Now that she finally commented about it, I was at a loss for words. There were just no words to justify her father's absence in a way she would understand. "Sweetheart, your father misses you too. He and I are just taking some time apart to understand and appreciate each other. Sometimes adults need a little space to examine things."

She remained looking out the window. My words were hollow to her innocence. "Do you still love him? You used to tell him all the time." My heart skipped another beat. Franklin and I were always open with our feelings around the children. It was important to the two of us that they witness a loving relationship in their own home. He and I feared that we failed in that effort. To my astonishment that was far from the truth. Here today, I found validation in our efforts as parents. Tamara had observed our loving. She had seen us kiss and say I love you. There were no words to soothe her curiosity so I reached over to grab her hand. "Sweetheart regardless of the changes your father and I are experiencing we both love you dearly." "Do you still love him?" I looked in the rear view mirror for any hint that Tia might be equally curious. She had the headphones on listening to her CD player. "It's not that simple sweetheart. I care for your father deeply but we're working through some issues." She released my hand resuming her blank stare out the window. "We'll discuss this later okay sweetheart?"

My heart began to sink as I made the turn to our home. Tamara had expressed to me a sadness I wasn't prepared to handle. Franklin and I hadn't divorced and I guess we expected to reconcile but why hadn't we done so. It had been a year and we seemed to be communicating perfectly but somehow still remained apart. We definitely have some important decisions to make…

When we arrived home, I checked the mailbox. Tia went next door to play and Tamara waited at our front door for me to open it. After discovering there was nothing in the mail, I looked next door to locate my younger daughter. "Tia I'll have lunch prepared shortly so don't go too far." "Yes mam." I was relieved that Tia had found something to occupy her time. When I opened the door Tamara walked directly to her room. "Tamara, would you come and help me make lunch?" "Yes mam." To continue our talk, preparing lunch seemed like the perfect catalysts. Realizing my plan might work, I checked the answering machine for messages. "Clarissa, hey girl Miles and I are spending the afternoon at Braxton's. I'll talk with you later. BEEP Clarissa this is Brenda. Give me a call when you get a chance. BEEP, Tamara, this is Tramane call me." "Mom was that a call for me?" "Yes sweetheart, Tramane wants you to call when you get a chance." She entered the kitchen and began perusing the pantry. "Okay, so what's for lunch?" "Well I thought we could make *BLT's* with tomato soup. How does that sound?" She nodded her head in agreement. "Okay, I'll start the soup and slice the tomato." She removed a can of soup from the pantry placing it on the counter then grabbed a tomato from the refrigerator and stood next to me slicing. "So, would you like to finish our discussion we started in the car?" "No mam." I wanted to discuss it further but decided against any pressure. "Okay baby, whenever you want to talk just let me know." "I will mom." Pulling my daughter close to me, I kissed her forehead. "I love you baby."

"So, are you going to have a friend meet you at the skating ring?" "I had talked with Tramane about it earlier but I'm not sure if she can make it. I'll have to call her back." "Well if she needs a ride, I'm sure your father won't object."

When Tamara finished slicing the tomato she opened the soup and poured it into the pot. Meanwhile I micro-waved the bacon and toasted the bread. Tia came inside breathing erratic and walked directly to the refrigerator. "Go to the bathroom and wash your hands young lady." She opened her eyes wide and shrugged her shoulders. "OOPS, I'm sorry mommy." "Lunch will be ready shortly little lady." "Okay mommy." "Tamara sweetheart, why don't you set the table?" "Okay."

As Tamara set the table I made the sandwiches. "Mom what do you want to drink?" "I'll have water thank you." Tia entered the kitchen with one hand on her hip. "I want diet coke." I turned around and laughed. "What do you know about diet coke girl?" She looked at me and shrugged her shoulders. "I want diet coke." "Okay, that's fine with me." I would often order diet coke whenever we dined out but had no idea she paid attention.

Once the table was set and the food served we sat down. I offered a prayer then we began eating…

Following lunch, Tia returned outside to play and Tamara returned Tramane's phone call. I decided to relax with *Sidney Sheldon's* latest novel on loan from a friend. Since I had no plans prior to the kids and I going skating now seemed a perfect time to read. Walking into the den, I kicked off my shoes. As I began to enjoy the carpet beneath my feet Tia entered the house. "Mommy, can I go inside Leslie's house?" "Is it okay with her parents?" "Yes mam." "I don't mind just behave yourself." "Okay." When Tia exited, I picked up the book from the coffee table and sat in the recliner. Slowly lifting the control arm, I tilted backward crossing my legs then entered the world of *Sidney Sheldon.*

When the phone rang, I peeked at my realizing I had been reading two hours. Captured by the plot of the book, I continued reading expecting Tamara to answer the call. "Tamara, will you answer the phone please?" "I'm still on the phone." "Okay…put them on hold and answer the other phone." It was times like these I regretted giving her a private line. She ignored everything around her except the frequent ringing of her own telephone.

"Mom, dad's on the line!" "Dang, I definitely won't be able to get back into this book now." I got up and entered the kitchen to get the cordless phone. "I have it Tamara, thank you." I could hear her say I love you to Franklin as she hung up. "Hello." "Clarissa I forgot to ask if you wanted me to choose a restaurant for tomorrow evening." "No!" "Are you sure? You seem a little testy about it." "Oh I'm sorry; I was enjoying a good book when you phoned." "I'm sorry to have interrupted." "It's no problem. Listen, if it were your suggestion that would be expected but since I offered allow me to handle it birthday boy." "Are you sure?" "I've got a handle on it. Anyway, there's something I think you should know." "What is it?" "Tamara said something to me this afternoon." "What?" "She said that she missed you not being home." There was a brief silence that seemed like several minutes. "Franklin did you hear what I said?" "Yes, I'm just not sure how to comment." "Well it's been long overdue. I expected her to have mentioned it earlier but when she didn't my assumption was that she understood what was happening." "What did you say to her?" "Honestly I couldn't find the words. She caught me completely off guard…Anyway, I don't want to get into this over the phone. I just thought you should know what's on her mind. We can discuss it over dinner." "Sure, I agree with you. Are we still on for tonight?" "Yes unless you have another engagement." "No, I'm looking forward to tonight. I'll be there at 6pm." "Okay, we'll see you then."

After hanging up the phone, I began thinking about the reasons Franklin and I weren't together. He had made me feel like a tramp. I'm not sure if he was even aware of it but things just changed for us intimately. We were completely out of sync and combined with this mess about some *floozy*…well, times were challenging. It was too sickening to consider so I did what I had been the last year. I blocked it out.

"Tamara! Would you clean the kitchen once you're off the phone? "Yes mam." "Thanks sweetheart." It was close to 3pm when I looked at my watch. "Tamara! Make sure you and your sister take a shower and get dressed by 5pm okay?" "Yes mam." I needed to get myself ready so I picked up my book and walked into the bedroom. There was slight tension in my body and since there was time, I entered the bathroom and started a bubble bath. When the tub filled, I undressed picked up my book and stepped in to soak and relax. "Ah! That feels good." I removed my bookmark and continued reading.

Franklin

"Son your father and I are going to Long Island for the weekend." "Where am I going mom?" "You'll be staying here with your Aunt Sheila." "Aw mom, why does she have to keep me?" I hated it when Sheila kept me because she was weird. "She's your father's step sister and she doesn't charge." My mother didn't know at the time but the no cost sitter she boasted of changed everything in me.

After speaking with Clarissa my mind was in Centennial Park...

It was 1962. I was a happy nine-year-old playing basketball with the neighborhood crew. There were little girls circled around playing double-dutch and on the streets leading to the park were guys rolling dice screaming about who won the money. Of course, there was Mr. Deuce. He drove a fancy car and wore all the jewelry. Mr. Deuce seemed to always be surrounded by pretty ladies.

Times were tough in Brooklyn but we always found solace on the court. My best friend was Brandon. We called him Clyde because of his skills on the court. He reminded us of Walt Frazier. We would play two on two all day long.

One particular afternoon my aunt called me in for lunch. "I'll be there in a minute," I said. "Franklin you better get yo butt up here now." "Man! Hey fellas, I'll see you guys later. Can Clyde come in for lunch?" "Tell Brandon to take his little ass home for lunch." "Heifer, I don't want to eat her nasty food anyway." "I gotta go man." "Alright, just leave the ball." "Cool, I'll be back after I eat." When I entered the house Sheila had cheese toast and water on the table.

After sitting down, I began eating. The sandwich was so stale I frowned reaching for the glass of water to quickly wash it down. Once the sandwich was washed down, I placed the glass on the table and noticed an empty Gibleys bottle on the counter. Sheila entered the kitchen carrying another bottle in her hand. She spoke but her speech was different. She seemed very happy but she walked slowly, swaying her hips side to side and sliding her feet as she approached me. "Sheila your gown is open." I could see her balloons and some furry stuff just below her stomach.

She didn't say a word, just kept drinking from that Gibleys bottle. I quickly turned away after she threw her head backward taking a long gulp. Sheila had tossed the second empty bottle on the floor as I finished my last bite. I was nervous listening to her feet sliding across the floor closing in on me. Unsure of what would happen next, my hands began to shake as I picked up the glass washing down the last of the stale sandwich. "You're going to be a lady killer boy." She shoved me on the head and stared at me with a strange grin on her face.

I wasn't certain how to comment because of the awkwardness of the moment. "What do you mean Sheila?" "Shit...you already too cute." She stepped closer to me and began rubbing my head. "Auntie Sheila gonna show you something. It will be our little secret. You can keep a secret right?" I said a nervous yes. "Well close your eyes and give me your hand." Extending my right hand, she guided it into some cotton like stuff.

I wanted to open my eyes but was afraid when she began moaning or mumbling something. "Are you okay Sheila?" "Shut up! Just do what I tell you." She moved my hand all over and through the cotton. After the cotton began to feel slimy, I told Sheila I didn't want to play anymore. "Shut yo pretty ass up and do what I say! I'm your auntie." My eyes were still closed but they were beginning to water as I started to whimper. "You little punk! Bring your ass here." She jerked my hand away from the cotton turning me around. Shoving my face in the slimy cotton, she commanded me. "Stupid ass boy, start licking!" Nearly suffocating from the strange scent I couldn't do what she demanded. "Use your tongue and lick it! You'll like this candy." "No Sheila." "Lick it! I said." I was crying and trying to breathe as she held my head tightly. "Damit boy! I'm gonna have to do everything." She pulled me but I wasn't sure where because my eyes were still closed. Next thing I knew my face was in the slimy cotton again. "Lick boy!" I cried and attempted to do as she said.

I must have eventually done what she wanted because she stopped yelling and began shaking. Releasing my head, she then pushed me away. I opened my eyes after being freed from her grasp. She lay there with her gown open. "You better not tell our secret." I rubbed my puffy eyes nodding in agreement but didn't say a word.

She leaned in towards me opening my zipper. In fear from uncertainty, I closed my eyes again but could feel her touching my wiener. Feeling wet and warm, I began to notice a sudden familiar stiffness. The feeling was similar to what happens in my sleep. "You're hurting me Sheila!" She just kept doing whatever she was doing until I started shaking. "Sheila! I'm dying! I'm dying!" I could feel something coming from my body and since her mouth was around my wiener I had to be bleeding. "I'm gonna bleed to death from my pee pee!"

She swallowed hard then pushed me away laughing. "What the hell are you talking about boy? Take your little ass to the bathroom and clean this shit up." I ran to the bathroom crying and holding my wiener. "Boy, remember what I said, keep your damn mouth shut about our secret."

Tears welled up in my eyes from recalling the memories of those days. I endured that shit until I was 16 years old. Since it happened, I had never been with a woman on my own terms. She robbed me of that experience, making me hate what should be one of life's most natural actions between people that love each other. It was then at a tender young age that I learned what it felt like to truly hate someone.

Clarissa

I felt a gentle touch on my left arm. "Mommy, is it time to go yet?" "Tia, I'm sorry sweetheart mommy must have dozed off." I hadn't seen or heard her enter the bathroom. "I see you've gotten dressed? Is Tamara ready?" "She's combing her hair." "Okay, why don't you go into the den for now while mommy finishes bathing and gets dressed?" "Okay girlfriend." "I beg your pardon." She laughed and skipped out of the room. I laughed and mumbled, "I need to be careful about what I say around her. She's a little tape recorder."

I finished bathing then stepped out of the tub. My body felt relaxed but also drained from soaking in the hot water. After drying off, I put on some lotion and perfume. Standing in the closet, I placed my forefinger against my cheek perusing my wardrobe. "Now, what shall I wear?" After about 10 minutes in the closet, I opened a drawer finally deciding on a pair of yellow shorts and a horizontally stripped yellow and white golf shirt. After getting myself dressed, I stood in front of the mirror and turned to the side. "I've still got it." With that thought, I turned off the lights and walked into the den to wait for Franklin.

"Girls, do you have your skates?" "Yes mam, we're ready to go." *(Ding Dong)* Tia ran for the door. "Who is it?" A faint voice replied; "It's your father." "Mommy daddy is here." "Okay sweetheart, open the door. Tamara let's go sweetie." "Okay mom, I'm coming."

"Wow! Look at you three beautiful ladies. I feel like I'm in a music video." I flipped my hand in the air. "Oh Franklin stop being so silly." "Are you ready?" "Yes we are." Tamara and Tia raced towards Franklin's car. "I'll be out as soon as I lock up." "Okay, we'll be in the car. Girls make sure you buckle up." "Okay Daddy." I made a quick sweep of the house then walked out the door feeling a little nervous. Franklin would likely be sitting in the car watching me walk towards him. When we were together he would always wait in the car and whistle at me as I approached. He loved the way I walked and given the similarities, I wasn't sure if there would be any whistling today. Surprisingly, I was just as unsure if I even wanted it. My palms started to sweat when I heard faint whistling from his lips. After entering the car, I acted as though I never heard the whistling and neither he nor the girls ever spoke of it. For all I know they probably didn't hear a thing since they were singing. And maybe I just imagined the whole thing out of some sense of nostalgia. Whatever happened or didn't happen, I indulged in a brief moment to remember my yesterdays.

We arrived at the skating center 45 minutes later. The girls seemed excited and quite frankly I was too. "We're here ladies." Tia screamed, "Yeh!!!!" "Tia, sweetheart you don't have to be so loud." "It's alright, she's just excited." "Mom there's Tramane." She pointed at someone about forty paces from us. "I'm going to meet her." "That's fine sweetheart just make sure you check-in with us from time to time."

Franklin assisted Tia with her skates then she took off. I smiled as she zipped past people. "I hadn't realized she became so good." "Yeah, she's much improved since the last time. Have you been bringing them here?" "Not really, they've come with Tyler and Miles a few times." "Well there's a definite improvement. So, how are those two these days?" I put on my skates and stood up. "They're doing fine." I held my arms out to balance myself. "Franklin it's been a while. So you better not let me fall." "Ha, Ha I was about to say the same thing." We both laughed. "Okay, here goes. I took off and it all came back to me." Tia zipped past yelling. "Hey mommy! You go girl!" "I beg your pardon young lady? We need to talk." I laughed pointing my finger as she past me grinning.

I waved at Franklin who hadn't yet put on his skates. He just stood there smiling watching the kids and I. Tamara and Tramane rolled around slowly with two boys not far behind. Time had been racing by and my daughter's growing up reminded me daily. I only hope we prepared her or at least gave her the proper foundation for being a responsible young woman.

Franklin finally made his way to the floor. He raced behind me and put his arm around my waist. "Were you looking for me?" "I knew where you were-you've never been too far." "You're right about that lady." The music had picked up and everyone started zipping by at faster speeds. "So, do you think you can keep up?" "I don't know but I can try." I took off swaying side to side. "Catch me if you can!" I zipped past Tamara waving. "Go mom!" I looked back to find Franklin hustling to catch up. "So you think you're pretty fast huh?" "No, I just wanted to see how long it would take you to come after me." As soon as those words exited my lips, I wanted them back. I was becoming too comfortable and feeling too good but Franklin and I were not the way we used to be. "I'm sorry for saying that Franklin." "Why are you apologizing? I'm not a stranger you know." "I know but the comment seemed a little awkward."

"Hey listen. Do you hear it?" What are you talking about? "The D.J. is about to play something slow." "How do you know because I don't hear a thing?" "Well, I asked him to play something for me and my lady friend." "Oh really, what did you request?" As soon as I asked the question I heard *KC and JoJo* echoing in the background. We didn't listen to hip-hop enough to know the artist but when I heard Tamara playing the song in her bedroom it moved me. I've loved it ever since and Franklin knew it. "Oh Franklin, that's…" "Shhh, Don't say another word just skate with me." He wrapped his right arm around my waist and held my left hand.

Slowly rolling around the rink, I began thinking. Franklin and I had gone through a great deal the last year but here, on this night, it was a distant memory. I was happy and I could think of no better place or time than right now.

Once the song finished I took off again. "Hey Franklin catch me if you can." He smiled and waved me on. "You go ahead I'll get us something to drink." "All right I'll meet you at the counter." I rolled past the girls. "Tamara, Tia your father is buying some drinks. Let's meet at the counter." "Yes mam." "Tamara you can bring along your friends." "What about me Mommy?" "So can you Tia. I didn't intend to exclude you sweetheart." "Come on Chelsea. My Daddy's buying slushies."

After we all met at the counter Franklin's mouth dropped when he realized he was buying eight soft drinks. "Okay, let's have everyone place their order and I'll pay." He whispered in my ear. "Clarissa, you should have warned me." "I had no warning myself." "So who are the young men?" Tamara hasn't introduced us. "Tamara, why don't you introduce your friends?" "Okay. Come on guys. Mom, Dad this is Michael Banks and Jamal Richardson." "I'm pleased to meet you." Franklin said, "So am I." "So, who are your parents?" I looked at Michael signaling that he should answer first. "My father is Michael Banks Sr. and my mother is Loretta." Shifting my attention to Jamal he chimed right in. "My father is Justin Richardson. My mother is Juanita Richardson." I don't think I've met them. Looking again at Michael I asked, "Where do they work?" "My father is an insurance agent and my mother teaches at the high school. Jamal chimed in without being prompted by my stare. "My father is a loan officer and my mother is a manager at Carlyle & Company. "That's nice. Well it was nice to meet you two." "Yes mam." "Come on Justin. The D.J. is playing *XSCAPE*." Tamara grabbed the boy's hand and zipped onto the floor.

"Clarissa have you listened to the words of that song?" "Yes I hear it Franklin." "Well it seems our Tamara is growing up." "Apparently she is doing just that." *(Background: Just Run, To the Arms, of The One Who Loves You, Just Run, To These Arms and These Two Arms Will Keep you warm...)* "Mr. Green, would you roll around the rink with me once more?" He chuckled. "You know I was thinking the exact same thing. It would be my pleasure Mrs. Green..."

"Thanks for the roller skate dance." "The pleasure was mine." "I'm getting a little tired. Can we sit for while?" "Sure, if that's what you want." We maneuvered our way to a vacant table in the corner. "That was fun but my feet are aching." "Why don't you sit and I'll take off your skates?" "Thanks but I can manage." "Did you finish your discussion with Tamara?" After removing the skates, I crossed my legs rubbing my feet. "No, she didn't want to discuss it further so I decided not to pursue the issue. She'll let me know when it's time to talk." "How do you feel about what she said?" "I don't know. It seems we're in limbo. I know we both needed some time to ourselves." "I guess that's a fair assessment." "Of course there are still some things I don't quite understand. You owe me some answers after all the time I've given you..." "I know." "You always say that but I never get answers." "Clarissa let's just change the subject before we ruin what's been a wonderful evening." Franklin appeared dismayed but he didn't argue and I hated that sometimes. He would never argue. Just permit me to conjure up all kinds of conclusions. The only thing he would say is: I know Clarissa; I'm sorry Clarissa, and all right Clarissa. I just wished he would argue for once then at least I would know he cared.

"Mommy, will you skate with me?" "Sure Tia. Excuse me Franklin." "I'll be out there shortly. In the meantime don't get yourself run over." I looked back and smiled realizing I could never stay angry with Franklin. That's part of the reason he had to leave. Otherwise, I would never understand what went wrong. We would be living together pretending he didn't make me feel like a tramp and pretending he didn't mention that *floozy*. I love him but he'll be the last to know. "All right Tia, show mommy your stuff." "Okay, watch me mommy." She had mastered tight turns and even began skating backward. "All right, you go girl!" Dang! I need to stop saying that around little Miss Tape Recorder. "Go Tia!"

"Catch me mommy, catch me." "All right Tia I'm coming to catch you." I raced quickly towards her. "Watch me mommy." "Okay but slow down baby." She turned skating backward and before I could reach her she bumped into another child and fell. "Oh my God, Franklin!" Tia immediately began crying as others began to circle around asking if she was okay. "I'm coming baby."

Franklin ran across the floor and arrived before me. "Excuse me please that's my daughter." When I arrived he was by her side checking for injuries. "Are you okay sweetheart?" "No daddy, my arm hurts." "Is she okay Franklin?" "Her arm hurts." "Can you move it baby?" She moved it slightly but the pain caused more crying. "Yes mam but it hurts." "Don't move it sweetie." "Okay Daddy." "Excuse me, excuse me, I'm a doctor. Let me have a look little girl?" With tears in her eyes she looked at me in search of approval. "It's okay Tia." "Does it hurt here? What about here? That's good. It seems she just bruised her arm. She'll be fine." He patted her on the head. "Slow down on those skates okay?" "Thank you sir, I'm Franklin Green her father." "No problem I'm Dr. Pete Borowicz Pediatrician."

"Dad is she okay?" "Yes Tamara she just bruised her arm during the fall." "Franklin I think we should be going." "I agree, Tamara go ahead and say goodnight to your friends. We're about to leave." "Okay Dad."

Franklin removed Tia's skates while I removed mine. We then made our way to the car...

Franklin

"How does your arm feel Tia?" "It's much better Daddy…Can I have some ice cream?" "Sure you can sweetheart. We'll be near Dairy Queen in about 10 minutes." "Thank you Daddy." "You're welcome." Clarissa touched my shoulder and whispered so low that all I could do was read her lips. "Franklin you're being played." "I know but it's cute." We both snickered.

Tamara had been quiet since we left the skating ring. So after we pulled into the Dairy Queen Drive-thru, I asked if she would like some ice cream. "I'll just have a chocolate milk shake." "Clarissa what would you like?" "A strawberry/banana milkshake would be nice." "Tia you do want a cone right?" "Yes Daddy." "Welcome to Dairy Queen may I take your order please?" "Yes. I'll have a small ice cream cone, a large chocolate shake and two large strawberry/banana shakes. That will be all." "Okay, I have a small cone, a large chocolate shake, and two large strawberry/banana shakes. Is the order correct?" "Yes, that's perfect." "Your total is $7.51 please drive forward to the window."

"Dad can you play some music?" "What would you like to hear Radio or CD?" "I have the *Soul Food* soundtrack." "Well pass it to me baby. That's a good CD." "Franklin, speaking of CD's, the ones we bought for the girls will mature this month. We need to decide if they should roll forward." "I intended for them to roll forward if the interest rate was equal or greater." "Well I checked on-line yesterday and the advertised rates are higher." "Well that's an easy decision."

"Sir, your total is $7.51." I handed her $10.00. "Out of ten, your change is $2.49. Here's your ice cream cone." Here Tia. "Thank you daddy." "One Chocolate shake and two strawberry/banana shakes thank you and please come again." "Thank you. Here's your shakes Tamara, Clarissa." "Thank you. Thanks dad."

We arrived around 9pm. "All right everybody, we're here." "Daddy will you carry me to my room?" I looked at Clarissa. "Is that okay?" "Of course, do you think I'm going to carry her?" We both laughed. "Come on Tia." She put her arms around my neck and rested her head on my shoulder. "Franklin just put her to bed please. She can bathe in the morning before we go to church." "Okay but do you think you can unlock the door first?" "Oops! Tamara will you open the door for you father please?" She ran ahead of me unlocked the door and went directly inside.

I carried Tia into the bedroom and lay her on the bed. "Do you want me to tuck you in after you change clothes?" "Yes." "Okay, call me when you've changed." "Okay, Daddy." After exiting her room, I had gone no more than two paces when she called out. "Daddy you forgot to close my door." I smiled then reached back and closed the door. "Thank you Daddy."

Voices were coming from the den. I walked in and saw Tamara sitting in the corner of the couch with her feet tucked under her thighs. I cleared my throat to get her attention. "Oh, hi Dad, what's up?" "May a join you?" "Sure" "It seems you didn't waste time kicking off your shoes?" She giggled "No sir." "What are you watching? "It's called *The Parenthood*." "The Parenthood...that's with *Robert Townsend* right? "Yes sir." "Well I won't bother you with talking." "Dad...when are you coming home?" A lump developed in my throat when she asked. I had listened to Clarissa describe how awkward she felt but I never imagined...

"When are you coming home?" Her question pierced my heart because she never looked at me. She just starred at the Television and fired the question. It was as though she had heard the same answers time and time again and didn't want to see the face of indecision. Tia's call was timely giving me an opportunity to break away and give some thought to Tamara's question. "Hold that though while I go and tuck in your sister..."

"Hey precious are you ready for me to tuck you in?" "Yes and I've already said a prayer." "That's great! Well get ready here I come with a tuck to the right and a tuck to the left." She just laughed and smiled as usual. "Are you comfortable little lady?" She adjusted her head on the pillow. "Yes." I kissed her forehead then got up to leave the room. "Alright then, sleep tight." "Don't let the bed bugs bite." "Don't let *em* don't let *em*." Just before I closed the bedroom door she asked me to remind Clarissa to visit.

Passing Clarissa in the hallway, I sensed she already knew from experience that Tia had summoned. "I'm on my way." She spoke as we shared what seemed a brief intimate visit in the hallway.

When I entered the den Tamara was still seated. Upon clearing my throat she turned towards me to acknowledge my presence but said nothing. "Now, where were we?" "When are you coming home?" "Tamara, your mother and I need to discuss it but..." She used my pause as an opportunity to chime in with what seemed like sarcasm. "I know! I know! You love me!" "That's right sweetheart I love all of you." "Mom included?" "Yes absolutely, I never stopped loving either of you." "So why don't you tell her? Does she know?" "It's not that simple Tamara." "Why isn't it Dad?" "Sometimes adults aren't as smart as we think. We know that we should talk to each other but some of the things we need to say hurt those we love. I guess we foolishly leave those things unsaid." "That sounds cowardice. You and mom always told me to never be afraid...that love conquers everything." "I know sweetheart but..." "May I be excused?" "I think we should talk some more don't you?" "Yes but I'm tired so may I be excused?" "Okay." She pressed the remote to turn off the television then stood and walked over to kiss me on the cheek. "I love you dad." "I love you too Tamara." I stood there staring at the blank television screen. I had definitely mishandled this situation. As she walked past me I heard her say good night to Clarissa.

"Franklin, are you okay?" Clarissa approached me from behind touching my shoulder. "No I'm not. Our daughter just..." "I know I was standing in the hallway." "I felt so inept talking with her. It was like everything I said was interpreted as a convenient excuse. The sad part is that her perception is accurate. I mean why...can we legitimately say why I am not home?" "Let's not discuss this right now. Tamara may still be awake." "I know I'm just a little frustrated." "I understand but we can talk over dinner tomorrow. There're quite a few things we need to discuss without distraction."

"You're right...tomorrow we'll talk. Catching a glimpse of my reflection on the television screen I was suddenly saddened. "Clarissa, I should be going." "You don't have to leave." Oh my God what am I saying? The words seem to flow off my lips quite naturally without reservation. "Since tomorrow is your birthday, I'm sure the girls would enjoy having breakfast with you. And...so would I." "Are you sure?" "You know, I haven't been sure of many things lately but I can't recall a time I've been surer than I am right now."

Clarissa

The next morning, I awaken to Tia's voice. "Mommy, Mommy!" "What is it sweetheart?" "There's a stranger in Tamara's room." I looked at the clock. It was 7am and I had planned on sleeping until 8am. How foolish of me to even consider I might sleep late because Tia always wakes up at 7am on the weekends. "Come on mommy, I'll show you the stranger." I rolled out of bed and put on my housecoat. The likelihood of a stranger was nil considering the alarm had been activated before going to bed and Franklin had stayed the night. So before setting foot in Tamara's room, I knew whom I would find.

"Okay baby show me the stranger." She stood behind me and pointed. "Look! I told you there's a stranger in Tamara's room." "Silly, that's no stranger it's your father." Franklin raised his head with one eye open. "What's all the fuss about?" "Tia awakened me raving about a stranger. She was afraid because she saw you lying next to Tamara's bed. Come on out baby. See! It's your father. She thought you were a stranger." "Daddy I didn't know it was you." Her face brightened when she realized it was Franklin. She ran over and lept into his arms. "I guess your arm is no longer hurting?" When Tamara awakened, I wished for a camera to capture her delight. If ever there was a morning glow on someone's face she had it.

"Good morning Dad." "Good morning girls." "Happy birthday Franklin, I guess you couldn't ask for a better gift?" He winked and smiled at me. "You're right about that lady." "Happy Birthday Daddy!" "Thanks Clarissa, girls; a man could ask for nothing more than to be surrounded birthday morning by the most important people in his life." He kissed the girls on the cheeks one after the other. He then wrapped them both under his arms looking up at me and whispered thank you. I smiled then left them to enjoy each other.

Entering the den, I turned on the CD player. There was nothing I enjoyed more than listening to *Mahalia Jackson* on a Sunday morning. It always seemed to prepare my mind for church. Following the first note, I entered the kitchen to start breakfast. After a few minutes of laboring, I had prepared Franklin's favorite meal-cinnamon waffles with strawberries and crisp bacon on the side. "Franklin! Girls! Breakfast is ready." "Mommy did you make pancakes?" "No Tia, I decided to make waffles since it's your father's birthday." Tia scoffed and poked out her bottom lip. "I wanted pancakes." "Young lady I think you had better go back to your room and leave that attitude." "Yes mam." Tia walked away with her head down. She had gone only five seconds when I noticed her walking in behind Franklin. He walked in laughing and stood next to the refrigerator as I handed him a cup of coffee. All I could do was laugh at Tia's antics. "Good morning Clarissa." "Happy birthday Franklin, did you sleep well?" "Thank you, I slept perfectly. I can't think of any better place to have been for the night."

Tia was hiding behind him. "So young lady did you leave your attitude in the bedroom?" "Yes mam." "Well have a seat. We'll eat when your sister joins us." "Tamara! It's time to eat!" "Tia, you don't have to yell. She'll be here in a moment." Franklin seated himself then I sat across from him. He took a sip from his cup then placed it on the table. "You still make the best cup of coffee I ever tasted." "Thanks." Tamara came in seated herself and said, "Good morning everyone." "Franklin, would you please bless the table for us?" "It would be my pleasure." We all joined hands as Franklin offered the prayer.

While Tamara and Tia chatted about the previous night, I took the opportunity to engage Franklin about his plans. "So Franklin, how do you plan to spend the remainder of your day?" "I assume we'll still have dinner." "Tsk, besides dinner silly." "Well, I know you're probably going to church so I intended on joining you, if it's okay?" "Oh really and when did you intend to discuss that with me?" The girls zeroed in on his comment. "Please mommy. Let's all go to church together." The thought was lovely but I couldn't prevent my temperature from rising. As usual Franklin had sold the girls on an idea before he discussed it with me. I picked up my cup of coffee holding it up to my face as I stared across its rim directly into his eyes. I wanted him to see my displeasure. If my stare were lethal, I'd surely be wearing a black dress next week.

Franklin looked at me and almost stumbled over his words. "Ah, Lets' not get too excited girls. Your mother and I haven't discussed it…" He glanced at me as he continued. "I don't have a change of cloths anyway." "Mommy has your suit in her closet." My stomach dropped when Tia uttered those words. After I asked Franklin to leave he had taken all his cloths except the gray suit I had given him. I loved that suit and since I had bought it the thought of taking it to the Salvation Army never crossed my mind. "That's nice sweetheart but I still need to discuss it with your mother." Tamara looked at the both of us then got up grabbing her sister's arm. "Tia, come on. Let's get dressed for church." "Thanks Tamara I'll be there to comb her hair shortly." "Forgive me Clarissa, I should have told you last night." I waited until Tamara turned the corner. "You should have told me what Franklin?" "I-I want to spend my birthday with you Clarissa." My heart warmed from his words. His eyes had conveyed more to me than any words he could say. I exhaled and whispered, "Me too." I then stood without looking him in the eyes. "Please excuse me while I get the girls ready. Your suit is in the back of the closet." "Thank you Clarissa."

Franklin

I finished my breakfast then pondered over what had just happened. During the course of our marriage, I had only gone to church a hand full of times. Clarissa had always gone but she never forced the issue with me. I wasn't sure if my determination to be with them was influenced by a need for family or desperation to attend the sanctuary I had avoided for so long. Regardless of the motive, I was on my way.

After finishing my cup of coffee, I got up and walked into the bedroom. It had been a year since I stepped into this room but things appeared the same. The king sized master bed was adorned with silk linen. The cherry dresser and chest were accented with photographs of family members and Clarissa's stuffed animals. She always kept the bedroom fresh and pleasantly decorated. Entering the bathroom the fresh garden scent entered my nostrils circulating my entire body. "This is definitely home."

Opening the shower door, I started the water then undressed. Upon entering, the hot pulsating spray began to soothe my tired body. When I exited the shower Clarissa was seated at the vanity styling her hair. The awkwardness of the moment caused my body to perspire. I wasn't sure if she took notice of me so I quickly grabbed a towel and dried myself.

"Clarissa, what time do we need arrive at the church?" "Morning worship begins at 11am." I smiled glimpsing at the clock realizing she hadn't gotten dressed. In fact she still wore her housecoat. We had about 60 minutes to dress and make the 10-minute drive to church. "Clarissa, do you think we'll make it?" "Of course we will there's plenty time." I snickered recalling the many times we had been late for engagements because of how slowly she dressed.

It felt strange dressing in her presence. Though we were married the last year had crumbled the comfort that used to exist between us. There was however another small token of my existence reflected in a bottle of cologne on the counter. She, just as I, had not erased the details of our lives together. I only wished that we hadn't arrived at our present state. "Clarissa, I'm happy that you kept my suit but I think you might find it a little embarrassing if I entered the church wearing sneakers." She turned to look at me and began laughing. "Franklin dear, it doesn't matter what you're wearing." "Well, I insist on stopping by my apartment for shoes." "Okay, if you must but you had better get going if you intend to go with us." "Okay, I'll be back before you're ready to leave." "That's fine I'll be ready when you return."

After gathering my things, I walked towards the door passing the girls as they were dressed and seated in the great room. "Girls, I need to stop by the apartment and get some shoes, I'll be back shortly." "Can we ride with you daddy?" "Sure Tia, just go and ask your mother." "I'll stay here dad." Tia took off towards the bedroom and asked Clarissa if she could leave with me. After getting permission she took a detour to her room and returned with a walkman. "Okay, I'm ready daddy." "Tamara, are you sure you don't want to go?" "I'm sure."

On the way to my apartment Tia started singing. I was amazed how lively she had become. Tamara was quiet and reserved but Tia courted attention. Her new artist of choice to mimic happened to be *Brandy*. I couldn't think of a more positive teen idol for my little angel. Her mother had mentioned that she never missed an episode of the sitcom. "Daddy, do you like Brandy?" "The music sounds nice sweetheart but you know I prefer jazz. I'm a bit too old for hip-hop." She looked at me smiling. "Did you kiss mommy last night?" My mouth dropped so wide I could taste the dryness in the air. "Tia, what makes you ask such a question?" "You were talking and smiling last night. It was the same way you used to before you moved away." I smiled knowing her observation was on the mark. "Okay, not that it's the business of a ten year old but I did not kiss your mother last night." "Well you should have. I know she wanted you to kiss her." "Okay, I'll play along. How could you possibly know young lady?" "Mommy said...Never mind." "What did mommy say?" "Never mind." I started laughing. "It's only because you're a ten-year old that I won't pressure you for an answer."

"Okay sweetheart, we're here." "Daddy, do you have some ice cream?" "Yes sweetheart but we don't have time for ice cream." "What kind?" "Tia, come on now, we don't have time." "I just want to know what kind you have Daddy." "Well, you know I love strawberry so take a guess." She smiled and poked out her bottom lip. "Ooh, can I have some?" "Tia, are you trying to sweet talk me?"

She blinked her eyes. "Please?" "Maybe later sweetheart, besides your mother is waiting for us."

When we returned it was 10:55. "Tia why don't you stay in the car I'll get your mother and Tamara." I walked quickly towards the door but before my hand could touch it the door opened. Clarissa was standing there waiting with her purse in hand. She wore an ivory colored dress accented with the pearl necklace and earrings I had given her five years ago. Her hair was tied in a bun highlighting her cheekbones and flawless skin. "You're late Franklin." "Only five minutes." She scoffed. "Well we're ready. Come on Tamara." She zipped past me then quickly looked back observing me from head to toe. "By the way Franklin, you look handsome." "Thanks for the compliment and I must say you look absolutely gorgeous."

After finally finding a parking space, we all exited the car and walked briskly towards the entrance. "Good morning Sister Green, how are you this morning?" "I'm doing quite well and you?" The woman smiled and said, "I'm blessed." "Mr. Green it's wonderful to see you too." "Thank you mam." The ushers were extremely pleasant. They were the first to meet us and genuinely made me feel welcomed.

Once we entered the sanctuary, I leaned towards Clarissa's ear as she walked to be seated and whispered. "She seemed very nice and cheerful." Clarissa smiled at the usher leading us then turned to me and whispered as we navigated the pews. "That's her purpose Franklin. This is the house of the LORD and everyone wants you to feel welcomed." The church was a beautiful sight. It had the feel of a theater with velvet carpet, bright lights and plush seating. The anchor of the sanctuary was a pulpit accented with silk foliage. All the pews flowed from the anchor in a horseshoe fashion. You could actually sit down without having to turn your neck to see the choir or the pastor. It was different from any other church I had visited. Each person we had passed smiled and whispered good morning. I hoped Clarissa and the usher wouldn't move too close towards the front because I didn't want any attention. "Franklin we're going up front." So much for wishful thinking-I couldn't remember many things about my previous church visits but one thing seemed the same. Even though a church is filled you can bank on a reserved seat for the latecomers nestled in the front pews conveniently located in the pastor's line of vision. So if you happen to be a visitor harboring any reservations about being identified your cover was blown. Luckily Clarissa was a regular so I wouldn't have to go through the drill.

An elderly gentleman stood in front and greeted everyone. "How's everybody doin? GOD has blessed me with another day. Um glad about it. GOD is good." The church responded in unison, "All the time." "And all the time." "GOD is good." He had a Ray Charles look about him, wearing dark glasses and smiling as he spoke but since he was standing alone, I felt assured he wasn't completely like Mr. Ray Charles. As he smiled, you could see his single gold tooth. He was bald with a deep baritone voice that reminded me of Barry White. After a few words of reflection he began singing. "*Can't No-bod-y Do me like Jesus…*" Clarissa stood and began swaying and clapping. I felt slightly embarrassed until I noticed that she wasn't alone. All around me people began standing one by one. It was as though they had received some secret cue from the music, the lyrics and his voice which all combined to create an uplifting spiritual mood. The atmosphere was euphoric.

Following the singing the Deacon proceeded to read the lyrics of a song. He then sang them as everyone followed. "*Father I stretch my hand to Thee. No other help I know…If thou should withdraw thyself from me…Where Shall I go…*" I was surprised when I felt a burning in my chest as the song progressed. The delivery of the song and the words tugged at something within me. The old man ended the song with some improvisational lyrics that stirred the entire congregation. "*I need-thee-O-I need Thee…*" Everyone faded off with the lyrics and began humming as another Deacon stepped forward and began praying. I bowed my head and heard the words "*Thank You LORD*" bouncing from every wall. Although I would never admit to it, I found myself welcoming the word Amen. I believed in GOD but I could never grasp what seemed to me as nothing more than a ritual.

The church quieted to the point you could hear a pin drop. This lasted about 5 seconds when this vocal and vivacious woman strolled down the aisle shouting: "Praise the Lord Church." Everyone responded in unison. "Praise the Lord." "I said, Praise the Lord Church." She welcomed everyone to the service and reminded us that we were considered family in GOD's house. There was a resounding Amen from all quarters. She then walked towards the back of the church and out of sight.

The pastor stood and asked: "If there is someone visiting here with us for the first time would you please stand?" His eyes were so fixed upon me that it felt like a touch which I later realized was Clarissa nudging me. "Or if you've just been away for a while, would please stand and say good morning to us?" I just sat there feeling as though all heads had turned towards me even though that was not the case. Clarissa rescued me from the embarrassment when she stood and said that she brought her husband along with her and the girls.

Afterwards, the pastor extended further greetings then began singing. As the words flowed from his mouth, people got up from their seats and walked around exchanging hugs. *"There's a sweet-sweet spirit-in this place. And-I know-that it's the spirit-of the lord...There's a sweet expression-on each face..."* We sang and prayed some more followed by tithing and a soul wrenching altar prayer that was highlighted by song from the male chorus. I enjoyed the prayer but was becoming restless by the time the pastor read the scripture.

"There is a sweet spirit in this place. I want to thank our visiting ministers and pastors for sharing with us this morning. It's amazing how GOD works. Sometimes we have trouble on every side. The male chorus said; *Pass Me Not O Gentle Savior.* Now that is very personal. *Hear my humble cry.* We're not angry when the LORD blesses someone we just want to receive a blessing. Amen."

"There is a word from the LORD that comes from the Old Testament." He read from *Daniel 3:17–18* and offered as the thought for his sermon; *even if He Don't...* I can't explain it but somehow my restlessness subsided as I read along with him and listened to the sermon. His words flowed from his mouth with purpose and I felt as though they were directed at me. "Shadrach, Meshach and Abednego let the king know that even if HE doesn't save us-That's our message-we will not serve your Gods. Even if HE finds pleasure in our suffering or mistreatment, Even if HE wants to make examples of three Christians, Even if we burn to death and HE looks the other way ignoring all we've stood for and have done. Even if HE don't deliver us we will still not bow down. My brothers and sisters there comes a time in life that we simply have to take a stand and say to Satan, Even if he don't, We know HE's able. So we're not going to submit to you" (Yeah!) He went on with a personal testimony then followed with his main thought. "Even if he Don't, I believe it's not because HE can't. Sometimes when situations enter our lives and we don't understand the reason, don't think GOD has exhausted all his power. GOD allows things to happen in our lives sometimes to make us a better person or strengthen our faith. (Amen!) This is a faith message. I'm reminded of Abraham, you know the story. He was told by GOD to go over yonder."

His words stirred memories deep within me. I began recalling a tape Clarissa had been playing once when I visited the girls. The message was about forgiveness. "You know some people can't handle GOD's blessings? Spend so much time complaining and drowning in self-pity they can't see GOD's goodness. Walking around saying I've been hurt or mistreated. So busy drowning in pity can't realize they woke up this morning. (Thank Ya!) Can't realize they got food on the table. Some folk can't appreciate the husband or wife at home. Just dying inside from being wrapped all up in anger and self-pity. We even have people right here in the church that have been mistreated and exhausting precious moments in life trying to figure a way to get even. The only person hurt by hanging on to anger is you. Truth is told the very person you're angry with is moving on with their life and here you are unable to receive your blessings because of anger. You know I can hold my hands to my face and I see ten blessings (Yeah!) You ought to be able to say Thank you Jesus! Thank You Sir! (Thank Ya!) You ought to be able to love somebody in spite of. (Yeah!) You ought to be able to forgive. Oh I tell ya! There's a man name Jesus. (Yeah!) You know the story. Luke 23; 34 He said father forgive them for they know not what they do. Every now and then you got to let go of some things, you got to forgive sometimes to see your blessings."

All this wisdom came from the same man and now I was merging the messages. He then proceeded to paraphrase the story relating other stories from the bible (Philippeans 4:10–12). "There's a story of a man that prayed for a car. He asked GOD to bless him with a car so that he could attend church. He finally got the car but forgot to pay for it. The entire time he had the car he couldn't find the church. The car was later reprocessed. He began praying again and asked the Lord to walk with him to church. We need to be more appreciative."

I looked at the ceiling contemplating the two messages and drifted to some other existence. The next thing I knew the pastor was singing and inviting people to join the church. *"I thought number one-would surely be me, I thought I could be-what I wanted to be, I thought I could build on light sinking sand-but I can't even walk without you holding my hand. LORD help us. I thought I could do…"* Clarissa was standing with her arms outstretched from the elbow and her palms toward the ceiling. I glimpsed at the tear flowing down the left side of her face then reached for her right hand gently squeezing when I felt her softness. She looked at me and whispered "GOD bless you Franklin."

Clarissa

The drive home was tranquil. Tamara was reading a vibe magazine that was left on the backseat and Tia listened to her walk-man. Franklin had been distant since we left the church. When he touched my hand during service, I had noticed his eyes were filled. I wanted to talk but it seemed the silence was what he needed more than anything. So I just reached towards the door pressing the switch to recline my seat and meditated on the pastor's message. I loved Franklin and it was time I let him know. After all he is my blessing.

Once we arrived in the driveway, I returned the seat to its upright position and picked up my purse. The girls had already exited and started towards the door. Franklin just sat there. I had one foot inside the car and the other on the driveway when I turned towards him. "Franklin would you like to join us for lunch?" I was surprised at the nervousness in my voice. He looked at me and before he could speak his expression had already conveyed his thoughts. My heart sank from disappointment but I was determined to conceal my feelings. I conjured up a nonchalant tone and quickly retorted. "That's if you don't have prior plans." "Thanks Clarissa, I would love to but I'd like to have some time alone." I wanted to ask if something was wrong but didn't want to seem overbearing. "Okay, just know that the offer still stands if you are hungry later in the afternoon." "Thanks, there're just some things I need to sort."

There was a long pause. The kind that let's you know something needs to be said but the words and time are still out of sync. Then like a snap of the finger he took a reprieve from his trance and spoke. "I'll pick you up later this evening for the show right?" "Yes, I'm looking forward to it." The girls had already gotten out and were waiting near the door. "Mom, can you open the door? I want to change and go over to Tramane's house." "Tamara I gave you a key. Where is it?" "I left it on my dresser. Can you let me in please?" "Well Franklin, I'll see you in a few hours." He nodded then waved towards the girls.

"Okay, bye girls." When he backed away, I walked briskly towards the door grimacing with each step. I needed to get out of these pumps and my dogs were reminding me with each step as they began to ache.

"Mommy will Daddy be back?" "Yes Tia, we're going to a concert tonight." "Who's going to sit with us?" "I'm sorry sweetheart I thought I told you Miss Tyler will be with you this evening." "I like Miss Tyler. So, can I stay up as late as I want tonight?" "You must be kidding? According to the calendar you have another three weeks of school and tonight's a school night. That reminds me, I need to make sure Tyler didn't forget."

Tyler was like a big sister to the girls. They loved being around her partly because she could dance. When I told her the girls danced she got excited and began telling them about her days on the college dance team. She even showed them some moves, which Tamara wove into her own solo routine. Her dance instructor even gave her permission to use the routine in competition.

With that thought, I picked up the phone and sat on the sofa. "Hey girl how are you doing?"

Franklin

Driving down the freeway, I began recalling what the preacher had said about going through some terrible times and not understanding the reason. It happened to me and I cursed everyone. There seemed no logical reason to accept the notion of being used to fulfill some higher purpose. The only purpose the situation served was my forced submission to Sheila's sick sexual demands. I recalled the times Sheila touched me and I asked myself if GOD was present why did he allow this to happen to me. He had to have heard my cry or seen my tears each time she pulled and handled my juvenile body. Surely he knew I found no satisfaction in Sheila taking my body for her selfish pleasures.

I had never read the book of Daniel much less known of Shadrach, Meshach and Abednego, but the way the preacher described their courage made it apparent they believed GOD knew their peril. Yet the three men held on to something more powerful than could be explained. They revered and trusted so faithfully that nothing could break their strength or spirits. Not even fire.

My mother often spoke about that kind of faith and unconditional trust. For all practical purposes she even raised me to believe the same but Sheila changed all that for me. If she only knew what Sheila had done to her son, I wonder if that would have changed or challenged her faith.

After arriving home, I reflected on an audio sermon Clarissa had played. It was a sermon about Christians that hang on to baggage. The message went on to explain how doing so causes someone to miss their blessings. I couldn't recall the scripture but the theme was *turning things over to Jesus*. After shutting off the car's ignition, I sat for a moment to consider the message. The thought of missing or not seeing a blessing because of anger was beneath my character. I would never permit anger to obscure my view. Besides, I had made some good decisions and done quite well in spite of Sheila. Colleagues even seek me out for advice in reverence to my success. I cried and called for help once but it never came when I needed it. So whatever faith I had is now stretched beyond any foreseeable repair. As far as Sheila goes, I really hadn't given it much thought. I just hated with a passion and felt completely justified.

For years this had been my thought process. I would have convinced myself again had the sermons not kept ringing in my head. *(Faith, Turning Over to Jesus, Meshach, Shadrach and Abednego)* Did something pass me by without my knowing? I've always considered myself disciplined and the rewards have been many. I completed college, retired from the Navy, I'm a successful businessman with two wonderful children and...I snatched the keys from the ignition and opened the car door. "That's some bullshit! Clarissa asked me to leave." After exiting the car, I slammed the door then pressed the button to activate the car alarm.

"Good afternoon Franklin." I nearly tripped when Brenda Livingston spoke. I turned to see her walking along the driveway. She waved with her right hand and held a newspaper in her left. On any other afternoon, I would have been flattered to see her flirtatious smile but today was not a typical afternoon. "Oh! Good afternoon Brenda." "Are you alright? You nearly fell." I put on a 3-cent smile and said; "I'm fine thank you, just a little preoccupied." "Well you have a wonderful day." "Thanks and you do the same."

After entering the apartment, I checked for messages then walked towards the stereo and searched through my CD's. Had I been blessed and blinded by anger? I pondered that question as my eyes surveyed every CD. I wasn't certain what my body needed musically but as far back as I can remember the prescription to clear my thoughts had always been embedded in song. My CD's were arranged alphabetically so as I perused each one, I recited the melody in my mind. Several melodies had passed when I reached the "C" section. The *Commodores* featuring *"All the Great Love Songs"* wow...it's been a long time since I've heard these tunes. I removed The CD from its case inserting it into the CD player. My thoughts were heavy and my body too weak to stand so I sat on the sofa kicked off my shoes and extended my legs. With one click of a button, I began meditating on all that I heard as *Lionel Richie* romantically echoed the lyrics of *Still* in the background.

What had brought Clarissa and I to this point escaped me. There seemed no apparent connection to our separation and my childhood. Deep inside, I held onto some personal issues but in my mind that had nothing to do with our relationship. Clarissa was assertive and smart but certainly no Sheila. So why were we apart? What had I done? Where had we gone wrong? We have two wonderful children, a home and a comfortable lifestyle. Our lives had been beautiful until she asked me to leave under the guise that I was the reason. I had never treated her in any of the ways she claimed. At least I felt certain at that time.

My degree of certainty diminished as I sat there recalling all those stolen moments. Unspoken thoughts of Sheila would creep into our intimacy and steal from me just as she did when I was young. Feeling weak and pitiful, I needed some control-needed to feel strong even at the expense of someone who had no idea what I felt inside. "Goddamn baggage!"

Clarissa and I had been married 17 years most of which I spent away at sea or some other assignment. Although we met in New York where she had been working, she loved the southeast so we decided to buy our retirement home in Jacksonville. I lived most of that time as a geographical bachelor so Clarissa never experienced my rare moments until after my retirement two years ago. Nightmares about Sheila were sporadic but they did occur leaving me trembling and uttering in my sleep.

Prior to my retirement my visits home were anticipated and extremely exhausting upon arrival. There was always a long *Honey Do* list to accomplish not to mention spending time with Clarissa and the kids. After all that, I would be too tired to dream of sadness. Of course after leaving the Navy that all has changed. I'm home every day and the anticipation and excitement to see one another is different.

I leaned my head back, looked towards the ceiling and closed my eyes. It was the summer of 1996 that I revealed some baggage in a way no wife ever wants to discover. The chiming of the clock disrupted my journey back in time. At that moment I realized why my home had been an apartment for the last year.

After a few moments of simmering thought, I reached for the phonebook and began scrolling. Thompson, Thompson, where is that number? Once I located the number, I stood and picked up the phone.

"Hello." "H-H-Hi Sheila, this is Franklin. Please don't hang up the phone. I won't take up much of your time." To my surprise she wouldn't slam the phone in my ear. As ghetto as she is, I could phone to tell her off but never get the chance. I never bothered trying to see her because of fear I might end up incarcerated after putting her through the torture I had contemplated. "What do you want Franklin?" "I-I-I'm not sure. I've been thinking about some things. You know, I can't forget what you did to me and I really don't' understand why you hurt me but…" "Franklin that was over 30 years ago and I don't have time for your shit!" I felt tears flowing down my cheek. Lord please, give me strength right now! "Now I have to go, I'm busy." "I-I-I forgive you. I forgive you Sheila for hurting me-I hope that you have found happiness."

Following the third ring a female answered the phone. "Hello." I couldn't speak. Everything I rehearsed in my mind escaped me and I couldn't utter a word. I wiped my tears and cleared my throat. "I'm sorry I have the wrong number." The tramp didn't even recognize my voice. Not that she should have but after hearing hers I had no intention on forgiving. I was fuming inside and if she were nearby that would be her last breath. I hung up the phone and opened my mental suitcase returning the anger to its proper place.

Lionel Riche continued to fill the room slowly returning me to my safe haven. I had to question myself for allowing such sadness to enter my thoughts and change the mood I had been feeling. Moments later the telephone rang startling me. I was relieved when I answered and discovered it was not Sheila playing the caller ID game but my mother. I hadn't spoken with my parents in a few days and it was always a pleasure to talk with mom.

"I love you mother!" "Ohh, I love you too son. Is something wrong?" "No mother, I just thought you should know. Can I tell you I love you from time to time without cause?" She knew her son well but I just hoped on this occasion my response would suffice and she wouldn't press the issue. "Sure you can and if that's all you're doing I won't pressure you." I asked her about dad and if anything in particular was going on. We did a little more chitchat and said goodbye.

Following our conversation I jumped into the shower and began musing over my pending birthday celebration with Clarissa…

Tyler

My head began to throb as soon as my eyes opened. I instantly knew this would be another one of my bad days. I had been tossing and turning throughout the night. The dream coupled with Miles' familiar touch made me ill.

He held me tightly around the waist and I could feel him throbbing against my lower back. A deep sigh proceeded by a slight roll of my eyes, coupled with a subtle escape from contact took over my restless body. My stomach as usual began to boil. I wanted desperately to confront him about those letters but fear overcame my curiosity. So I just lay there searching my mind for some indicators anything that I may have missed or ignored that would have suggested something was wrong.

My quest was futile, nothing had happened. He wasn't different nor did he treat me as anything less than the most important person in his life. I pondered that thought as his warm body nestled against mine.

I knew he wanted to make love but offered no encouragement. My limp body just lay there hoping that he would leave me the *Hell* alone. I guess that was wishful thinking on my part because he began massaging my breast. I sighed then spoke softly. "Don't Miles, I need to use the bathroom." "All right baby, I'll wait for you." I wanted to gag but instead I reminded him that Lamar was in the other room. Most days I was okay but every once in a while, I would have dreams and thoughts that just irked me. My mother used to say that I had the memory of an elephant. I considered it a positive quality but she always said I would never learn to forgive anyone. I'm not sure about all that but I wanted to punish him and convinced my position would be justified.

I quickly made my way to bathroom planting my bottom on the porcelain throne. The cold surface seemed to trigger the release of that boiling sensation I felt when I had awaken. I could have powered the entire state of Florida with all that activity.

"Damn Tyler! Are you okay in there?" I scoffed and slammed the door. "Screw you Miles!" I could hear him laughing. "Don't forget to turn on the fan!"

(Knock! Knock!) "Tyler, I'm sorry are you okay?" "My stomach is just a little upset and my head aches other than that I'm fine." "Can I bring you something?" "No, I'll be okay…"

"I'm going to wake up Lamar and see if he wants in on some exercise. Would you like to tag along?" "He's leaving today right?" "Yes, sometime this afternoon." "You two go ahead, I'm going to read a book and relax. Maybe I'll be able to get rid of this headache." "Do you want to do anything special later this afternoon?" "Did you forget what I told you? I'm sitting with Clarissa's kids this evening." "Oh yes, It slipped my mind. She and Franklin are going out for his birthday right?" "Yes." "Alright, I'll be back in a few hours."

I sat and listened to Miles and Lamar talking as they walked through the house. After they left, I showered and got dressed. I hadn't planned on doing much so I slipped on one of Miles' oversized t-shirts, shorts and a pair of thick socks. Opening the bedroom door, the lingering smell triggered a hunger sensation. The lion inside immediately began to roar. When I walked into the kitchen breakfast and a magazine were placed on the table. I smiled examining the spread…Grits, eggs, bacon, toast and orange juice with an *Essence* magazine…

Once I finished eating, my mind began prioritizing my list of activities for the day. Wash the laundry, dust the house, vacuum the carpet, mop the kitchen floor and finish my book. I had always prided myself on having my priorities perfectly aligned so after entering the great-room I took a quick survey, picked up my book and sat on the sofa…

The images in my mind were shattered when the telephone rang. I took a quick glance at the clock and realized several hours had passed. "Page 367, Dang just a few more to go." I counted the remaining pages of my book as the phone rang a fourth time. "Shoot! I still don't know the identity of the murderer." I contemplated speed-reading but decided against it fearing I might miss an important clue. After all I had finished more than 350 pages and still guessed.

The phone rang a fifth time when I reached a good stopping point. After a few moments of mental deliberation, I put the book aside an answered the phone. "Hello." "Girl I was about to hang up the phone." "Well you should have. I was deep into this book." "Well excuse me Miss Thang! I just called to verify that you're still sitting with the girls." "Now Clarissa, I'm offended that you even feel the need to ask." "I'm sorry but you can never take anything for granted." "I'll be there between 5 pm and 5:30 pm." "Thanks. So, what are you reading?" "I was about to find out who the murderer is in *Nora Roberts* new book." "Well pass the book this way when you finish." "Okay." We talked for a few more minutes but I ended it when Clarissa asked about our conversation from the other night. I was definitely *trippin* and knew that she would feel the same. Besides, my headache was gone and my stomach had settled and I was determined not to allow anything to steal my joy.

After talking with Clarissa, I returned to my book. Ten minutes later I discovered the answer I had suspected some 4 hours earlier.

Miles

"Whew!!!" I stopped in front of Lamar and began running in place. "That was a good sweat." "It looks that way, so how far did you run?" "I try to run at least three miles every other day but I have to say you surprised me." "How did I do that?" "I thought you were giving me a head start like when we were kids." "Not me my brother, I stopped running since becoming a little short-winded these days." "With all the weight you've lost I would have assumed differently." I pointed towards an oak tree as I gathered my breath. "Let's take a seat on that bench." "That sounds good."

A squirrel was sitting upright near the bench nibbling on an acorn. As we approached it disappeared onto the tree. "That breakfast idea was nice Miles." I jerked my head. "That was abrupt." Lamar ignored my comment and began talking. "You've got a wonderful lady. You two have been together for five years right?" "Actually, it's been a total of six years." "Is that right?" "I know it doesn't seem that long but it has been." "It's cool that you do little things like that for her." I looked into the trees as birds begin to chirp. "It wasn't much I just knew she would be hungry." "Well it shows that she's in your thoughts." I nodded my head smiling simultaneously. "True!" "So, where did you learn to be so considerate?" "I guess some of Mom's goodness stayed with me." "I could have used some of that goodness in my own life." His face was stiff and emotionless so I slapped him on the thigh to generate some action. "Hey Bro, what's going on?" "Do you remember when we were growing up how you always tried to do the things I had done?" "Yeah, you objected and if my memory is correct you would always leave me behind." "Get out of here! I always included you." "Yeah right, do you remember when I was learning to ride my bike?" "Yes. What about it?" "You would always take-off down the street with your friends leaving me on the driveway holding up my bike. I was the coolest non-bicycle riding, standing in front of the house holding a new bike kid on the block."

Lamar shoved my shoulder and started laughing. "I'm sorry for laughing but the way you said it kinda *tripped* me out." I scoffed. "You knew I was having trouble getting the bike going. I accidentally got started one afternoon while cooling on the slope at the edge of the driveway. I was straddled with both feet on the ground holding the bike when I slipped and the bike started rolling down the drive. From that point on I've been riding." He motioned his finger in the air as though to suggest "Ahah, now you've got it!" "That's right, I wanted you to do things for yourself and not depend on me." "Well that's not the way I felt. To be honest I often envied you because everything you wanted came easy. Whether it was sports, friends or anything you wanted to attempt." I scoffed. "You could even get the ladies without effort. I on the other hand had a heavy burden. You were considered cute and I…Well I just existed."

He remained silent as I observed two elderly men jogging past. "I remember…People called you Dumbo because of your ears?" "Yeah that was some trifling shit. Remember that dude named Lenny? That brother hung out with all the popular fellas. When I walked to school he and those guys would stand near the entrance pointing and laughing. It seemed like they waited there every morning for six years so I could walk by and give them a morning laugh. I hated it and sometimes arrived late so as not to see them when I walked by. I was glad when they went to junior high believing their departure would give me a break for at least a year. But that was wishful thinking because the kids my age had picked up where he left off.

Remember that girl Victoria Cooper?" "Yeah, she was the bully." "Yeah among other things, you know that girl sat across from me in class. She must have had her sexual drive early because she would sit with her legs open sporting a short yellow dress. The girl would whisper at me during our individual reading periods and point to her twat. I ignored her and following that I became the subject of her jokes. And because the scrub had many followers the same shit Lenny had been doing continued. Then of course there was Portia. You do remember Portia Patterson?" "Yeah, she's on crack these days." "Well that's too bad but you know I talked with her over the phone back in the day. She thought I was the man until we met. The girl actually walked over gave me a hug and patted me on the back. Do you know how impersonal that felt? She might as well have kept that cheesy gesture to herself. She never called me again after that meeting."

"Well she wasn't right for you and besides you've got Tyler now." I gave him some *Dap* and said: "I know that's right but I still envied your ass." Lamar looked away in silence. "What ever happened to us Lamar?" "What are you talking about? You and I are straight." He uttered the words with very little conviction so I knew there was a definite validity to my curiosity. Picking up an acorn, he rolled it around between his fingers then tossed it onto the pavement. "What inspired you towards college?" I sighed, shook my head then picked up an acorn and rolled it between my fingers. "A need to get away, discover myself and make my own way. It's funny because my belief was that if I could attend college then somehow I would measure up." "Measure up to what exactly?" I stood and threw the acorn up into the tree. "People like Lamar, Portia and Victoria.

Do you know the most frustrating thing for a teenage boy?" "What would that be?" "It's a natural inability to generate or capture even the slightest interest among your female contemporaries not to mention male friends. To be considered an equal and not an outcast. I was so pathetic that the out crowd revoked my request for membership. And ladies…did you know I watched soaps with mom to understand what women want? I even read some of her Harlequin romance novels for tips and learned a lot but could never get to first base. Hell, there were times I wished I had a million dollars so I could change some things about myself and be more like you or one of those popular singers back in the day. Truth is told some of them were ugly but just had money and a record label."

I looked directly at him making eye contact. "Not any more though." "What's changed?" "I'm educated and I have money and that's the great equalizer." "Is that right?" "Damn straight." I started pacing around the bench. "There is no woman that wants a brotha without a J.O.B and an education. All I have to do is continue excelling and I'm in the house." "Miles…when will you become satisfied with yourself?" I stopped pacing then sat and looked directly in his face. "Satisfied? Please! I held my palm to his face. A brother can't get anywhere being satisfied." "You said you wanted to discover yourself which indicates to me you wanted to uncover your purpose, is that right?" I nodded my head in agreement. "That's true and until I find it I'm all about the knowledge and cash money my brother." "Well, maybe satisfied is a poor description but at some point you've got to learn to be happy with yourself." "What makes you think otherwise?" "Listen to what you said: "There's no woman that wants a brotha without a J.O.B and an education." "That's right!" "And let's not forget this juvenile need to equal or surpass people from junior high. Why after all this time do those people have power over you? Why are you concerned with all that shit as an adult not to mention married as well?" I scoffed; "Hey man, don't start *trippin* on me. I thought you wanted to talk about something?" "All

I'm saying is that until you're happy with yourself-nothing you do will make a difference." "What are you talking about? I'm straight you're the one with issues."

He rolled his eyes and held up his hand. "Listen, I love you and I'm proud to have you as my brother." "There you go changing again and what's with the touchy feely attitude?" "I just wanted you to hear the words from me. We allow too many days to go by without telling people how we feel." "Why don't you tell Brittany?" "Touché, touché you are absolutely correct my brother. But I tell her and junior daily so that they never forget. They both know." "Well if that's true then why are you two apart?"

"How's the music going?" "So, you're changing subjects again? I'm having a tough time keeping up with you but to answer your question the music is fine. In fact, we performed in a talent show at *Natilies* Friday night." "How did things turn out?" "It was nice but we didn't win." "Sorry to hear that." "No big deal we were just having fun jamming anyway." "Was it a tough crowd?" "Actually, they seemed to love us but that just wasn't enough." "Tyler must love the idea of having her personal sax man?" I scoffed; "she doesn't care much for that part of my life." "Why would you say that? I thought you two shared that experience." "Tyler asks me to play something for her but she never comes to hear it. She would rather remain home reading a book." "That's precious time wasted my brother." I picked up a small twig and tossed it across the grass. "Tell me about it."

"Did you know that Brittany lost her mother to cancer?" I threw my hands up. "Lamar you're killing me with all the different subjects." "She died about two years ago. Brittany went through hell and nearly had a breakdown." "Damn, I didn't know all that." "We kept it from everyone. After the funeral she talked about how much it irked her that people had the nerve to show up crying as she lay in a casket but never took the time to show up while she lived." He dropped his head. "A whole lot of moments wasted." "That's deep." "I promised myself my baby would never feel like that again." He frowned and shook his head. "Now look where we find ourselves." "What do you mean? You can still go back to her you know."

Lamar stood and began pacing. He looked as though he carried the weight of the world on his shoulders. "Do you remember telling me about Desiree?" "What! Where the hell did that come from?" "I don't mean to bring up the past but you do remember?" "Yes and as a matter of fact you started laughing. I believe you said something to the effect that…Slipping like that wasn't me and that I didn't have the look or the attitude of someone who would screw up in that way." He started smiling and nodded his head. "You were swept off your feet by attention. I didn't know what to say at the time but I can tell you now without a doubt. You can't love or define yourself through another person's eyes." "What are you talking about?" "Tsk. You don't get it." "Duh, I'm afraid I don't." "If you define yourself by what others say or think then what do you have when they're nowhere around?" "Please, that's simple just find some more people. Screw that being alone shit." He threw his hands up. "I'm not talking about being alone *brotha*. I'm talking about finding your purpose, loving yourself and being happy with who you are. I'm talking about remaining true to yourself and your purpose regardless what goes on around you." "Where is all this shit coming from? Is this what you wanted to talk with me about?" "I just have a new perspective and wanted to share it."

I sighed and looked down at the grass. "You know I hated myself for getting in that situation. When I started dating Tyler, I wanted to be her everything...but fell short. I can remember foolishly dreaming that I could scrub away that segment of my life and continue being the perfect man. She deserved it and I desperately wanted her to have it."

He smiled then slapped me on the shoulder. "Well I guess you missed a significant portion of mom's training after all." "Are we changing subjects again?" I used two Fingers motioning towards my eyes then him. "You've got to keep me connected do you understand what I'm saying?" "Mom used to always tell us to forgive someone when they make a mistake. Learn to love someone for what they have become not to base that love on the road they took to get there because people make mistakes." "Yeah I remember something like that." "Well every now and then that someone might be you." "Is that right?" "Absolutely but I'm not saying discount past indiscretions just examine the whole picture."

I stretched out in the grass and began push-ups. Lamar remained silent while I pumped out fifty. "Whew! That felt good." I rolled over to my butt and folded my arms across my chest. "You know this has been a strange conversation." Lamar stood then walked over to hold my feet. I pumped out 50 sit-ups then rested on my back. "What's going on?"

He stood and brushed the grass from his pant legs. "I just decided to take my own advice." "What?" I rose up and rested on my knees. "Lamar we are definitely not *feelin* each other. I must have missed something?" "At this moment, while talking with you I've decided to take my own advice." "Is that right?" He smiled and nodded his head. "I'm allowing precious moments to pass." "So, what are you going to do about it?" He extended his hand to assist me as I came to my feet. "Well you and I are going to leave here and I'm driving home to my family." "That's wonderful, I'm glad that talking to me helped you reach that decision." He wrapped his arm around my shoulder as we started towards the car. "So am I my brother, so am I"

Clarissa

When the doorbell rang, I rushed from the couch in anticipation and excitement but quickly decided to pause and gather myself so as not to appear anxious. A strange sense of nostalgia overcame me as I recalled my first date with Franklin…

Of all the places to meet someone, Franklin and I met in a bookstore. He had been shopping in downtown New York and I had been browsing most of the morning searching for a few books my book club friends suggested. I was carrying Toni Morison's "Tar Baby" and searched for "Song of Solomon". I can't recall how it happened but as I picked up one book the other slipped from my hand. Before I could react or kneel down, Franklin had already picked it up. I was so involved in my search that I had no idea he was near. He handed me the book, looked into my eyes and smiled.

"This is a wonderful story, I strongly recommend it." It seemed like a feeble attempt at a pick-up line. But I decided to play along since finding him attractive. I asked him to share with me the storyline. He gave me just enough information to ignite my interest without revealing the entire story. I liked that about him because some people can never do that, would start talking and reveal the whole book eroding the pleasure of reading. Especially if they're flirting which I felt reasonably sure he was doing. But since he avoided that mistake I determined he had to be an avid reader or at the very least had the smarts not to ruin a story. So for all practical purposes he gained bonus points with me.

Anyway, I told him a girlfriend recommended the books. We stood there talking for about half an hour when I complained about my feet hurting. He pointed towards the sitting area and asked me to join him. Surprisingly, I accepted and we talked another hour before I knew his name. After introducing ourselves he offered to buy me a cup of coffee. We sat there for hours discussing everything from books the two of us had read to Soul food. "So Ms. Jones, can you recommend an authentic Soul food restaurant?" "I most certainly can!" "Is that right?" "Yes, in fact it's absolutely the best in the city." "Where might I find this place?" "It's mine!" "Oh, so you're a business woman?" "Not exactly, but if authentic is what you want, there's no better place than to visit my kitchen." "Is that an invitation?" "No just a fact and maybe a little advertisement. I don't know you well enough." "Oh that's cold! Very cold! You tell me all about the best Soulfood then deny me, all in the same breath." We both laughed. "Well keep talking your chances are getting better."

Back then I had always made a conscious effort to shop early in an effort to outwit the crowds. However as the crowds began to thicken I realized it had to be late. It was around 2pm and neither Franklin nor I considered ending our first encounter. In fact, I surprised myself by accepting when he asked me to join him for dinner. I gave him my address and phone number and we agreed he would pick me up at 7:30pm.

While I awaited his arrival I prayed the evening wouldn't be a disaster. I wasn't accustomed to sudden dates, especially with someone whom I most certainly had never seen. But, there was a certain honesty and pleasantness about him that weakened my inhibitions. It was a fresh experience and the slight discomfort was not great enough to cancel. I seated myself, watching the clock as my body began to warm and my private thoughts settled on hopes that the warmth wouldn't spoil my fragrance...

Now here I am a little more than seventeen years later with my body all warmed the way I was that night. I exhaled adjusting my clothing then opened the door. "Oh it's just you. Hello Tyler. Why don't you come in and have a seat." "Watch out girlfriend, don't make me tell you about yourself answering the door with that attitude. By the way you look nice." I hugged her tightly and thanked her for the compliment. "I'm sorry I thought you were Franklin, the anticipation is killing me." "Sorry but you did ask me to sit with girls." "I know, I know, but don't read me too much girlfriend. Can I offer you something?" We both sat on the loveseat.

"I'm okay for now but you need to relax." "Girl it is 5 o'clock and you said that you would be leaving at six. So why are you looking for Franklin now?" "Well I was reminiscing and lost track of time and reality." "Tsk, you're acting like this is your first date or something." "It's funny you should say that, because that's exactly what it feels like."

"So, where are the two of you going?" "I'm sorry I thought I mentioned it to you." "Duh, I would have remembered." "Aw forget you girl." We both laughed.

"I bought tickets to the Jazz concert tonight." "Oh, that should be nice. I'm surprised Miles didn't buy tickets for the two of us." "So am I-you couldn't imagine my surprise when you agreed to sit with the girls." "Well, we couldn't have gone anyway, his brother is visiting." "Oh really and how's he doing?" "He's doing fine; they took off to run earlier. So, are you giving Franklin anything special?" "Oh yes girl! Me." "Oh, I'm scared of you!" Reaching for my purse, I pulled out a small box. "Just kidding, I bought him this nugget ring." "That's nice, just make sure you get it insured you know how men can be sometimes." "I agree with you in part but you did say it with a strange emphasis. Is there some 1990's meaning that I've missed?" "Nothing like that it's just that I bought Miles a beautiful watch a few years ago. It was fairly expensive considering our finances at the time. Anyway, he lost it. Talk about angry, girl I'm still mad about that watch." "Wow, I had no idea but I can certainly understand your feelings."

I adjusted and kicked off my shoes. "So, how are you Tye?" She looked at my feet and laughed. "Girl, don't get too comfortable Franklin will be here soon." "I'm perfectly aware of that thank you. I'm just resting my feet while I wait." "Okay, you know what happens when you take your shoes off to get comfortable." "What are you talking about?" "Let's just say the kids may start to think a pig farm is in the den." I shoved Tyler's shoulder and started laughing. "Girl you *ain't* right. Why did you have to go there?" "Oh I'm just speaking the truth from experience my sister and look at you trying to be ghetto." "Yeah right, seriously though, how are you?" When I saw you last it seemed like your thoughts were heavy."

She stopped laughing, stood up and walked towards the kitchen. "I'm getting something to drink." "Tye, is everything all right?" I could hear the refrigerator open then close. "Oh yes, I'm fine I just needed to sort some things." The cabinets opened then closed. "Clarissa, where are the snacks?" "Take a look in the pantry, you'll find your favorites." "Okay, I see them. Why did you move it?" I walked towards the kitchen. "Chile you know I like to change things around once in a while." "Yeah, but what's up with relocating the *ginger snaps*?" "To be honest you've influenced Tia. She gets up in the middle of the night and satisfies her craving. So, I stopped putting them in that cookie jar you gave me." "Girl, that's silly." "Not when you consider that she eats them all before I can get some." We gave each other high five and started laughing. "I know that's right." "So, I guess you found the new cookie jar?" "Yeah but I thought you were beginning to slip on the snacks." "Not me girlfriend," I said holding out my hand for a cookie. *(Doorbell rings)*

"Oops! Girl, that has to be Franklin. Answer the door while I go and brush my teeth." "Girl isn't it a little late in the day for something you should have done already?" "That was true before I ate cookies." "I know you can't be *trippin*. The man is your husband and he knows you like *ginger snaps*. It should be no surprise if your breath smells like cookies." She started laughing and I felt certain she was getting her kicks at my expense. "Besides he would probably figure you're just keeping it real." "Just answer the door silly."

From the bathroom, I could hear the exchange between Tyler and Franklin. His voice sounded pleasant as it filled the rooms. I could hear his wonderful laughter and began to wonder if he was as nervous as I. After brushing my teeth, I dried my mouth and freshened up my lipstick. The reflection in the mirror had a glow I hadn't seen in quite some time. I looked beautiful and felt like a million bucks.

Franklin

My palms began to sweat as I stood at the door waiting for Clarissa to answer. I only rang the doorbell once because twice always seemed aggressive, impatient even. It was neither required nor desired to appear in either of those ways. So I anxiously stood for what seemed like hours waiting. As the sound of footsteps neared the door, I began to gaze at the pavement. When the lock disengaged and the door opened I slowly raised my head to greet this beautiful woman with a smile.

"Hello Franklin, you look handsome." I hugged her then kissed her cheek. "Thank you Tyler, you're looking as beautiful as ever." She raised both shoulders toward the ears placing her index finger over her lips. I was reminded of *Mike Myers'* mischievous grin from *Austin Powers.* "Shh! You'd better keep quiet. Does Clarissa know that you check out other ladies?" "Oops, I'd better keep it on the *DL*, huh?" We both laughed.

I liked the fact that I didn't have to be pretentious around Tyler. Even though she knew Clarissa and I were apart she never treated me differently. It was as though we were still together. Tyler motioned towards the den and began walking. "Clarissa is still getting ready so why don't you make yourself comfortable." "Thanks, would you let her know I'm here?" Tyler burst open in laughter holding one hand in the air and the other across her abdomen as though attempting to catch her breath and stop the laughter all at once. "Franklin, believe me, she definitely knows you're here but I'll go and tell her anyway."

As she walked away, I sat on the sofa looking over the pictures on the wall. So many wonderful memories I thought to myself. Tamara was my first-born and I'll never forget this one time she scared the life out of me. I had driven to pick up Clarissa from the gym. Tamara and I parked out front and remained in the car. I was sitting there playing with her when she started crying. Having no clue why, I offered a pacifier which she quickly spat out. Reaching into the diaper bag, I then there was no milk. Clarissa had often remarked how it takes a mother to remember all the things required for a baby trip. I brushed it off as an attempt to make women the authority in caring for a baby-Men can do it too.

I tried singing and making funny faces but Tamara continued crying. I was about to begin a diaper check when I noticed her little naval appeared severed. Tamara was only a few weeks old so I panicked and began praying. My prayer was that I wouldn't lose my daughter and that I was sorry for being a bad father and forgetting the milk and disturbing her little naval. When Clarissa arrived, I was crying and so was Tamara. She took the baby and began changing the diaper as I explained the severed naval. She nodded to acknowledge me but continued her efforts. Suddenly there was quiet then Clarissa held up a soiled diaper informing me that Tamara wanted to be cleaned. In my panic, I never verified her diaper. Clarissa informed me that the naval had not severed rather, the part that remained after birth was no longer needed and had fallen off. To my dismay this was a natural occurrence after a few weeks. Even to this day my Tamara doesn't like to be dirty. Over the years some have called her a child super model but I know the secret.

Although I wouldn't trade any of the experiences and lessons on parenting I learned with Tamara, Tia was my chance at redemption. But all those things I thought I knew and learned were out the window after Tia's birth. Her arrival demanded a whole new learning curve. Let no person ever convince you that rearing all siblings is the same.

I smiled as the memories flowed through my mind. Tia's arrival was quick as Clarissa was in labor less than an hour. She entered this world with her eyes wide open and if I didn't know any better I would concede she was already dressed and grown up. Fearless from the start, she began walking and talking well ahead of peers.

"Daddeee!" "I stood with my arms opened wide as she came running towards me then tightly wrapped my arms around my little angel. "Hi pumpkin, how are you?" "I'm good." "So, how was your day?" I released her and sat back down. She walked towards the coffee table picking up the remote control then turned to the Nickelodeon channel just in time for Keenan and Kel. "It was fine." "Well I see you're preoccupied." She didn't say a word but instinctively walked backward with her eyes affixed on the TV and sat next to me. After seating herself, she pulled my arm around her waist resting her head underneath my shoulder. "Where's your sister sweetheart?" "She's on the computer." She spoke the words but never looked my direction.

"Hi Dad." I turned to find Tamara walking towards me. I extended my left hand as she reached down to hug my neck. "Hello young lady and how are you doing" "I'm fine Dad." She said happy birthday as she handed me a card. "It's from the both of us." "Thanks sweetheart." Tamara stood next to me as I opened the card.

On the outside cover were the words; Wisdom, Integrity, Wit and Compassion. My heart began racing as the words settled on my mind opening the card to view the passage inside…

"These aren't the virtues of youth. They're qualities earned through years of hard choices, brave decisions and bold ideas. And when these qualities are present in a man others see a life well lived. They see a man very much like you." Happy Birthday Daddy, we love you, Tamara & Tia…

All I could do was hug them as my eyes welled up with tears. I was so preoccupied that I hadn't noticed Tyler and Clarissa enter the room. "Alright birthday boy, I'm ready." I quickly wiped my face then looked to discover Clarissa and Tyler standing there holding a cake. They both yelled "Happy Birthday Franklin" in unison. I was so overcome with joy that I couldn't move or say a word. "Make a wish" Clarissa said as she floated across the room and placed the cake on the coffee table. I closed my eyes making a silent wish and said thank you. "Alright, let's cut his cake so you two can get out of here." "Alright, Tyler has spoken ladies." I grabbed the knife and cut everyone a slice. Clarissa and I devoured our pieces in record time after which Tyler and the girls cleared the table leaving Clarissa and I alone. She kissed me gently on the cheek and whispered "Happy Birthday." I gave her a peck on the lips and whispered "thank you."

"Well, we should be going." We both stood and walked towards the door. "Tyler! We're leaving." "Okay!" "Goodbye girls! I'll see you later. I love you." "Okay mom, have a good time."

"You two have a wonderful time okay," Tyler said as she met us at the door. Clarissa gave her a hug and whispered something in her ear. They both snickered. "Alright you two, let's not get started."

Tyler

After Clarissa and Franklin had left the girls and I put away the remnants of cake. Tamara slowly walked towards the sink as she placed the last bite into her mouth. Tia scraped off the frosting and smeared it all over her plate then she jumped up and headed to her room leaving the plate on the table. I cleared my throat to get her attention. "Oops! I forgot." She ran back to the table grabbed her plate and dropped it in the sink. "I'll wash the dishes Tamara if you'll sweep the floor." Tamara surveyed the sink then turned towards me with a grin. "Okay, do you know where the dishwashing liquid is kept?" "I think I can figure it out." Tamara walked over to the laundry room and retrieved the broom. As she began sweeping she motioned towards the cabinet beneath the sink. "You'll find the dish soap underneath."

After cleaning the kitchen and washing all the dishes Tamara picked up a magazine and started towards her room. Tia had already gone and from the silence I assumed she must be reading or coloring. "Tamara, would you take a peek in your sister's room on your way back?" I adjourned to the den and turned on some music. As the sultry voice of Sade filled the room I began to browse…"Miss Tyler Tia is coloring." "Thanks sweetie."

Clarissa's home was absolutely beautiful. The huge den invited guests to come in and relax. It was arranged with a sitting area near the bay window that illuminated with each morning sun. The center portion of the room boasted a beautiful fireplace accented with wing back chairs and a sofa. The far end of the room had a wall mounted television and two chaise lounges large enough to accommodate two people comfortably. Authentic African art was nicely placed around the room. She also had some African American art and a few pieces from other countries she and Franklin had visited. The room spoke volumes about them as a couple.

I was proud of her and felt truly privileged to be a friend to the two of them. Clarissa and Franklin offered encouragement and guidance all of which I surely needed. They're friendship was priceless and timely following my mothers death. Miles was supportive but he still had both parents and I convinced myself he couldn't possibly understand my feelings. However it meant a great deal to me that he cared enough to continue trying. Clarissa had lost her parents so, when she spoke I listened. The irony of it all is that the things she either said or did Miles had done also. After allowing that thought to simmer a few moments, I continued browsing until I reached the bookcase. There were several to select from politics, religion, love, friendship, investing, entrepreneurship, fitness and parenting to name a few. I settled on *Friends and Lovers* then sat down to begin and enjoy the author's journey.

The last of all the lively characters was being introduced when Tamara entered. "What are you reading Miss Tyler?" She startled me at first but I managed to settle my nerves and conjure up a smile. "Hey you, come on over and sit down." I patted an area on the sofa next to me. "It's one of your mother's books, *Friends and Lovers.*" Tamara was a splitting image of her mother with dark brown shoulder length hair and chestnut skin. Her eyes were slightly canted upward with eyebrows so naturally perfect they appeared arched. She had long narrow fingers with short French manicured nails. Not that I was checking her out but her mother definitely schooled her in femininity. She seated herself on the sofa with her legs curled underneath her thighs then leaned into my shoulder. Oh my God…I was never able to do that at home much less at fourteen. "Miss Tyler is the story good?" "It's still developing but I have a good feeling." She had perfect little toes and of course they were professionally treated as well. I was *trippin.* "Tamara-I know you don't shave your legs girl?" She rubbed her leg then looked at me and nodded. "Yes mam, my mother taught me." "Wow! Does she take you with her to do your nails as well?" Little Miss Prissy started giggling. "Nooo, we do that kind of stuff together. My mother bought everything to take care of my hands and feet. She said we could bond more as mother and daughter." "I see, rather than learning from friends and messing up a few times Clarissa teaches you?" "Yes mam." I couldn't help but notice the pride in her tone.

"Miss Tyler, my girlfriend Tramane would like to come over for a while, is that okay?" "I don't see why not. Is it okay with your mother and her parents?" "Her parents don't mind and mom knows that she and I are close friends. We're just going to be in my room." "Okay then, would you like a snack or something when she comes over? She got up and walked towards the kitchen picking up the cordless phone as she passed. "No thank you, I can take care of it."

Clarissa

The waitress took our orders as I canvassed the surroundings. *Angelioque's* was just as romantic and exquisite as Amber had mentioned. Now Amber was our resident expert for dating in the 90's. She was a petite white woman that had been with the company for about four years. The lady was classy, confident and enjoyed her sexual freedom. Two weeks ago she waltzed into the office boasting about an evening she spent at dinner with her new beau (the new guy). I mean the new guy had only been at the office two days. If the truth is told he was a fine something. At least that was the talk around the water cooler when he arrived to fill a vacancy in our marketing department. Amber went on to say that she would have him eating out of her hands in only a few minutes. That was two weeks ago and from the looks of this restaurant he must have found some sweet treats in her palm.

Angelioque's was located on the top floor of the Marriot overlooking the St Johns River. The view itself was both beautiful and classy with an ambiance that could be enjoyed by patrons seated anywhere. For starters, when you entered each female guest was given a rose as a professional and courteous waiter escorted her to the table. The tables encircled a waterfall that was the centerpiece of the restaurant. To reach our table we walked down the stairs towards the waterfall passing 4 rows of circular patterns leading towards the center of attraction. A pianist was neatly tucked away in a spacious lightly lit corner playing all kinds of romantic instrumentals. Each table had a candle and the city provided the perfect romantic backdrop from huge continuous windows overlooking the river. There was even a balcony for those that wanted to feel a breeze while overlooking the city.

Franklin ordered shrimp with angel hair and I selected the eggplant Parmesan. We both decided on garden salads to begin our meal. "Madame yours is an excellent choice of entrée, as well as you sir. May I suggest a Merlot?" Franklin agreed, the waiter nodded then smiled as he did an about face and walked away.

"Clarissa this is a beautiful restaurant." "Yes it is, Amber, one of the ladies from work recommended it." "Well, from what I can see she has excellent taste but we'll reserve final judgment until the food comes." We both laughed.

Franklin's brief laughter changed to more serious when the waiter returned pouring two glasses of wine. "Sir, I've placed your orders with the chef, is there anything more I can do for you before your food is served?" Franklin nodded at the waiter thanking him. "Mrs. Green, would you mind if I offered a toast?" I raised my glass to take in the aroma. "Sure, that would be nice." "How about we toast to a promising evening, good company and our darling children?" I tipped my head and smiled in agreement.

Franklin took a long sip and smiled in delight after he swallowed. "Speaking of the girls, did you have a chance to revisit the subject Tamara broached yesterday?" I paused and began rubbing the rim of my glass. Sensing my uneasiness Franklin reached across to take my hand. I looked at him and muttered a reply. "Not exactly, she didn't want to discuss it further. However, I did some soul searching afterwards to consider our current state…but we should discuss those things later. It's your birthday remember?" With that last comment I mustered a fake smile. Luckily the waiter had returned with our salads, because Franklin's expression told me he was not convinced.

Once the salads were served Franklin thanked the waiter then reached out for my hands. In all the years I had known him his relationship with church had been distant at best. He visited church sporadically but he always took time to thank the lord for a meal no matter what the surroundings. I liked that about him and felt certain that GOD had a special plan for him whenever he stopped running.

As we sat quietly eating our salads, I looked up after each bite to observe his demeanor. The salad with fresh crisp vegetables was a delicious and the service exceptional but he clearly seemed pre-occupied. There were things that needed to be discussed but I was afraid we might ruin the evening.

Franklin gently placed his knife and fork on the plate then took his napkin from his lap wiping his mouth as though he were finished. "Clarissa, there's something I need to share with you." In my heart I knew we needed to rekindle our relationship. In fact I was certain he would confess the same. We had been apart long enough and I had long ago forgiven him for his indiscretion. He just didn't know it but in my heart of hearts I knew. After all, for the last year all of his free time had been spent with the girls and me. There was no way he could possibly have feelings for that Sheila bitch *(Lord forgive my choice of words to describe one of yours)*. "What is it Franklin?" "Well I didn't intend to discuss this matter but somehow I feel there's no better time than now."

The pauses were killing me. I wanted to reach across the table and shake him until every detail was revealed. Then again, maybe details would be too difficult to bear. My thoughts began to return to that evening I first discovered his betrayal. It was 2am. I remember because I had planned to surprise him with some of the love games Amber and I had discussed.

Now there was no clock to awaken me, it's just that I always awaken at 2am to visit the bathroom. I'm not sure exactly why I discussed lovemaking with Amber. Anyway, after my return from the bathroom I stood over Franklin, as he lay prone. The sneakiness turned me on as I slowly pulled back the cover revealing his huge hairy chest and silk pajama trousers.

Once the covers were removed I leaned over to kiss his chest and explore his lower body with my hands. He breathed deeply and shifted his hips. I kissed his nipples then reached into his pants massaging him gently. As I began to feel the swelling and throbbing pressure in my palm my juices started flowing. Amber had said that I should swallow him up while he slept. So I shifted my kisses from his chest down his abdomen stopping just above his jewels then navigated my way up the side of his sweet wand. I squeezed then slowly stroked accepting him into my mouth. I had to admit my skills were raw but I followed Amber's instructions to the letter and from Franklin's response I didn't seem to be too far off the mark. Franklin began to mutter and push at my head. I responded by working him even harder. And that's when I heard it. Right at the very moment I was swallowing him up he called me Sheila. At first I thought my imagination was going wild from sexual excitement but that quickly changed. "She-e-ila, you bitch!"

Following that he snatched my head pulling my hair. "Sheila you bitch!" I pulled away from him in tears. Franklin was not what I considered a rough lover but the way he reacted signaled that someone was satisfying my husband in a way I had never known. I nearly choked from his aggression. "You bastard how could you?" He had the nerve to rise up looking innocent. "What's wrong Clarissa?" "Leave this house Franklin! Just leave for God's sake!"

Well, that was then and even though he has denied it to this day I was prepared to forgive him. I hoped for an admission but my heart desired some explanation other than cheating. "Clarissa, something happened that I should have told you long ago." Oh my God! I thought, while fighting to prevent tears from welling up in my eyes.

"Clarissa something happened that I've been ashamed of for a long time." No kidding Sherlock, because of that Trick we're not together. I wanted to say it aloud but feared it might bring an end to the revelation. "She took advantage of me and..." What! The nerve of him to suggest that she took advantage of him...Who does he think he's talking to, a teenager? He's the married man and it's his body so if anyone took advantage of the situation he did. My instincts were telling me to get up and walk out but my heart got in the way. I needed this to complete its course, so I sat there shattered heart and broken promises listening to his words.

"I didn't want it but she forced me and there was nothing I could do." I knew the name of the person but decided to ask anyway. "Who are you talking about Franklin?" My body trembled inside hoping I would be wrong but so far my worst fears had been true. He had cheated and there was no reason to believe he wouldn't say it was that trick. "It was Sheila she robbed me of my innocence and destroyed everything that you and I could have ever shared." I looked straight into his saddened face and muttered as low as I could without causing a scene. "You bastard! How could you do this to me? How could you do it to the kids?" He began to mutter a response. "Clarissa, what are you talking about? There were no kids." Another dagger ripped what was left of my heart. He actually did this before the children were born? Wasn't I enough for him? "What does that mean Franklin?" "Clarissa, there were no kids and there was no you or I. Baby I was nine years old!"

The waiter returned to check on us. "Sir, how are your salads?" We both stared at each other ignoring his question. Sensing the tension he did a quick about face and walked away. I couldn't believe my ears. Was Franklin actually saying he slept with Sheila at nine? This whole matter confused me even more. "Franklin what does that have to do with us? And for that matter why are you telling me?" "It has everything to do with us. The way I treated you and the way I responded to you sexually." The more he talked the more confused I became. "Franklin I don't understand." "Just listen and it will make sense to you." As he revealed all the details my stomach turned so much I wanted to just throw–up. All kinds of questions entered my mind as I listened. What kind of an adult would do such a thing to a child? Where were his parents and how could they have not known? And why the hell is Auntie Sheila still alive. I'm saved but I felt a rage in me that wanted to choke that hussy to death. Aren't we supposed to be most safe with relatives? I had read and even heard on talk shows that child molestation occurs often in the home or among relatives.

Now that in and of itself was a shock to me but I never in a million years would have conceived of something so disgustingly ugly this close to me.

Franklin's voice faded as his eyes saddened and welled with tears. I reached for his hand to offer comfort but he pulled away making a feeble attempt to gather himself. He inhaled deeply clearing his throat while holding his chest high as though to proclaim he would not be conquered.

"Clarissa, I've always loved you but I didn't tell you sooner because I didn't believe it mattered. However the events over the last year and the message from our recent church service challenged my thinking. After attending services with you, I realized that I've carried a secret between us for too long. An entire year has passed with us apart. Things are very different and I now know that what happened really did matter. It's too heavy on my heart and today I was forced to consider that it might have subconsciously impacted the relationship I've had with my family. Kinda like what the reverend said about missing or not seeing your blessing."

My heart felt relieved and confused all at once but his eyes told me that he spoke the truth. "Franklin dear I've been a fool because I had known of Sheila for a long time now. Mind you, I never considered she is your aunt rather I was quick to assume you were having an affair" "My God Clarissa! What gave you such a foolish idea?" I felt so ashamed I could hardly speak as I reflected over the last year. "You called her name in your sleep…and…while we were being intimate. I was trying something new and you called me Sheila. Can you imagine how you made me feel as a woman…as your wife?"

We both sat silently until the waiter arrived with our dinner. He gently placed the meals in front of us without making eye contact. "I have a delicious Eggplant Parmesan for the lady, and for you sir, shrimp and angel hair, may I offer you anything more?" He stood and looked directly at Franklin finally realizing that he had walked into a serious moment. "Sir and Madame I'll excuse myself until you signal for my return. Please excuse me." He nodded performed an about face and vanished. Neither Franklin nor I had spoken or acknowledged him at all.

I mustered as compassionate a tone possible and conjured the courage to articulate some of the questions that had been entering my mind. "Have you told your parents?" The way he scoffed I knew his answer would surprise me. "Hmph I told my father and subjected myself to ridicule. At first he asked me if I were gay. He said that most young boys my age were mannish and dreamed of having an older woman sometimes fancying the idea so much that they told tales. He started telling me about how he and his boys would lie about being with girls to gain respect. I was so shocked by his reaction that I completely shut down. He went on to say that since I broached the subject it was time to discuss the birds and the bees because my hormones were creating a vivid imagination."

"Did he confront Sheila?" "Oh yes. The day after I told him we had another talk. He said that Sheila told him it never happened. She said she recalled getting up for breakfast wearing a robe and I was staring. Claimed that she never imagined I had eyes for her but she would be certain to dress more appropriate in the future so as not to arouse my imagination.

God I felt so betrayed…my father who should have been protecting me…his son. It shattered my heart to hear him explain away the things she had done to me." "I'm so sorry Franklin; I would have never conceived that sort of response from your father." His eyes were filled with sadness and disappointment. "I felt alone and ashamed because Sheila had taken advantage of me and the person I felt would protect me failed. As a matter of fact, my parents continued to take me there after I told him. So I guess he never discussed it with my mother. Because she never mentioned it and nor did I…personally I had no desire to go through another let down. After a while I blocked it away and felt numb to the whole situation. I had resolved that maybe I did look at her in some particular way causing her to hurt me." I reached out for his hand again. "Franklin sweetheart, you can never accept for a moment the idea that you caused this to happen. You were only a child and she was the adult that should have known better." Inside I was angry with his father but decided against berating him. I needed to be strong for Franklin and since he had always seemed to cherish his father I didn't want to risk alienating him with negative comments. He wiped a tear from his eye and took a sip of water. "I know Clarissa but the real tragedy is that my father is clueless how this has affected our relationship."

He smiled as he placed the glass on the table. "I guess you never expected dinner to turn out this way?" Even though his remark seemed out of place I loved the way he always found humor in the mist of turmoil. "It's okay, dinner is fine." "How do you know when the only thing you've eaten is a salad?" He signaled the waiter. "This is my birthday celebration, so let's celebrate." He began wiping his eyes with the napkin just as the waiter arrived. "How may I help you sir?" "Well, it seems that while we were talking our food got a little cold. Would you mind returning it? I'll compensate you for the inconvenience and the cost of the meals." "Right away sir, will there be anything more?" "That will be all."

Miles

"Lamar! Do you want to get a quick bite before hitting the road?" "No, I'll just take a cup of coffee because food will cause me to become drowsy." As I entered the kitchen, the aroma from breakfast welcomed me. Tyler had left the dishes in the sink and a note on the refrigerator. *"Miles, I was running late would you take care of the dishes and start the laundry for me please? Love Your Boo."* I pushed the faucet to the side and turned on the hot water. "Damn! Why didn't she wash this stuff?" "Hey what's up?" Lamar walked in and seated himself at the table. I turned on the kettle to heat some water for coffee. "Oh it's nothing just Tyler and the dishes." He started laughing. "So she left some extra work for a brother after that fine meal?" I turned around in annoyance and held up my palm. "Step off Lamar! Just step off!" "Hey how about that cup of coffee, can you make it a little faster?" "Watch yourself there are no servants up in here." "I'm sorry man, I'm just *trippin.*"

When the whistle blew, I removed the pot from the burner and pulled two mugs from the cupboard. "Hey *Bruh* your comment earlier brought back some old baggage." "Let me give you a hand with those." Lamar took the mugs and placed them on the table. I poured the water then returned to the cabinet for the instant coffee. "What old baggage are you talking about?" "It can wait. Let's see, we have French Vanilla, Hazelnut and Maxwell House, what's your pleasure?" "Please, you know I'm not into *Foo Foo* coffee, just give me the Maxwell House." I started laughing and returned to the table with the Maxwell House and Hazelnut coffees. "You should broaden your taste." Lamar snatched the Maxwell House jar opened it rolling his eyes and took two spoonfuls. "My tastes are broad enough thank you." I stirred my cup then inhaled the sweet aroma. "Umm! You just don't know what a treat you'll be missing." "Save that for someone you want to impress or worse yet someone that wants to impress you." I took a sip and swallowed hard. "Now that was cold Lamar. You ruined the taste of the first sip." He laughed while stirring his cup. "I just wanted to get a rise from you and it seems I did." "Yeah kick a man when he's down." "What's that suppose to mean little *bruh?*" I got up from the table and walked to the sink to start the dishes.

"So Miles, what old baggage were you referencing?" I cleared my throat but continued the circular motion of the dishtowel around the plate I held in my hand. "You know while I was in college it was easy not keeping in touch with you. Since I didn't enjoy hearing about you, your lady friends or the money you earned I took the easy route. It seemed like you had it all going your way and I didn't." "That's not true. Everyone was supportive of you realizing you would reach your potential after college." I shook my head in disagreement. "Naw man! Everyone talked about you and what you were doing with your life. I felt inadequate around others and now the feeling was among family. It was easier to distance myself for my own self-preservation." "Damn Miles, I never knew you felt that way. I'm sorry man." I motioned my head and shoulders as if to shake off what I perceived as pity.

"Hey don't sweat small stuff! Anyway, I've everything going my way now." "Are you happy?" "What is that suppose to mean? Of course I'm happy. I've got a good job, a bad ass lady and friends who look up to me. Not to mention the ladies. I can't tell you how many times I've gone home to find that all the honeys from back in the day are sweating a *brotha*." "Is all that really important to you?" After washing the mugs, I drained the sink and wiped down the counter. "Hmph it does sound shallow huh?"

"Hey little *bruh* keep in mind what I said okay?" "Sure, I've got it filed away right here!" Rolling my eyes I pointed towards the base of my head. "Look little *bruh*, it's getting late and I should get on the road." I turned towards the table and hugged him as he stood. "All right, do you have everything?" "Yes, I put my things in the car this morning."

When we walked outside, Natasha James from across the street had just returned home. She wore a lime pantsuit that accented all her curves. It was as though she put those curves on display reaching for something in the rear seat of her red Mitsubishi Eclipse. Lamar and I both looked at each other. "Who's your neighbor?" Her greeting interrupted me before I could respond. She waved her narrow hand in the air and gave us her best smile. Natasha was the homecoming queen at her alma mater in Atlanta. She had been away from college three years but when you saw her wave and smile it was as though she was riding on a float with her homecoming court. "Hello Miles how are you today?" I signaled Lamar to follow then walked towards her. "I'm fine thank you. Hey if you're not in a hurry, I'd like to introduce you to someone." When she put her hand on her hip I could hear Lamar clear his throat. "As long as you're not trying to fix me up, I don't mind." We both started laughing. As the dimples in her butter colored skin posed she extended her hand while I introduced the two of them. "Natasha James this is my older brother Lamar." I'm pleased to meet you Lamar." Lamar gently cupped her hand as he admired her. "The pleasure is mine Ms. James." "Now I never would have guessed you are the oldest." "Now Natasha, why are you *trippin?*" "I'm just kidding, how's Tyler?" She released Lamar's hand turning her attention towards me. "She's doing great, I'll tell her you asked." "Okay. Well Miles you must excuse me, I need to get inside. Again it was nice to meet you Lamar." Lamar nodded then turned and walked away. I followed until we reached his car. "Nice lady." I took a quick glance in Natasha's direction and smiled. "That she is my brotha that she is." The nudge on my shoulder interrupted my stare as she entered her home. "Remember what I said about living through someone's eyes other than your own. Find your inner happiness all right." "Yeah-Yeah-whatever." I turned and hugged Lamar. "Drive carefully and call when you arrive."

The car started and as he backed up, I waved and yelled to him. "Kiss my little nephew for me and say hello to Brittany." He held up the okay sign, smiled then drove off. I figured this would be the last I saw of him for another six months because I had no immediate intention on visiting. Too many things were on my plate, work, marriage and this *freakin* house. Besides I can hook up with him when my plate is cleared.

The phone started to ring as Lamar vanished around the curve. I raced towards the door to beat the answering machine. During my dash to get inside I tripped over the bricks edging the sidewalk. "Damit!" Oh well, the only damage is my ego. I got up brushing off my hands and knees. Luckily my body didn't slide otherwise I'd be nursing a cherry.

When I entered the house the answering machine had picked up. Tyler was leaving a message and since I had already fallen due to haste I let her continue making a mental note to phone back later. Walking into to the bathroom I picked grabbed the Neosporin, peroxide and cotton balls from the medicine cabinet. After cleaning and applying ointment to my bruise I phoned Tyler.

"Hey sexy, I missed your call by a few seconds. Lamar had just left and I was outside. You know, I nearly busted my ass to get to the phone." "Nearly huh? So that means you're okay? Just think if you had tried a little harder and busted your cute little butt…well never mind." The words she uttered seemed insensitive but the sultry way they flowed from her lips told me otherwise so I decided to play along. "Would you rather I had hurt myself?" "Not exactly it's just that you would have given me an excuse to invite you here for some T.L.C" We both laughed. "Actually, I'm considering a double-take. "Miles you can't recreate a moment once it's gone. But I'm more than willing to consider other opportunities." "So, you seem more amenable compared to this morning." "I've had some time to read and relax." "What's bothering you?" "Not a thing."

So tell me, what are you doing the remainder of the evening?" I expressed my interest in coming over then proceeded with a synopsis of my afternoon with Lamar. Subconsciously, I was still annoyed by her nonchalant attitude when I asked what had been bothering her this morning. "How about, I stop and pick-up a video and something to snack?" "That would be fine just remember the movie should be appropriate in case the girls want to watch." "Aw! I wanted to get an adult flick." "Ha hah, I don't think so, I'm babysitting remember?" "I know, I was just kidding. I'll get a shower and see you within the hour."

While in the shower, I began reflecting on my discussion with Lamar suddenly realizing he had gone without telling me what was on his mind. "Damn!" I had been talking so much that he hadn't gotten the opportunity to share. Now that I think of it he did seem troubled. Mental note-I'll make a point to call him next week.

Franklin

After we entered the driveway, I placed the car in park but left the engine running. "Clarissa, even though I brought up a sore subject, I want to thank you for a beautiful evening. She smiled extending her hand towards mine. Her touch was warm conveying a sincere connection with me. "Franklin, I too had a wonderful evening and I want to apologize. "What could you possibly have to apologize for Clarissa?" After the words left my mouth I regretted interrupting her thoughts besides it made perfect sense that she was referring to our discussion at dinner.

"I'm sorry we left before Gerald Albright concluded but it was getting late." I laughed from embarrassment. "What's so funny?" "I just thought you would say something different, forgive me for laughing. "Thanks for sharing with me tonight." I looked into her face and nodded in agreement. "Well, it's been long overdue, my regret is that the secret has cost us so much." With those words, I turned away feeling unworthy for not trusting her enough to have shared this before now.

Peering at the neighbor's house, I felt the emptiness that comes along following the realization that you've been the lead character in destroying your own happiness. I was about to drift into another world when the engine shut off. I turned to find Clarissa holding the keys and opening her door. "I would like you to come in Franklin." "Do you think that's a good idea?" She smiled as she stepped out then turned around looking directly at me. "Franklin I couldn't think of a more appropriate time. Come on, I'm sure Tyler is ready to get home." I looked towards the street gathered myself and stepped out of the car. "Okay, but it seems Miles has joined Tyler already." Clarissa looked around then shook her head. "Oh my, I hadn't noticed Miles' car. Anyway, I'm sure they both would love to get home."

I walked tentatively behind Clarissa stopping four paces as she held out the keys attempting to open the door. "Oops!" She turned and handed a set of keys to me. "I think these belong to you." She then rambled through her purse. "I know they're in here somewhere. Ah Hah! Got them." When she opened the door I hesitated for a moment until she turned and cleared her throat. "Did you change your mind about my request?" I mustered a quick smile then quickened my pace behind her. "Not at all, I'm right behind you."

"Hello…I'm home. Tyler, Tia, Tamara…I'm back." I followed as she walked into the family room where Miles, Tyler Tia and Tamara were all sitting watching a movie. The scene reminded me of the times we used to do the same thing. I smiled at the thought of those wonderful days. Tia was the first to notice us. "Hi mommy, hi daddy you're home?" Clarissa kissed her on the cheek then walked over to Tamara and kissed her forehead. "What are guys watching so intensely?" "*Dr. DooLittle*…it's about over. I thought the girls would enjoy it." "That was nice of you. So, how are you doing?" He stood and walked towards me extending his hand. "I'm just *coolin* with my baby and your babies. What's up Franklin? How was the show?" "Yeah girl, how was the show? Tyler said. "It was great but a certain someone wanted to leave early." Clarissa slapped me on the shoulder. "Franklin! I told you I wanted to get home so that Tyler could return home to her husband…but I see you guys had it all under control." She winked at Tyler and they both started grinning mischievously.

"Hey Franklin, Tye and I are going to head out." Tyler began walking towards Clarissa and waving her hand in protest. "I don't think so. Not until Clarissa tells me about dinner." Pushing Clarissa towards the living room, they immediately began whispering. "Tye you guys can chat tomorrow, let's give them some space." I just stood there perplexed by all the drama. Tyler did however concede to Miles' wishes. She and Clarissa returned to the family room as Tyler strolled over to Miles and kissed him. "Alright boo, let's go home. Goodnight you two. Goodnight girls, I'll see you later." The girls took a reprieve from the movie credits and said goodnight. "Clarissa the girls can keep the movie, it's a five night rental. I'll pick it up later." "Oh thanks Miles, but I can return it for you." "That's cool…It was good to see you Franklin." I extended my hand and replied likewise. Clarissa thanked Tyler and the two hugged once more before she exited the door. "I'll call you Tyler." "Yeah and give me all the details…good night Franklin." I kissed Tyler's cheek and thanked her for sitting with the girls. "No problem, you know I love them."

When the two of them drove off, I closed and locked the door. It felt familiar yet awkward given the last twelve months. I smiled then turned and walked into the family room. Clarissa must have already given the girls instructions because they were clearing away everything. "Are you two getting ready for bed?" "Yes sir." "Well, I know you're not going to bed without hugging your dad." Tia hugged my neck but Tamara finished cleaning then started towards her room. "Tamara, can I have a hug?" She paused and gave me a look I had never seen. "Sorry, it's just I haven't gotten a hug from you before bed in a while." That comment stung but I dismissed it as I hugged my daughter. "Goodnight sweetheart." I held onto to my daughter closing my eyes to reflect on her comment realizing that she was right. The thought saddened me to near tears. I gathered my emotions then slowly opened my eyes noticing Clarissa observing the two of us. Tamara left my arms and walked over to her mother. "Goodnight precious, I'll see you in the morning."

After Tamara exited Clarissa walked towards the kitchen. "I'd like a glass of water can I offer you something?" I sat on the sofa and crossed my legs. "No, I'm fine thank you."

I sat nervously awaiting Clarissa to join me. When she entered the room she looked as beautiful as the first day we met. "I didn't realize how thirsty I had become." She sat with one leg folded under her hip then exhaled and pointed towards the kitchen. "I think you know the location of the glasses." I laughed. "So you're definitely not sharing?" Since she didn't respond I, knew the answer. "On a more serious note…can I assume you heard Tamara's comment?" She inhaled deeply releasing a sigh. "I had a long discussion with her and found out some things you may not know." Shifting my head in dismay I asked for clarity. She pointed towards the bedrooms. "We can discuss the details in a more private setting. I assure you that waiting until tomorrow will be okay." She smiled to offer assurance so I put the discussion to rest.

"Thanks for sharing your birthday with me." "I should thank you…your presence made it special." My palms moisten as the mood seemed to take a life of its own. It reminded me of days past when everything in me ached for this woman. Something in the mood would happen triggering emotions that grew slowly and methodical. At the present time it would have seemed logical to hold her in my arms, maybe even kiss her lips. But how could I presume such intimacy given our current situation. We sat in silence for a few moments until I couldn't take it anymore. "Clarissa, I should be leaving. The girls are in bed and I'm sure you want to get some rest as well." "Franklin, although I certainly appreciate your consideration, I'm perfectly capable of making my own decisions. Besides, I don't want this night to end quite yet." I was taken by surprise with those words. I couldn't be certain of her meaning but one certainty is that

I also wanted tonight to continue. With that thought came more silence until Clarissa surprised me by taking my hand and leading to a place we hadn't been in twelve months. I wanted to speak but she pressed her finger against my lips preventing any words from escaping. She smiled then whispered. "Don't say a word. Let's just continue this wonderful evening."

Tyler

"Oh my God! What happened? It was just three weeks ago that we saw him." I couldn't believe what Mrs. Stewart was telling me. Cancer was taking his life. There was a period of remission following the radiation treatment. At least that's what the doctor had told her. She had been treating him for several months now and assumed he had told the family. He was feeling pain and checked himself into the hospital. After being told the cancer had spread and nothing more could be done he called his mother and Brittany. They were with him at the hospital and wanted us to get there as soon as possible. She asked if I would be okay then said she had to go because Mr. Stewart had not been reached yet.

"Okay mom, is there anything I can do? Where is junior?" She indicated that junior was with Brittany's sister and would be okay. "Just get here as fast as you can." Then she hung up the phone leaving me to ponder how I would reveal the news to Miles. He hadn't spoken with Lamar since his recent visit and would be devastated. This was certainly something I had to tell him in person.

Miles had been putting in extra hours on Saturday mornings working on an important business project. So unlike his mother, I knew exactly how and where to reach him. The phone rang three times before he answered. "Hey Boo, how are you?" I purposely paused to gather my thoughts on how to keep from breaking the news over the phone. "I'm fine baby, just working on this project. What's up?" I cleared my throat…"Well sweetie, I was considering dropping by your office…Would you mind?" The excitement in his voice told me all I needed to know. "I would love to see my baby." I opened the telephone book searching the yellow pages for Southwest Airlines. "Great, I'll be there within the hour. Can I bring something for you?" We exchanged a few comments then I hung up the phone and clicked over to the other line.

The woman on the line informed me that the earliest we could leave would be 4:55pm. "Dang, that's 5 hours from now. Alright, I'd like to reserve two open round trip tickets." After making reservations, I packed two days worth of clothes for the both of us. "Let's see…am I forgetting anything?" I slapped my hand against my thigh then phoned Clarissa to let her know what happened informing her that we would be away for a few days. Then I left for Miles' office.

The traffic was heavy as usual but flowing steadily. When I got off the downtown exit traffic was backed up bumper to bumper. I had forgotten about the baseball exhibition game otherwise I would have taken the back roads. After stopping at the traffic light about 10 blocks from Miles' office I reached into my purse for the cell phone calling Mrs. Stewart to give her our flight information. She was disappointed that we would be arriving so late but given the available flights and the fact that we couldn't arrive sooner even if we drove she understood. The traffic began to accelerate and moments later I entered the parking garage of Prudential. Miles had been blessed to manage a section in the credit and financial services department. I was happy about the promotion but the hours he worked the last few weeks were stressful for the both of us.

As I entered the building elevator my thoughts shifted to Lamar. I rehearsed his appearance in my mind from his recent visit. Recalling he was bald and a little thin but seemed happy and full of strength. My thoughts were shifted when the bell sounded indicating I had reached the 6th floor.

Miles was smiling and standing near the office entrance. As I approached he walked towards me with his arms extended. His hug was gentle and reassuring. I kissed his lips then wrapped my arms around his neck as tightly as I could. "Wow, I need to have you meet me here more often." Released him from my embrace, I stared into his eyes. "Miles…I spoke with your mother today." He began to usher me to his desk. "Oh yeah, how is she?" "Can we sit down sweetie?" He stared at me strangely as though anticipating some bad news. "Sure, you can sit here." He reached for a wing back chair and pulled it closer towards his desk then we both sat down. "Is there something wrong with my mother?" I reached for his hands while shifting my head from side to side. "No baby, she's fine…It's Lamar. He's in the hospital." He had a look of disbelief. "Lamar? What happened?" "Its cancer…I'm not certain of the type or where but he's in the hospital and your parents want you there as soon as possible. I've already made plane reservations." He got up from his seat and walked towards the window. "Damn! Could that have been what he tried to tell me?"

"What did you say sweetie?" "When Lamar visited with us…he tried to tell me something. Actually he told me several things but not this, not cancer." I walked up next to him calling on all the strength in me. "Miles his prognosis is uncertain so we need to leave soon. I packed some things and they are in the car." He looked at me with a piercing stare. "What are you saying Tye?" "Miles baby, I'm not saying anything. I'm telling you everything your mother told me." "Alright, let me close up shop and we'll get out of here."

On our way to the elevator Miles called his mother. He was silent through most of the conversation, which meant she had a great deal to tell him. Several minutes had passed before he parted with silence. "Can I speak to him? Okay, we'll be there in a few hours. I love you too." When he closed the phone I reached for his hand. "Is everything alright?" He hesitantly replied. "I guess so, Lamar is resting…I can't believe this is happening." "We'll be there soon baby."

The drive to the airport and the subsequent flight were silent. Miles extended a few courtesies at the ticket counter and to the flight attendant but only to the degree required. He wasn't standoffish, rather preoccupied. When we touched down in Birmingham he quickly gathered himself and walked directly to the rental car counter. As I waited for our baggage my thoughts drifted towards Brittany.

Brittany had lost her mother to cancer and I could only imagine her anxiety during this time. Then there's Miles and his complicated relationship with Lamar. I recalled all the times he postponed visiting with him under the guise of working or money is tight. Certainly in the last few years money had been of less concern but maybe all those early years of using the excuse just made it habitual. I remember once telling Miles we should never allow such things to keep us from visiting because quite frankly the only money required would be for gas to make the trip. It's not like we would have been visiting a friend rather it would have been family. But all of those would've, should've, could've scenarios are insignificant at this point.

I felt a tap on my shoulder and turned to view my darling husband in his somber state. "I'm going to get the car and will meet you out front." I smiled and nodded in agreement. "Alright baby." My attention turned when the bell sounded indicating the luggage from our flight was being loaded on the conveyor.

After getting our bags, I looked at my watch *(4:45pm)* then walked outside near the taxi pick-up. There was no sign of Miles so I adjusted my watch to local time. Moments later, I looked up when a horn sounded as Miles approached the curb. He stopped the car then stepped out to load the bags. I seated myself and began preparing my mind for the silence that would come during the 20-minute drive to Birmingham Memorial.

Once we arrived at the hospital the atmosphere seemed twice as tense. The people in the lobby looked mentally drained much in the way Miles appeared. There was a mother holding snuggly her crying infant as she rocked back and forth. In another corner was an elderly couple holding hands as a woman dressed in white spoke with them. In every inch of the lobby someone's life was unfolding for better or worse. Miles and I stepped up to the nurse's counter where the receptionist appeared intently focused on the computer monitor.

"Good evening, can you tell me which room I can find Lamar Stewart?" The receptionist looked up from her monitor and cleared her throat. "I'm sorry sir, are you next of kin?" Miles huffed. "As a matter of fact I am. He's my brother!" He made a failed attempt to mask his annoyance as the receptionist stood and began to speak softly. "Sir, I'll have to ask you to wait while I get the attending physician. "What's the problem? I'm his brother…just tell me the room number." "Please sir; it will only be a moment." Miles slammed his fist against the counter as she walked away. All eyes were now focused in our direction. I grabbed Miles' hand and squeezed gently to comfort him. I had watched enough hospital dramas to know that when a family member is told to wait for the attending physician bad news would likely follow. I kept the thought to myself and held my husband's hand hoping my assumption would be proven wrong.

Clarissa

The last three weeks had been therapeutic. Franklin and I discussed his child-hood and all the feelings he had about it. His birthday had marked a transi-tional period in our relationship giving it the feel of something fresh and new. We talked and shared daily as though we were dating for the first time. I began to revisit old feelings and thirst for new ones.

With that thought, I jumped out of bed to begin my day. It had been a long time since I felt so energized on a Saturday morning. After brushing my teeth and washing up, I put on an oversized shirt a pair of shorts and house slippers. The girls had been invited to a sleepover so I had the house to myself. I made the bed and spruced up the bedroom then headed to the kitchen for a cup of coffee.

When I entered the kitchen, I opened the blinds welcoming the rays of sun. The warmth of the rays penetrated my body reminding me that I've been blessed with another beautiful day. I pushed the button on the coffee pot then walked outdoors to retrieve the newspaper. Mr. Harrison from across the street was out pruning his flowers. "Good morning Mr. Harrison." He wore a straw hat with a light blue shirt and tan shorts. After hearing my greeting he raised his hand above his head waving side to side. "Good morning Clarissa, how are you?"

Mr. Harrison was a retired school principal, an elderly gentleman with a wealth of academic experience and three books to his credit. He and his wife were both products of Howard University and active participants in the civil rights movement. They both retired from academics and now enjoy most of their time gardening and traveling. "I'm fine thank you. I'm surprised the Mrs. isn't in the garden with you." He shook his head and chuckled. "She's in there on the phone talking to our daughter." I looked quickly over my flowers then picked up the newspaper. "Alright, well you two enjoy this beautiful day." "We sure will and you do the same."

When I entered the house the aroma of fresh Colombian coffee welcomed me. Briefly, I thought of how wonderful it is that Mr. and Mrs. Harrison have managed 50 years of marriage. I recalled a conversation between Gertrude and I where she said the key to a successful relationship is to temper perils of the heart. "Child life is a journey of choices…each one you make shapes who you are and who you'll become. Don't allow issues to victimize you, confront them head-on because they don't go away by avoidance or pretending." It's funny because there is no way she could have known the peril that challenges Franklin and I but somehow what she said so long ago was very relevant. And given what I know now Franklin and I have truly impeded our relationship because of avoidance and pretending.

Mr. and Mrs. Harrison, God Bless them, they were like surrogate parents to the community. They reminded us from *whence we came* and challenged us to reach for places we hadn't been. I poured a cup of coffee then walked onto the patio to enjoy the sun, a paper and thoughts of reconciliation.

My stomach began to turn as I read the latest in the Lewinsky saga. The last few days had been filled with innuendo and omissions. In the latest development the secret service was being asked to offer testimony regarding the allegations. *A national embarrassment some were saying…I knew he couldn't be trusted…my heart goes out to his wife and I applaud her strength others would say.* Then there was that terrible event in Jasper Texas that had everyone on edge. *How could this happen in the 90's? Nothing has changed? It's an isolated incident involving three sick people. I would lose my religion if, I were those parents.* The topics occupied conversations everywhere and opinions were all over the place.

My thoughts shifted when the telephone rang. I folded the paper under my arm and raced indoors. "Hello." My heart quivered when I realized Franklin was on the opposite end. "Have you had breakfast?" I thought to myself how perfect his timing had been. "No, I've just had a morning cup of coffee." "Well how do you feel about *IHOP?*" I smiled at the gesture. "Franklin dear that would be wonderful, I just need a half hour to get ready." We talked a few more minutes to finalize the time. As I cradled the phone I noticed a red number one in the window of the receiver.

Franklin arrived less than an hour later. He was dressed in blue dock shorts, a yellow golf shirt and sandals. "It looks like someone is ready for the Florida sunshine. I don't blame you considering the wave of heat the last few days."

Franklin simply smiled and from the roam of his eyes I sensed that my comments weren't the only catalyst to my observing all thirty-two of his teeth. I wasn't flashy or simple for that matter. Just tan shorts and a cranberry blouse. We embraced after he entered the doorway. I could feel his breath then his lips on my cheek. "So, are you ready Mrs. Green?" I spoke while walking towards the bedroom. "I just have to get my purse. Give me 60 seconds."

On the drive to *IHOP* we discussed the girls. He and I had spoken with Tamara after I shared with him the things she revealed to me. The girls had been the other subject occupying my thoughts and our discussions lately. Tamara had blamed herself for our separation. She thought that Franklin was disappointed in her and wanted to get away. Thank God we talked with her. She was still occasionally distant but all her feelings were now in the open. Since discussing her feelings we were at least more conscious of dealing with them.

Miles

The physician returned holding her clipboard in both hands and looking down. But she didn't have to say a word. Just a few steps behind Brittany followed with her arms wrapped across her chest and head bowed. She raised her head as though sensing my presence. Tears were flowing down her face and upon seeing me she cried out running towards my direction. "Miles he's gone! He's gone!" My heart dropped. The only thing I could do was reach out to console her as the finality of those words pierced my consciousness. Moments later my mother and father appeared. Mom was devastated and Dad held her as tightly as he could. He ushered her towards Brittany and I then wrapped his arms around us all. A tear travel down my face as I looked to find my wife standing a few feet away next to the doctor. When I motioned for her the physician remained standing quietly waiting for the opportunity to explain what happened.

I gathered myself then walked towards the doctor. She expressed her condolences then explained all that happened. After giving me the details, she quietly walked away. "Twenty minutes! I'm twenty freaking minutes too late!" If I had arrived sooner I would have been able to speak to him. I should have called from the airport or in the car at the very least.

Not knowing what more to do or say I mustered the courage to see my brother. As I walked past Tyler she asked if I wanted her by my side. I nodded and told her I would be okay. Mom and Dad were now seated outside the room consoling each other while Tyler stood next to the wall holding and comforting Brittany. When I opened the door to his room it felt cold. If I hadn't known, I would have thought he was asleep. There were flowers and get-well cards all over the room. All these people responded within a few hours. I didn't know for certain but it seemed all these people had the chance to offer a gesture before he left this world. "Everyone except me...his only brother had no chance to…" Tears welled in my eyes as I began think of all the hellos, how are yous and I love yous that will never be shared. I kneeled down to his side taking his hand in mine. "It's just not fair! It's not fair."

Franklin

I kneeled down studying the terrain then the hole. One more look at the terrain then the hole. Just a little more concentration was all I needed to birdie this hole. Only 10 feet and I could walk away victorious. The competition had been surprisingly challenging or maybe I've been away from the green too long. I walked to the hole once more confirming the distance then kneeled to make sure the surface was free of debris. "Franklin this is not the U.S. Open and you're not Tiger Woods." I held up my hand to silence my competition. "Shh, don't interrupt my concentration." Only 10 feet to go and that will be the end. After verifying everything was in order I tapped the ball and observed its movement towards the hole. Keep straight, straight, straight, that's it. *Cling Cling!* "Yes!" I pumped my fist in excitement then looked over at Clarissa. "Now, I'm ready to go." She shook her head in laughter. "Franklin I had forgotten how childishly serious you can get at putt-putt golf." I huffed. "You weren't feeling that way while you had the lead." She ignored that comment and walked away.

"Hey lady, can I offer you some frozen yogurt to soothe the loss?" It took every ounce of energy in me to mask the gloating. "It will be my treat." She turned in her club and walked to the refreshment counter. Once there she leaned over the counter placed an order then proceeded to a table. I signaled the person behind the counter and asked them to double what she requested then walked over sitting at the table. "You were off of your game today?" She snickered. "I let you win because you always whine afterwards. At least that's what I remember." "Wait a minute! I know we haven't played in a while but I never whined. In fact, I am the one who let you win all those other times." She held up her hand. "Please Franklin don't even go there, we both know you always whine. I just decided to have a little mercy on you that's all there is to it." The attendant approached with two small strawberry yogurt parfaits. "That will be $5.75. Is there anything more I can get for you?" I nodded my head and handed the attendant $10.00. "Keep the change." "Thank you sir." The attendant nodded then walked away.

Clarissa began her usual methodical ritual of savoring every ounce. She took her spoon and slowly scrapped around the edges to fill the tip. Then she would slowly open her mouth extending her tongue beneath the spoon to sample the sweetness. I don't know if it was purposeful but it sure did appear sensual and mere watching always aroused something in me.

I snapped from the hypnotic setting when a woman yelled from excitement following a hole-in-one. She danced around her companion like she was performing the funky chicken. Observing her made me realize that my feeble and uncreative attempts at celebrating were no comparison. Shifting my attention to Clarissa, I scooped a spoonful of frozen yogurt from my cup and shoved it into my mouth.

"Oh Shit." I muffled pressing my temples shaking my head side to side. "Franklin! Are you alright?" Rocking back and forth I felt a tear roll down my face. "Brain freeze…I have a brain freeze!" Clarissa immediately began laughing so hard tears welled up in her eyes. She pointed the spoon in my direction as though to instruct me on how to eat frozen yogurt. "You should take smaller bites, you'll enjoy it more and there won't be a brain freeze." As the sensation faded away, I gathered myself and decided to follow her instructions.

"Hey lady there's something going on that I think you should know." She paused a moment then braced herself for the unknown. "It's nothing terrible I just wanted you to know that since our discussion about my past I've been visiting a counselor." She nodded then took another small spoonful of yogurt. "Is it helping at all?" "Well it's early in the process but talking about it helps me understand things." "What things do you mean exactly? What happen to you is despicable but I can't help wonder why you didn't trust me enough to share it sooner. When you shared it with me, I blocked the question out because it seemed selfish but the more I considered it the more troubling it seemed." I reached across the table to take her hand. "It wasn't a matter of trusting you sweetheart, I just couldn't share it. Maybe we both should attend the sessions?"

A few moments later Clarissa's cell phone rang. I didn't know whom she was speaking but whomever and whatever they shared caused her demeanor to change abruptly.

"I'll let everyone at the office know, take as much time as you need. Give our condolences to the family." I was alarmed when she said condolences. "Is he going to be alright?" I wanted to interrupt the conversation to satisfy my curiosity but opted not to be rude. Whatever she was discussing and whoever it was deserved her complete attention. "Make sure you call when the arrangements have been made. Okay Tyler, you two take care of yourselves. I'm truly sorry." The family involved was identified by the sentence she spoke but I had no details.

"That was Tyler...Miles' brother passed away today." "Oh my God! What happened? Was there an accident?" "No, apparently he had been battling cancer and the family never knew." "That's tragic. Is there anything we can do for the family?" She muffled a response as her chin dropped towards her chest in sadness. "Not right now, they still have to make arrangements." I reached for Clarissa's hand to comfort her. "Yes, of course they have to make preparations." I looked at my watch to access the time. "Well I think we should get going." She raised her head and nodded in agreement. "Okay...I just can't imagine what they are going through right now."

Miles

The day before the funeral, I visited with Brittany. She had finalized the arrangements after discussing with my parents the proposed date of internment. Her desire was to bury him before the Fourth, so they all agreed on the Thursday July 2nd. When I arrived she opened the door and hugged me at the entrance. Under the circumstances she seemed to be holding together fairly well.

"Hey Sis, I picked up the suit you wanted for Lamar." She stepped aside and pointed towards the living room. "Thanks Miles, can I offer you something?" I sat on the sofa and began surveying the flowers and sympathy cards that filled the room. "No, I'm okay." She stood with her back to me looking out the window.

"You know he must have known he would leave us. Just last week he told me everything." It sounded as though she just wanted a sounding board so I remained silent only making the necessary response to assure her that I was listening. "He explained about the money he used for radiation treatment. And to think, I thought he was tipping." She shook her head in disgust over the thought of her reaction. "He was trying to spare me a repeat of the anguish and misery I felt following my mother's death." She huffed then turned and looked at me. "That was Lamar, always concerned about others even when you couldn't understand his reasoning." I smiled and agreed with her as she continued. "He made me promise not to tell anyone. I'm not sure exactly why he wanted it that way, surely there was some justification." She turned her attention back towards the window gazing outward.

"Brittany, I know the timing may be off but I just want to know if Lamar took care of everything." She turned with a perplexed expression. "What do you mean exactly?" Embarrassment circulated my entire body. I felt stupid for asking given the way Lamar had always handled his affairs. After all he had been the esteemed fireman in the family. Chewing on the leather, I had managed to insert into my mouth, I composed myself and apologized speaking with a little more sensitivity. "I'm sorry; I just wanted to make sure you and junior would be okay financially." She nodded and returned to peering out the window. "He left us plenty. There's a term-life insurance policy that pays off the house and an additional policy that provides us more than enough cash. We'll be okay."

She turned from the window walking towards the pictures on the wall. "You know Miles he always talked about the two of you and how he wished you could have spent more time together." Those words cut me to the core. I had been doing my own thing having very little time for my brother. As I recalled, I rarely contacted him. In fact, the only time we talked is when he initiated it. My moment of self-pity was interrupted when I observed her pulling an article of some sort from a desk drawer near where she stood. "He wanted you to have this." She extended her hand towards me holding a key. "Brittany, I can't accept that from you. She walked over to me reaching for my hand then placed the key inside my palm and closed it. "He wanted you to have this because of your love for Jazz. That was one thing the two of you had in common." I was surprised because I had no idea Lamar had an ear for Jazz. "Are you sure?" She nodded her head pointing towards a closet in the corner. "There's a shelf filled with albums he's collected."

I walked to the closet inserting the key. Upon entering, I was completely amazed that he actually had vinyl albums of old standards. Billie Holiday, Nina Simone, Etta James, Coltrane, Byrd, Cole, Turrentine, Wes Montgomery and much more...I couldn't believe my eyes. Overwhelmed with emotion, I quickly exited the room. Tears had filled my eyes as I looked at Brittany and thanked her for the key. She reached for my support then we both embraced and cried together. She cried over her loss and I cried over loss and guilt...

"I always found it difficult to be in his presence. It was like having to measure up and not being able to do it..." Brittany lifted her head from my shoulder looking at me in amazement. "Miles you never had to measure up to Lamar. He loved you and I'm surprised you didn't know." I felt silly all over again. "I hear what you're saying and don't misunderstand me he never did anything wrong...it's just a feeling that stayed with me." She released her arms from my shoulder returning to the window. "He always talked about your spunk. Said you were driven and would do great things when you finally discovered your purpose...but for reasons he couldn't explain you just didn't know how to be pleased with yourself." The words sounded vaguely familiar to my last discussion with Lamar...

The afternoon of the funeral was surprisingly pleasant considering the last few weeks of scorching heat and humidity. Guests were dressed in the traditional somber colors. Mom and Dad were doing well considering just last night she was praying, crying and asking why God had taken him before either herself or Dad but she quickly proceeded to ask for forgiveness for questioning God's will. Brittany sat next to them quietly holding little junior's hand.

The funeral was celebratory as several people stood to say wonderful things about Lamar. Most talked about how he himself or he and Brittany had entered and touched their lives. I punished myself as I sat there realizing that most of the guest held an advantage over me. They actually knew my brother...the man. Tears rolled down my face realizing the only memories I have of my brother involved his childhood. I had never thought of it before but somehow subconsciously convinced myself that just knowing his childhood was enough. That is until this hour, this very moment while listening to people saying wonderful things. I had wasted precious opportunities to know my brother. Lamar, from the sentiments I heard, enjoyed a kind of happiness and inner peace I never experienced. And now he was gone before I had the chance to ask him the source.

Clarissa

Arching my back and extending my arms backward I released a yawn. Stuffed beyond belief, I began feeling drowsy. Franklin had barbequed chicken, pork ribs and hamburgers and everyone managed to put away more than their fair share. I'm not complaining because that means no leftovers to put away and aside from that Franklin could make some delicious barbeque. During his time in the Navy he had collected cookbooks from all the countries he visited. Those that weren't in English he had translated and has been experimenting with every chance he gets.

Our guests were family, friends and co-workers and a few friends of the girls. Raising myself from the chair, I surveyed the room walking towards the kitchen. Everyone had either taken a seat or a spot on the wall with his or her eyes fixed on the television and frequently bursting into laughter as we watched *The Best of the Chris Rock Show.*

The Independence Day celebration had turned out perfectly until Franklin's father shifted my thoughts. He approached me from behind wrapping his hands around my waist. "Hey daughter, the food was absolutely delicious but mother and I have to get going." As the memory of Franklin's revelation emerged in my mind I cringed. "Wow, I didn't mean to startle you." He could never imagine what I was thinking at that very moment but I found a fake smile somewhere deep inside and thanked him for the compliment. Slapping him across the mouth is what I wanted to do but managed to thwart the desire.

This man was a huge part of why my husband and I were separated. If he had been a true father and handled that trick maybe Franklin...God! I don't know but he should have done something...he should have been there...how could he have been so nonchalant? "Well I'm sure Franklin will be disappointed that you're leaving so soon." I on the other hand cheered. For the life of me I couldn't understand why or how Franklin managed to keep a relationship with him. Lord please forgive me for having that thought but I don't understand. He smiled then kissed me on the cheek. "He'll understand. Now where are my grandkids? I want to see them before we leave." I reached for the intercom and dialed in Tamara's room. "Tamara your grandparents are about to leave. Bring your sister and come to say goodbye please."

"Excuse me I need to return to the other guest. The girls will be here in a moment." Terrible thoughts raced through my mind as I walked away in frustration. Franklin had completed a few sessions with the counselor but the subject of my going never occurred again and I was happy he didn't pressure me about it. Besides there was nothing to be gained being there to listen to all the details of what happened. Especially given the fact that I had some matters to sort that definitely shouldn't be mentioned for the first time in that setting. Quite frankly, the only details I had up to this point were my own images that infuriated me. If I were to hear details I'm not certain what my reaction would be so it's best I support him outside the counselor's office…at least for now.

When I reached the family room the credits were scrolling and everyone moved around laughing commenting on *Chris Rock's* jokes. "Clarissa the food was good girl. You must bring some of that apple pie to work on Monday." Amber sashayed towards me gently swaying her hips. The girl was a trip. She wasn't threatening just bold and confident about her womanhood. She hugged me saying that she and Brett (the new guy) had to leave. "Girl I don't think any will be left but if there is I'll save a piece for you." "Sounds good…thanks for inviting us and I'll see you at work." Brett smiled and shook my hand then they both left.

I smiled thinking of the many times Franklin and I had been in a group setting patiently waiting for the first couple to leave signaling it was okay to excuse ourselves. Of course there was only a small parallel because our guest weren't required to attend, but the way everyone seem to take Amber's departure as a silent cue it reminded me of those times just the same.

After saying goodbye to the last of the guest, I closed the door and walked towards the kitchen. Franklin and Tia were standing over the sink rinsing the dishes unaware that I entered. My feet came to an abrupt halt as I took a few moments to admire him. It felt a little embarrassing but something in me couldn't resist. Besides after all these months I had almost forgotten about his attractive endowments.

At that moment all my physical inhibitions had escaped me. I looked at those two recalling all the wonderful moments and smiled. My trip down memory lane was overshadowed when a sound escaped me that had been bottled up the entire time the guests were here. Franklin and Tia turned in unison when they heard the fart. Now I would normally classify my flatulates a poot but I had been holding it so long it graduated to the male category of fart with a capital 'F.' *Oh my God! Not an odor!* I thought to myself. I was so embarrassed that I simply turned and quickly raced toward my bedroom. I could hear Tia and Franklin snickering. He cleared his throat and called out sympathetically. I had no idea what he said and at that moment it really didn't matter.

After entering the bedroom, I closed the door picking up a magazine from the nightstand. As I thumbed through the pages pretending to look for an article Franklin knocked calling from the door. "Clarissa I'm sorry for laughing are you alright?" I sat in the chair next to the window and crossed my legs. "Yes, I'm fine thank you." "May I come in?" I could hear the laughter in his voice even though he tried to mask it. "Sure but only if you make a promise." He paused for a moment then responded. "Okay, what do you want me to promise?" "No jokes, okay?" "That's a reasonable request."

When he entered the room Tia slipped in behind him. "Ooh, Mommy you didn't say excuse me." Franklin and I both burst into laughter. "Come here young lady." I extended my arms to embrace my little muffin. "Excuse me for passing gas...So young lady, can you tell me why we celebrate the 4th of July?" She removed herself from my arms sashaying with as much confidence as a teenager then stopped in front of the full-length mirror. "I don't know." Then as suddenly as she answered she put her index finger against her temple turning towards me as though having just realized the answer. "Wait! Let me check my mental camera...Click! It's a celebration of America's independence from England!" After giving the answer she sashayed over to her father wrapping her arm around his waist. Leaning against him with one hand on her hip she managed a dancer's pose. "Right daddy?" We both looked at each other and smiled. "That's a good answer for a 10 year old."

"So, did you two finish cleaning the kitchen?" Franklin looked at Tia then at me and laughed. "Actually, we came to see if you would consider helping us out." "What did you say?" "Hmph" I got up and started towards the door. "I thought you two had everything under control." "Yeah we did but it became a little stuffy so we took a break." "Ooh Franklin! That's so mean." I slapped him on the shoulder but couldn't help laughing because I knew he was right.

Tyler

Clothes were piled up in all three hampers. The last few weeks had been busy and neither Miles nor I had thought about dry cleaning. So when I looked into the laundry my hands slapped against my side dreading the task. Miles had been quiet and distant since the funeral so I didn't ask for his help. The only thing giving him peace was his music. He played the records Lamar had left him for hours then he would play his horn mimicking or making his own sound.

I sifted through every pocket stacking dry cleaning in one pile and washables separated by colors in another. Miles had dry cleaning that had been neglected for weeks. I silently chastised myself for letting that happen because my mother taught me better. There was something different in nearly every pocket I emptied. I found spare change, a few dollar bills, ATM receipts, buttons, paper clips and business cards. It seemed I would never end this tedious task.

For five years I had been complaining about clearing pockets before dropping clothes in the laundry room. Strangely for some reason Miles was deaf to this demand…but it didn't matter because I truly enjoyed doing things for him. A smile emerged as I considered how wonderful a man he is and to think just a few weeks ago I had been *trippin* over some nonsense. As I pulled out the last pocket a business card fell to the floor. Normally I would have just put it aside with the others but the black arrow on the face and the words *look on back* captured my curiosity.

The name didn't faze me one bit but when I read the back my heart dropped recalling the day I bought that watch. My heart split recalling the reason I chose those words to inscribe on the back of the watch's surface. My hands trembled recalling the reason I had been given for the watch no longer being in our lives. What is this and how could this woman possibly cite that inscription unless she saw the watch? How could she and where could she? All these questions were circling my mind when I dropped everything as my stomach began reacting causing me to race toward the bathroom.

Everything spilled from within me as though I had eaten a box of laxatives. Twenty minutes had passed when I began washing up. The image reflecting in the mirror appeared worn out. I wasn't sure if my appearance was caused by the chores or the business card but considering I had just begun the chores the answer was obvious. Compounding the stress were recollections of a letter I had read from Margo. I could kick that bitch's ass!

With that thought, I made an effort to block it all acknowledging that there had to be some reasonable explanation. I turned on the fan returning to the laundry room. Fanning my hand in the air, I spoke aloud to convince myself that I was overreacting. "I need to stop *trippin!*" As quickly as the words escaped my mouth, I felt a light pat on my butt. "What do you need to stop *trippin* on?" When I turned and saw him my mouth couldn't move. He started helping with the laundry and I forced myself to recall all the wonderful things he's brought to my life. He cooked; cleaned, co-managed our finances and he never once raised a hand at me. The man was my partner, my friend, my confidant and my lover and God knows he could make love like nobody's business. It's funny how a woman recalls certain characteristics or qualities when she wants to convince herself of something. "It's nothing, I was just complaining to myself about all this laundry." "Well, a *brotha* is here to offer some support. Besides, I haven't exactly been fair to you since the funeral. Its time I get on with my life you know what I mean?" I smiled and kissed him on the lips. I'm sure he thought it was an expression of concurrence but I know that at that very moment I resolved that I was *trippin* and that Miles was the best thing to come into my life. I dropped the clothes cupping his head in my palm pulling his head towards mine. Since I'm usually not the aggressor I expected no resistance. I kissed him deeply and before I knew it we were making love in the laundry room…

Afterwards we rested against each other. I thought to myself how my body wanted him but couldn't brush off feeling like a teenager trying to prove the man is mine. In the back of my mind the thought lingered that I may have pursued him because of feeling threatened. Damn Tyler! You can be so stupid. "Wow! What got into you Tye?" I pushed him away resuming the laundry. It wasn't a violent push nor was it passionate…just cold enough to signal things had changed. "I thought you just did." It was not my intention to sound miffed but it came out that way. "Is there something wrong? Don't tell me you didn't reach your peak?" I rolled my eyes. "You know we can go again." Typical man, always thinking of himself and his sensitive manhood, I turned to see him hungrily looking over my body. "It's okay as long as you got yours I'm happy." I lied…Miles could always take me to my peak and beyond…truth is I made it there twice but I didn't want him to know.

"Miles sweetie, what ever happened to the watch I bought for you?" The words flowed so nonchalant I had to wonder if I hadn't just received a clue from the business card. "What? I told you what happened years ago. Don't you remember? I lost it." Oh no! I know he didn't just brush this off with a straight face! I wanted to throw the card in his face but decided against it. "What brought that up after all these years?" I smiled as the idea for my next move settled in my mind. "No particular reason, it just suddenly entered my mind so I decided to ask."

I must have scratched the surface of something because his demeanor quickly changed which made me even more concerned about my discovery. He left the laundry room entering the kitchen. I remained there loading clothes but could hear the cupboard open and close. Then the refrigerator opened followed by rummaging through ice. I just shook my head because it was clear he was making a drink. At that moment I knew there was something more to this story. Some people fidget and others sweat during anxiety or nervousness but Miles would sip a little scotch. Now, I'm not assuming or accusing him of anything but there is something more to this lost watch and I intend to find out. I peaked outside the laundry room observing him tilt an 8OZ. glass of dark liquid into his mouth. Hmph, no cola's in the house was all I thought.

"Miles dear, would you finish up the laundry? I have to run to the store and I'm going to stop by Clarissa's along the way." "Sure, I'll take care of it."

I walked into the bathroom took a quick shower dressed and was out the door in 15 minutes. Now that was a record for me because I normally need an hour. Things are much simpler when a lady throws on a baseball cap, shorts and a tee shirt.

During the drive several thoughts entered my mind the last of which I apparently took onboard. I made that conclusion after driving into the shopping mall parking lot for a brief visit at the travel agency. Call it impulsive or insecure but I needed to know how this person was able to cite my personal inscription…

"Hey Tye, how are you doing girl?" I walked past her only briefly pausing to kiss her cheek as she motioned for me to enter the door. "I'm okay thanks." I knew that her motherly instincts would prompt more questions and considering my drab mood I braced myself for interrogation. "Who do you think I am some stranger? I've known you long enough to detect when something is bothering you. But I'm not going to press the issue." She held up her hand as though to silence anything I might contemplate. Walking into the den she dropped herself on the sofa picking up a magazine. I just stood in the foyer. "You're no stranger so find yourself a seat." I followed her instructions like a child that had just disappointed a parent. I hated that she could make me feel that way but she always had my interest at her core so her antics were bearable. I sat down telling her about the business card and the mysterious loss of the watch I purchased. As usual she didn't judge only listened. Sometimes that frustrated me because a part of me wished she would incite a little fire and vengeance when I felt I had been wronged. Of course that is the immature part of me. Certainly there were other friends I could talk with and they would do me the favor of offering advice and later top it off by spreading my business all over Jacksonville. No Thanks!

I told Clarissa that I had made reservations to Virginia Beach and planned to make an appointment with this lady. I wanted to find out how she managed to know my husband and happened to know what had been inscribed on a watch that I bought. "Do you think it's innocent?" I wasn't sure how to answer that question but given my reaction I hadn't ruled it out as being less than innocent. "I'm really not sure. But when I asked Miles about it his answer wasn't convincing." I began to rub my temples in frustration considering my reaction.

"You know something? After I asked the question he went into the kitchen and poured a drink." I made a few gestures for effect. "He actually made a drink and that's something Miles never does unless he's nervous and I've only known him to be nervous on a few occasions." Holding up my right hand and extending my fingers I started to name the occasions. "He wasn't going on a job interview, he wasn't playing any music, and he wasn't being presented an award so that leaves me to think he's hiding something." "Well what ever you decide to do be careful and don't rush to judgment." She leaned over and hugged me. "Thanks Clarissa. I'm not planning anything...only to gather a little more information..."

As I waited in line to check in for the flight my thoughts drifted to what I was about to do in deceit. The previous night with Miles was pleasant and he held me tight the entire night. Thank God my monthly visitor had stopped by because I certainly didn't want him inside me with this other woman occupying my thoughts. And considering how pleasant the day had been it would have been a challenge to resist him without exposing what I've learned. I knew there were good reasons for that monthly visitor…

I told Miles that a prospective client wanted to meet and review some proposals before signing on with our office. It was just a little white lie and who knows maybe I could generate a client or two while I'm in Virginia Beach…

"Good morning, where is your destination?" I smiled and without a word reached into my bag and pulled out the ticket. "Miss, where is your destination?" I was still a little uneasy with the idea of making this next step but managed to respond. "I'm sorry, Virginia Beach is my destination." The lady just smiled as she took my ticket. She then began punching the keyboard and talking at the same time. "Would you care for a window or aisle Ms. Stewart?" I had always loved the aerial view of a city so it was no question where I wanted to sit I just had to convey my desires to this woman who had begun to annoy me. "Will you be checking any baggage?" The woman had an unnatural smile and to top that she especially irked me by talking without the courtesy or decency of looking in my face. I understand that I'm one of many customers but she could at least appear more sincere. "No baggage and I'll take a window seat please." "Okay Miss, your flight departs from gate C-21 seat number 5F." She handed me the boarding pass and I could swear she understood my signals because she spoke with just a little more sincerity or maybe I just convinced myself. "Please enjoy your flight." I nodded taking the pass. There wasn't much of a delay and by the time I reached the gate they announced that boarding would begin in five minutes.

The flight was tranquil culminating into a beautiful view of the ships moored in Norfolk. As I looked out the window Clarissa and Franklin entered my mind…My thoughts were interrupted when the captain announced that we would be touching down in ten minutes. The flight attendants were scurrying to make sure all seats were fully upright with tray tables in the stowed position. After the plane landed, I said a silent prayer and waited as we taxied toward the gate.

Once I disembarked the plane my stomach started to flutter. There was still time to turn around especially since I had no idea what revelations awaited here. However once I exited the airport the fresh air and a gentle breeze were a pleasant calm to this unpredictable circumstance. Taxis lined the roads everywhere and the people were briskly walking trancelike with little bags rolling behind. No one said hello or even acknowledged one another. It seemed as though I was an observer in a robotic demonstration.

I signaled for a taxi and the driver nodded then pulled up making a stop at the curb. He quickly exited then zipped around the rear popping open his trunk then stepping towards me standing erect. It reminded me of those military movies where a subordinate comes to attention when encountering a senior officer. Of course I'm no officer but the gesture certainly made me feel special. He then opened the rear door and snapped back into an erect position. "May I take your bag?" I extended my carry-on and stepped into the car. He closed the door and quickly returned to the driver side entering the car. "Where is your destination?" "Would you take me to the Waterside Omni Hotel please?" He chuckled and cleared his throat. "There's only one Omni in the area." I felt a little silly but since I hadn't been here my only recourse was to laugh it off. "I knew that, just checking to see if you're on your toes." We both started laughing as he pulled away from the curb traveling down the road. I called Miles to let him know I had arrived safely. The conversation was intentionally brief so that I wouldn't lose my focus. Today would be a day for answers...

The hotel had a circular access road leading to the main entrance with beautiful glass doors and pillars. A handsomely dressed gentleman was stationed outside wearing a rustic overcoat with gold shoulder boards and a matching hat. He reminded me of Captain Kangaroo but much more regal. When the cab stopped the driver turned and smiled. "That will be $15.00 dollars mam." I realized I had been staring when he stated the fare again. He had the most beautiful dimples to form when he smiled and I just happened to notice. "I'm sorry do you have change?" I handed him a 50. He pointed at the passenger side visor where it was clearly written that no bills over 20 would be accepted. I sighed in disappointment and explained that I had no smaller denomination. He showed those dimples once more and offered to make an exception. "You're a beautiful woman that seems trustworthy so I'll let it slide." "Oh, that's sweet of you." I smiled but regretted the words that escaped my mouth because it seemed so flirtatious. He handed me the change exiting the car to retrieve my bag. I stepped out and exhaled, "This is it!" He extended my bag towards me. "Excuse me?" "I was just talking to myself out loud, pay me no attention." I picked up my overnight bag and said goodbye. "Have a wonderful Day." I turned to find him waving and displaying those beautiful dimples.

The receptionist was taking care of another customer so I decided to browse. Near the elevator was a legend of where the conference rooms, restaurants and business offices were located. *Director of Corporate Programs, Ms.*

Desiree Bonet,' I cringed when I saw the name then walked to the elevator and pushed the button for the 9Th floor.

Her secretary escorted me into the office. The walls were covered with African art and pictures of sandy beaches with dark blue water. I purposely looked over her but the attempt became futile when she spoke extending her hand. "Good morning Ms. Stewart, how may we satisfy your corporate lodging needs" She had a sincere British accent and flawless skin. I extended my hand and felt as though I was touching myself as she was so soft. "Mrs. My name is Mrs. Tyler Stewart." I spoke with proclamation observing her response for a hint that she may have known my name. When she motioned towards a chair and continued smiling I figured she didn't know my name or had forgotten. "So what can the Omni do for you?" I slowly reached into my purse pulling out the business card. "May I offer you a beverage?" I stood and placed the card on her desk. "I found something that belongs to you." She paused looked at the back of the card then exhaled. I was nervous not knowing what to expect when she reached for her phone and pressed a button. My initial thought was that *sistah* was calling security to throw me out of her office. "Pam, would you please hold all my calls and see that I'm not disturbed?" "Well, I think it's accurate to say you're not here to discuss corporate lodging?" My face was emotionless I wanted to snap but decided the best course was to listen. Placing the card back on her desk she looked directly at me. "I was visiting Jacksonville on business and happen to stop in at *Natilie's* for a nightcap...and was quite surprised to see Miles performing on stage. Realizing that when he was here five years ago he unknowingly dropped his watch on the restaurant floor...I wanted him to know it wasn't a total loss and since I didn't have the watch on my person a note seemed to suffice. Surprisingly, he didn't recognize me although I have since changed my hair both color and style among other things." I could not believe the calm of this lady. There was a part of me that expected a scene. I had contemplated all kinds of scenarios along the way here but certainly not what I was experiencing. "You mentioned a restaurant-why were you dining with my husband?" I asked with just enough agitation in my voice to illicit a defensive response but there was none. "It was lunch time and all the other tables were taken so I asked to join him. He spoke a great deal about you and how special you are." Strangely, I no longer felt tense but a little more at ease as she spoke. "I'll take the watch if that's acceptable for you." She seemed a little startled by my response but agreed. "It's at my home but I can get it for you. Have you had lunch?" I told her I hadn't then she offered to meet for lunch in the hotel restaurant. I agreed realizing the mistake of coming to her office.

Fear entered my thoughts realizing that she was either expressing the truth or she cared enough for him to do what he hadn't…Protect me. Neither alternative was appealing and my body knew instantly. "Would you excuse me? I need to visit the ladies room." She called her secretary and asked her to show me to the ladies room. "I'll meet you downstairs at 1pm if that is acceptable to you?" I nodded in agreement then waltzed to the ladies room…

After leaving the bathroom, I entered the elevator and went downstairs. It would be an hour before lunch so I reached inside my purse for my cell phone. After checking for messages, I walked to the lounge pulling my overnight bag behind me. Clarissa had phoned and wanted to know if I was all right. I decided to return her call and inform her of what had taken place.

Clarissa spoke tentatively as though feeling me out to gauge my mood. "Tyler, are you okay? Have you met with her?" I sighed clearing my throat. "I'm fine and yes I've met with her. Surprisingly, she's been quite pleasant and that scares me." "Why is that? I don't understand." "I don't know exactly it's just a feeling. I mean she has either been honest with me or she cares about him enough to shield me from the truth." "Girl what did she say to you?" "She explained how he unknowingly lost his watch over lunch. Apparently it fell on the floor as he was leaving." "Hmph! That's interesting." "Yes, I thought so too but before I could comment she mentioned that all the tables had been taken so she asked to join him and he agreed. Apparently they talked to great length and discussed me." "Well, do you believe her?" I paused to allow the question to sink in before answering. "Actually she seems quite honest. I don't know if it's the accent or her unthreatening demeanor."

I rolled my wrist to check the time. "Look Clarissa, I'm going to meet her at a restaurant for lunch…thanks for listening." "You know I'm here for you. We'll talk when you return okay?" "That sounds good I'll talk to you tomorrow. I think I'll stay the night and do some thinking." "Call me if you need to talk and don't cloud your judgment." I wasn't sure of the meaning behind her advice but I hung up and walked into the restaurant. I had to see this woman make her entrance. During our meeting I hadn't seen much of her below the torso and even though she gave me no reason to feel threatened I couldn't shake the urge to make a quick comparison.

She arrived at exactly 1pm stopping for brief discussion with the hostess. Her hair draped just below her collar and bounced with fullness as she sashayed towards me. I couldn't help but notice her high cheekbones as she smiled and seated herself. "I believe this belongs to you" Pulling the watch from her she handed it to me.

Clarissa

The house was silent when I entered the door. Franklin had picked up the girls from summer camp giving me an opportunity to relax after a long day at the office. I placed the mail on the table and went directly to my bedroom. After kicking off my shoes I dropped my bag and undressed leaving my clothes on the floor. With the girls away I intended on soaking in the bathtub.

After filling the tub with hot water and coconut oil I turned on some music and stepped in to relax. I had been thinking about this moment all day and now it was finally here. As the steam circulated my body I began thinking about Franklin. He had asked if we could reconcile but I hesitated. Sure things were going quite well but he didn't know the true reason for my apprehension nor had he pressed the issue. My assumption is that he believed I needed more time to accept what happened to him but there was more. Given that fact, I had been stressed and felt unworthy of his patience. I had to tell him everything before we reconciled. The secrets between us had to be removed.

I had to put my own issues on hold when Tyler phoned. The change was welcomed and given her location and the uncertainty surrounding it she certainly needed my friendship.

I'm not sure how long we talked but I later heard a rapid knocking at the door awakening me from an apparent sleep. I can't be certain when the call from Tyler ended but Tia was knocking saying she wanted to come in and tell me about her day. Raising myself in the tub, I looked at the clock realizing I had been soaking for two hours. "I'll be out in a moment sweetheart." "Okay." After drying off, I put on some body lotion, my bath robe and then opened the door. "Hi sweetheart, how was your day?" I wrapped my arms around her shoulder then walked over towards the bed. She sat next to me extending her hand. "Oh, what's that sweetie?" "I made it for you. It's a picture of our family." Tia could surprise us sometimes with her thoughtfulness. The picture had four people, a house and two cars. Above the picture she had written *"My Family."* I hugged her tightly while staring at the picture allowing it's meaning to settle in my mind. "That is so beautiful Tia; you're going to be a female *Picasso*." "Ms. Greer told us to make a picture of the most important thing to us but I have three things." I felt so proud at that moment that tears formed in my eyes. "Mommy why are crying?" I squeezed a little more resting my head against hers. "Because I love you so much baby." "So why are you squeezing me?" I started laughing after that comment releasing her from my loving grasp. "I didn't mean to squeeze you so hard." She smiled then walked towards the door looking back before exiting. "I know mommy and I love you too."

After Tia left the room Franklin knocked entering with his hands behind his back. "Hello lady how was your day?" I sighed and subconsciously tightened my robe realizing I hadn't yet dressed. "It was long but not too bad. What about yours?" He walked slowly towards the bed then pulled his arms from behind his back revealing what he had been hiding. "These are for you Clarissa." "Oh my orchids, they're absolutely beautiful." Without much thought I instinctively stood, pulling his face towards me and kissed him. My sudden move had caught us both completely off guard as Franklin and I both breathed deeply in anticipation of what might follow. When I felt his arms around my waist I stepped back dropping my hand from his face. "Thanks Franklin I love them." The moment was a little awkward and when Franklin offered to excuse himself I was assured he felt the same. "Well, I should excuse myself while you get dressed." I couldn't speak a word. I just smiled nodding in agreement thankful that the bed was close enough to sit down because the spontaneous kiss had weakened my legs.

At that very moment, I begin to hear music escaping from the bathroom. *Donny Hathaway* was telling me about myself in his music. As I relived that kiss inside my mind, I was hoping that Franklin wouldn't find an excuse to return.

Dragging myself away from sensual thoughts, I quickly got dressed to join Franklin and the girls. Before leaving the room I turned off the radio and silently thanked Mr. Hathaway for the reminder.

When I entered the family room everyone was seated watching television. Franklin was the first to notice my entrance. "I thought we might have to send in the cops for you." I smiled but didn't respond walking over to kiss Tamara. "Oh, so you guys rented a movie?" The girls were entranced and didn't speak a word. After kissing Tamara I looked up and noticed Franklin pointing towards the living room and motioning that I join him.

When I entered the living room Franklin was already seated with a serious expression on his face. "Clarissa, there is something I want to discuss with you." He motioned for me to sit next to him reaching for my hand as I approached. "Why are you suddenly so serious?" As he held my hand, I could feel his thumb gently rubbing across my fingers. If it hadn't felt so good I may have assumed he was nervous. "Clarissa I've been doing some thinking and I believe it is now time." Since we weren't too far removed from the sensual encounter in the bedroom I had no intention of guessing the subject of his comments. "What exactly do you mean Franklin?" He then took my hands into both of his pulling them towards his lips softly kissing the backs. "Reconciliation…its time for me to come home to my family if you'll have me." Since I didn't know what to say at that moment I was careful not to retract my hand. I may have been at a loss of words but I didn't want to send a signal that might discourage him. "Franklin there's something we should discuss but I don't want to talk about it with the girls in the next room." He got up and started walking with me following since we still held hands. We passed through the family room unacknowledged by the girls stepping outside onto the patio deck. After closing the door, we shared a seat on the chaise lounger. "Whatever it is we can talk about it now." As I searched for the words to begin my confession my heart raced from anxiety. Images of all the conversations formed in my mind…so vivid that it seemed to have all happened today at this very moment. I kissed his hands and decided to share my secret. "Franklin I have not been completely true with you since our separation." After the words left my mouth I wondered why I hadn't been tactful in my delivery to preserve his feelings but that thought was quickly washed away by Franklin's response.

He tightened his hold of my hand and exhaled shaking his head in what I concluded must have been disbelief. Looking at him observing the disappointment in his eyes my thoughts drifted to the indiscretion.

It happened 6 months ago. Mr. Nelson Patton from the office had taken me to lunch. It was all very innocent because I had gotten to know him since my arrival at the company. We discussed books, our profession, our families and anything else that happened to strike our fancy. I can't be certain when it happened but somewhere along the line my inhibitions ceased. This was demonstrated to me one particular afternoon when we seated next to each other during lunch as opposed to across from each other as we had previously done. That was no problem at least it didn't appear to be.

We were talking and laughing when he noticed some food in the corner of my mouth. Rather than speaking to make me aware of it so that I could wipe my mouth, the man took his napkin wiping my mouth himself. When his hand touched my face the look in his eyes spoke volumes. The surprising revelation is that I heard exactly what his eyes conveyed and if we had been some place private my fear was that I couldn't be certain not to respond to him. The thought frightened me so much that I quickly got up and walked the five blocks back to the office alone. Along the way, I kept telling myself that it was nothing but after arriving at the office I was compelled to visit the ladies room and freshen up. Certainly it had been a while since I had been with a man, but that was no cause for what I permitted to happen. Most surprising is that I had no idea this man had touched me emotionally. For the life of me I could not point to the occasion when this had happened. But regardless when it happened, I had suddenly observed and thought of Nelson in a very different way.

I never thought of another man after marrying Franklin until now and only by grace have I been protected from the consummation of those thoughts. I was thankful but Franklin needed to know before we moved forward.

Tyler

For the life of me I couldn't understand my lack of anger. As I sat there holding the watch listening to her explain there was no indication of evidence to support my worst fear. Deep in my mind the notion that she was protecting him could not be discounted but strangely it didn't matter. I questioned her in the nastiest of tones just to get a defensive response. "So, why were you with a married man having lunch in the first place?" She surprised me by remaining calm and answering the question. In her voice there was no hint that she felt the need to be defensive and more important no indication of a romantic interest in my husband.

It was 2pm and we had been seated for about an hour talking quite cordially. The more I questioned her with my nasty tone the more she deflected it with calm unthreatening discussion. Sadly, I must admit her responses made my inquiries seem so unfounded that a sense of shame came over me. I can recall some friends other than Clarissa proclaiming that a *floozy* would always start trouble and wants to be discovered. But this woman was different she had no desire to start trouble regardless how much I tried to influence her with my comments and queries.

"Mrs. Stewart, I'm sorry for all this confusion but do realize I have no desire to disrupt your home." I listened and nodded in acknowledgement as she looked at her watch. "I do need to return to work but if there is anything more I can do please don't hesitate to call."

She signaled the waiter then reached into her purse removing her wallet and some cash then placed $30.00 on the table. "I'll take care of lunch." She smiled returning the wallet to her purse. "That's nice of you and thanks for sharing your time." "No problem at all, you're quite welcomed." As she walked away my eyes were fixed on her every move. Once she reached the entrance she stopped for brief discussion with the hostess. Afterwards they shared a brief laugh as she looked back at me. I shifted my eyes and pretended not to see her wave but I did. I saw everything and at that moment my questions were satisfied.

Surprisingly, I sat there without feeling the need for vengeance given my new revelation. There was no way I could know at this time what exactly happened but something did. I removed the cell phone from my purse and called my confidant. "Clarissa, how are you doing?" "Girl I'm just relaxing, how are things with you?" I exhaled as though the weight of the world was in the breath I breathed.

"We just finished lunch and she put my fears to rest thoroughly. I even talked nasty with her and she remained calm saying that she had no desire to disrupt my marriage." "You don't sound very convinced…if anything facetious is how I would describe you." The laughter couldn't be contained any longer. "I might have been if she hadn't looked back at me after leaving the restaurant. She was definitely surveying the effects of her work." "Are you certain she wasn't just saying goodbye?" "Hmph, you needed to be here to witness the performance but I can say that she wanted to protect me. If you want to know the truth about it she could've gotten ghetto on me but didn't." "Well, that's a good thing because you would have kicked her butt and I would have to come bail you out of jail." We both shared a brief laugh to break the seriousness of the situation.

"One thing the meeting convinced me of is that I shouldn't have come here at all." "So, are still planning to stay overnight?" "I'm not sure right now. There is a late flight arriving home tonight and I may take it." I heard a splash in the background. 'Clarissa, are you busy?" There was another slosh of water as she apparently adjusted before commenting. "I'm just soaking in the tub but we can talk." "I appreciate the offer but we can talk later. Besides there's some things I need to sort out." "All right, call me regardless whether you stay the night or not." "Okay."

After hanging up the phone, I sat a few more minutes to consider what I had learned…

It was early and since I had never been here taking the opportunity to visit was appealing. However the thought of staying the night at the Omni wasn't exactly comforting so I left the restaurant with my overnight bag rolling behind. Once outside the hotel a cool breeze comforted my face. I turned for one final glance at the hotel catching a glimpse of my reflection in the window. Reaching into my purse, I pulled out a pair of sunglasses then turned to signal a taxi. To my surprise it was the guy with the dimples.

"You've had a brief stay, may I take you bag?" I pretended not to recognize him and responded smugly extending him the handle to my bag. "I beg your pardon?" "Oh, forgive me I just recalled bringing you here earlier from the airport." "Oh yes, I'm sorry I didn't remember." He opened the rear door then walked to the rear loading my bag in the trunk. Upon entering the car, he turned his shoulders towards the backseat giving me a close up of those dimples. "So, where can I take you?" "Let's see...how about the Hilton?" He quickly turned placing the car in gear. "To the Hilton it is."

Once we arrived, I realized there was an added bonus. Mr. Dimples opened the door then walked toward the rear retrieving my bag. With a quick smile and a thank you I paid him and entered the hotel lobby. After checking in I went directly to the t-shirt shop I had noticed across the street. Humored by the convenience and the fact that I had no bathing suit my thought was to make a purchase. The walk from the hotel to the t-shirt shop and back had warmed my body so I went directly to the room showered and changed to take advantage of the beachfront amenity.

On the beachfront I relaxed and took in a few rays being careful not to exceed an hour thinking to myself that a sister has no business sunbathing in the first place.

Along the return walk to the hotel I stopped for a soft-drink at a tikki hut. The beach was crowded and people were definitely having a good time. I checked my watch then put on my wrap casually continuing my walk back to the hotel. Posted on the lobby marquee was an advertisement for a limbo contest and Mongolian Bar-BQ for guests. Since the cost was reasonable and I had no means of cooking the idea seemed attractive. Feeling a little tired I made a mental note of the start time then went up to my room.

Kicking off my sandals at the door, I entered the room undressed and took a long hot shower. My body needed a bath but there was no way I would ever sit in a tub that didn't belong to me. After getting out of the shower, I put on some body lotion then wrapped myself in a towel. Since my room was on the 16th floor overlooking the beach I turned off the air conditioning and opened the windows to embrace the ocean breeze. As the sea breeze filled the room with a hint of salted air, I lay on top of the bed listening to the waves and enjoying the natural cool...

Awakened by the sounds of cheers, music and the subsequent smell of food I rolled off the bed. As I came to my feet the towel that veiled my body fell to the floor giving my breast a sudden exposure to the cool air awakening them from their rest. Fortunately my nakedness was masked because the only light in the room came from the loom of lights that were 16 floors beneath me. I picked up the towel wrapping myself then walked to the window for a peak at what sounded like fun. Below people were encircled as they danced and clapped parading underneath a pole being held by what appeared to be two topless men. As the people danced underneath the pole it seemed as though they were looking up at me going lower and lower doing the limbo dance.

I had decided to get dressed and join the fun when my cell phone rang. The display screen illuminated inside my purse and after removing it I checked the green screen and placed it next to my ear. "Hello." "Tyler, I had expected a return call from you." "I'm sorry but after lunch I went to the store and bought a bathing suit then sat on the beach." "Is that right? Well I hope you didn't bake yourself." I laughed briefly. "I know my body already has a perfect tan. I was just enjoying the nice weather." "Is everything okay?" As we talked I went onto the veranda to see if my bathing suit had dried. "Everything's fine I just showered and got a nap afterwards. Apparently I'm missing some limbo and Mongolian Bar-BQ." "That sounds fun where is it happening?" I held the phone over the balcony for a few seconds then returned it to my ear reentering the room. "The hotel is offering it at their tikki bar." "That ought to be fun. Are you going?" "I think so, it's supposed to be good food and I have to eat."

Holding the phone between my right shoulder and cheek, I stepped into the bathing suit bottom struggling the entire time. "Girl you sound like you're having a difficult time doing something." I chuckled. "That's right I'm dressing myself while we talk." "Well, I'll see you tomorrow. I just wanted to let you know I'm here for you." I laughed and spoke sarcastically. "Thanks mom." "Don't try to be funny I'm just concerned about you." "I know and believe me it's very much appreciated."

Miles

After a long day at the office I was finally on my way home. The day had been challenging finalizing all the projects I had put on hold following Lamar's death. I was just getting back into the swing of things and after finally clearing my in-basket I felt a huge sense of accomplishment.

During the drive, I decided to treat myself to a milkshake. My plans nearly changed when I entered the *Sonic* Drive-In parking lot. Every bellhop station was occupied with young ladies scurrying back and forth on their skates with meals in one hand and cash in their waist belts. Since I wasn't in the mood to park to begin with the drive-thru caught my attention, as there were only two cars in line. I ordered a large coconut crème milkshake and some fries and was on my way.

I sighed in delight as the cool treat made contact satisfying my taste buds. Depressing the buttons on the steering wheel I began searching for some appropriate road tunes settling on *101.5*. With all the work on my desk I hadn't read the paper so radio would at least give me the top stories. When news about Jasper Texas began I turned up the volume. The events had angered people...reminding some of times they would like to forget and others a portion of evidence to suggest how little things have changed. After a few brief comments the station shifted to more music.

When I turned onto our street Natasha was standing near her mailbox. I assumed she had just arrived or was about to leave because her purse was strapped over her right shoulder. After parking, I got out and walked to the mailbox. "Hello Miles." She looked across the street waving with a letter in her hand. "Hi...are you just getting home from work?" After opening the mailbox and finding it empty I turned to find Natasha approaching. She extended her hand offering an envelope. "Miles I'm sorry about your brother. This isn't much but I wanted you to know that your family is in my prayers." After taking the envelope it seemed only natural to hug her. "Thanks, I appreciate the thought." "Well, I had better let you go. Have a good evening." She then turned and sashayed her way back across the street.

When I entered the house, I dropped my briefcase by the door and walked straight to the kitchen. The milkshake was tasty but it had done nothing to wash down the fries and now my mouth was in dire need of water. After pouring a glass, I finished it off then poured another. Returning the pitcher to the refrigerator, I noticed the answering machine lamp was lighted. Turning up the second glass of water, I walked over depressing the button on the machine. *(BEEP)* "Tyler this is Amber, I'm working on the Noland portfolio and there's some additional information I need from a file that you have. When you get this message please give me a call. Thanks. The next message was no message at all just a hang up. Once the machine reset I placed the empty glass in the sink and walked to my bedroom. On the way there I couldn't help but recall that Tyler was on a business trip. Ambers call was strange considering the office would surely know about her trip not to mention Amber...

Franklin

"Clarissa baby there's is nothing you could say that would make me feel any differently about you. I love you and it's time we ended this amicable separation." The words escaped my mouth with confidence. I had no idea what she was about to disclose but my thinking was that it couldn't compare to what I put her through. This whole business with Sheila had cost me dearly and now was the time for redemption. I was willing to shoulder whatever consequence resulted from my inability to share that horrible experience regarding Sheila much earlier.

Clarissa paused a moment with a look of disbelief on her face. "Well, Franklin I appreciate that but there's something you should know." "What is it sweetheart?" "You do realize that I interact with quite a few lawyers in my work?" Careful not to change the grip of her hands, I nodded and braced myself for what might follow. "After you told me about Sheila I discussed the legalities of such an issue with one of them." My body reacted squeezing her hands. "I didn't go into details or share your name just hers." "Why was that necessary?" "Well I wanted to know if there was a way to make her pay for what she had done." Observing the sincerity in her eyes, I raised her hands and kissed them. "He actually went a step further and checked out Sheila's history. Apparently she has an adoption case pending." Feeling uneasy with the change of her tone and uncertain about what to make of her comments I got up a walked towards the window. "I don't understand Clarissa...what does that matter?" I could hear her get up and her voice became louder as she moved closer towards me touching my shoulder. "Franklin it's obvious. I mean if she hurt you then she may do the same to this child." She stood next to me and extended her hand to my face guiding my attention towards her. She had a determined look on her face and I knew she was for real. "Clarissa in all the time we've been together you have not once sought revenge. I know that sounds irrelevant but somewhere along the line you've rubbed off on me and I can't go through with what you're suggesting." Once again she had a look of surprise on her face. I just stood there pondering how angry my wife must have become to set aside her values and consider revenge. There was a moment of silence then her expression changed. I can't explain how because she was teary eyed and jubilant at the same time. The only thing left for me to do was hold onto her…

"Mommy are you coming to watch T.V. with us?" After releasing Clarissa from my embrace, I turned to observe Tia standing in the doorway. "That's not fair young lady…what about me?" She smiled then turned walking away talking. "We want you to come too daddy." As Clarissa walked away I reached grabbing her hand for what felt like an urge to kiss. Instead we shared a brief stare and for the first time in a while I felt like we were in sync…

In the family room everyone was fixated on *Pocahontas*. "Clarissa, would it be okay if I made some popcorn?" She nodded then franticly fanned her hands at me. "Shhh!" "I assume the popcorn's in the same place?" "It's in the pantry daddy." My gut reaction was to thank Tia but after Clarissa responded to her in the same way she had just done with me the thought subsided and I said nothing.

I returned to the family room with two bowls of popcorn. Quietly I took a seat next Tamara on the floor while Clarissa and Tia were seated behind us on the sofa. Clarissa reached for and grabbed a bowl then I placed the other in front of Tamara. After stuffing my mouth with a handful of popcorn, I leaned back against Clarissa's legs enjoying the movie thinking how wonderful it is to feel like home again.

When the movie finished, Clarissa put away the bowls while I put Tia to bed. "Go ahead and change into your pajamas then I'll come back to tuck you in." She nodded her head then closed the bedroom door. Standing outside her room I could her Tamara gargling. When she came out of the bathroom I proudly observed how much she had grown. "Hey young lady are you too big for a good night kiss?" She walked over and hugged me then said goodnight. "I guess tucking you in is beyond consideration?" She looked back at me and with a slight nod of the head politely spoke. "I'm a little too big for that now dad but if you insist I won't stop you." I took off in a sprint towards her. "You never get too old for daddy my precious." Tamara kneeled next to the bed and said a silent prayer then climbed in awaiting my fatherly gesture. I pulled the cover over her then kissed her forehead. "Goodnight young lady." As I walked out the door my heart fluttered from what I heard. "Sleep tight…Don't let the bed bugs bite." Looking back into her eyes I turned off the light. "Don't let em."

Walking down the hallway I could see that Tia's door was open. As I drew closer her little voice became louder as she too was praying. Standing outside her door, I could hear her ask GOD to bless everyone that came to mind including people she didn't know. Then it happened, she asked a special blessing for us. "Please GOD...Bless my mommy and my daddy. Oh! And please bring my daddy back home so we can be a family in this house again...Amen." I couldn't move or speak so I just stood there pondering my child's prayer. "Daddy I'm ready to be tucked in!" Wiping my eyes I cleared my throat then entered her bedroom.

After tucking in Tia I joined Clarissa in the family room. She had kicked off her shoes and lay quietly on the couch. "The girls are something special you know?" She looked at me smiling then shifted her legs so that I could join her. "Tamara remembers that old night-night sleep tight rhyme and Tia just asked GOD to bring me home so that we could be a family again." We both sat quietly to consider what I had shared then for no reason at all we cried. We cried because of the years I hadn't trusted her enough to talk about the abuse, we cried because of the separation, we cried because the girls were the best gift we had been given, we cried because of being happy in the moment and we cried because there seem nothing else to do in a moment filled we so much love and emotion. We cried because we were in sync and we both could sense that Tia's prayer would be answered tonight.

Tyler

The next morning on the plane flight home, I reclined the seat to take a nap. My head was throbbing from a combination of too much limbo and margaritas. I had partied with the other guest until 11 p.m. Even though I had a wonderful evening 4:45 a.m. came along quickly giving me just enough time to make a 5:45 a.m. flight and now I was paying for that night of fun. With that thought I depressed the button with the little black and white stick lady...

"May I help you?" Rubbing my temples grimacing I hadn't said a word but she reached in her pocket and removed a package of aspirin. "Oh thanks, can I have some water to wash it down?" "Certainly, I'll return in a moment." Seated across from me there was a mother and child. The little girl just stared while sucking on her pacifier with no care in the world. She was so cute wearing a little pink dress with matching bows and white sandals. Even though my head had nearly taken me down for the 10 count I mustered up the energy to play with this innocent person.

Covering my eyes I whispered "peek-a-boo." She started wiggling and when the pacifier popped out of her mouth I knew she had not only played this game but she was ready for more. Her single tooth protruded beautifully through the lower gum as she smiled jovially jumping in her mother's lap.

Our fun was interrupted when the flight attendant arrived with some water. "Well, I see you've found a little friend? Here's your water." Taking the cup with my right hand, I smiled then popped the two tablets into my mouth washing them down with water. "Yes, I have and she's a cute one too." By this time the mother had taken notice of her baby's new friend. She smiled and said hello as I performed one last peek-a-boo. "Well sweetie, I'm going to rest a while and try to rid myself of this headache." The little girl continued bouncing in her mothers lap making all kinds of happy baby noises. Her mother kissed her whispering, "She's resting now Jessica, play time is over." I adjusted in my seat then lay back closing my eyes.

Two Hours later, I awakened as the plane touched the ground. The pilot announced that we would arrive at the gate within 15 minutes. While stretching and adjusting in my seat I took a look across from me where the little girl was fast asleep. The mother noticed my brief glimpse and smiled. "She usually takes a mid-morning nap but the plane ride just brought it on a little sooner." "She's so precious. How old is she?" "She's just twenty-six weeks." "Wow and she already has a beautiful tooth." As the plane taxied towards the gate the flight attendant went through the usual litany reminding everyone to remain seated until we reached a stop and to be careful removing items from the overhead compartment. In typical fashion people unbuckled adjusting in their seats and when the plane stopped it was like a gun went off to start a relay race. People were scurrying lifting bags over the heads and shoulder of other passengers and all the while the door to the plane remained closed. I decided to remain seated until most everyone left. No way would I become party to this confusion.

The mother and daughter of course remained seated as well. As the scurrying and movement of passengers continued the noise awakened the little girl. Once the mass crowd had vacated the plane the mother and I gathered our belongings. In typical motherly fashion she had a baby, her bag and the baby's bag. "Would you care for a hand?" "Oh that's nice of you. If you don't mind, I would be grateful if you could take this bag inside. My husband will be waiting." Taking the bag, I smiled walking out ahead of her. Once in the lobby she and the baby embraced her husband. I stood at a short distance so as not to interfere with their family moment. After kissing her husband she gave him the baby and escorted him my direction. "I'm sorry I don't even know your name. This is my husband Jeremy and you know Jessica, I'm Francesca Baldwin." Extending her narrow hand she smiled and thanked me again. "My name is Tyler Stewart I'm pleased to meet you." She went on to explain to her husband how Jessica and I were playing and that I helped her with the bags. Jeremy thanked me then took the bag. "Have a pleasant day Ms. Stewart." "Thank you." As they walked away I took the opportunity for one last peek-a-boo with the staring little Jessica…

Sitting in the quiet of the car, I arrived home in less than a half hour. I felt refreshed from the morning nap and briefly considered going into the office until the garage door opened. Looking at my watch, I knew it wasn't lunch time but Mile's car was parked in the garage. I hadn't yet decided what to do with the information or the watch Desiree had given me so I remained seated after shutting off the car engine. With all the dancing and such the previous night, I was care free giving little thought to the situation.

Before I could open the car door Miles had entered the garage. I watched his reaction for some indication that he might still be in contact with Desiree. When he smiled running out to hug me I knew. "Hello baby how was your trip?" I stepped out of the car and into his arms. "Dang Miles you act as though I've been gone for days." "I'm just glad you've returned home safely." He kissed me on the lips then released me staring in the backseat of the car. "I'll bring your bag just go on in and relax." "Okay but what are you doing home?" "I decided to work from home today." "Is that right?" He grinned then opened the door. I walked in proceeding to the den kicking off my shoes then sat on the sofa. "I've never used my sick days and yesterday our personnel office informed me that I needed to take them. Since I knew about your return today it seemed a perfect time to be sick." He walked past me going into the bedroom with my bag when I motioned to stop him. "Miles bring the bag over here there's something I need to take out." Giving me the bag he sat on the arm of the sofa while I rummaged through the side pockets.

"You know I got a strange call from Amber on yesterday." Not looking up, I continued moving things around searching the pockets. "What was so strange about Amber calling?" "Something about you having some files she needed. I just assumed that she would have known your schedule right?" After finding what I was searching for it dawned on me why Ambers call was strange. I had taken a couple days off so she had no clue what was going on and certainly not my flight itinerary. "I have something for you." Handing him the watch, I waited for some reaction that would confirm or deny her story about the watch falling to the restaurant floor. At first it seemed as though he didn't recognize the watch but after flipping it over his face changed.

"I talked to Desiree and she asked me to return the watch to you." "Tyler...I can explain." He stood reaching for my hands. My God the signals just didn't add up. "What's there to explain you lost the watch and she found it. Oh and she kept it safe for you all these years." I could feel my head throbbing as my neck shifted left to right while speaking. The drama was on and there was no stopping it. I threw the business card at him. "I've told you to clear your damn pockets before putting your clothes in the laundry room! That's how I found out about her." "Tyler it's not what you think baby. That was a long time ago." Thoughts were racing through my head. "If it was so long ago how did she come to possess something I had given you?" "It was nothing Tye." The look on his face and the sound in his voice gave me some strange vibes. "What are you talking about? Did you sleep with her?" He didn't answer but continued rambling. "I'm really not worthy of you Tyler. You've been so wonderful, I just don't deserve you." I don't know exactly when it happened but I was standing stiff, erect and about to explode. "Did you fuck her Miles?" He stood holding my shoulders looking intently into my eyes. Then the words flowed from his lips ripping my heart into pieces. "Yes Tyler...I made a mistake and...I'm sorry." "You bastard! Get your damn hands off of me!" I shrugged his hands off my body then drew my fist from the low depths where he had kicked my heart. After making contact with his face he shook off my pitiful punch and grabbed me pinning my arms on the side. "Let me go motherfucker!" Shaking my body to get loose with no success, I shoved my face into his chest and began biting. When he let me go I ran to the living room yelling. "Get the hell out of this house you bastard! I hate you!" He came after me pleading pitifully. "Tyler it only happened once and..." Before he could say another word I had thrown a candle holder. It struck his head knocking him backward. "I don't want to know the details of your betrayal. Get the hell out!" He tried to approach me again but I wasn't having it. Plates, vases and picture frames were flying through the air as I screamed ordering him to leave. "I want you out of here Miles!" I stomped breathing heavy with tears flowing down my face. "I hate you Miles...I wish you were dead!" The words surprised me as they escaped my mouth but he needed to know my anger and his expression told me he understood but he hadn't moved. I threw a book at him then ran to the kitchen. Rummaging through the drawer, I picked up a carving knife. "Get out Miles! I want you out of here...right now." Holding the knife above my shoulder ready to strike I pointed to the door. "Get your ass out of here!"

Chasing him out with the knife, I slammed the door and locked it. When the engine from his car started, I leaned against the door dropping the knife to the floor. "I hate you Miles, I hate you." Sliding down the side of the door, I cried and cursed the man I had given everything...only to discover he betrayed me.

Miles

Devastated by what happened, I drove through two stop signs. I wouldn't have known except that drivers were blasting their horns and cursing me. It was impossible for me to know what they were saying but I summed that it could not match the things Tyler had said. I wished now just as I did back then that somehow it could be erased. Sadly it could not and I would have to roll with the punches. "Why did I allow this to happen?"

Approaching the freeway, traffic progressed slowly. Not certain where to go, I abruptly changed lanes figuring on driving to Braxton's. Lamar was gone and Braxton was the next best thing to a brother. "Dammit! Why don't you watch where you're going?" This elderly man cruised by nearly causing an accident. Quickly I was becoming irritated with the traffic although the traffic was not the real issue. Cars were backed up to turn left and the line wasn't moving very fast. I turned on the radio to calm myself. "She is the best thing to come into my life and I screwed it up." I didn't realize that I was animated while talking to myself until by happen chance I observed the person in the car next to me laughing. For no good reason at all, I didn't care ultimately conveying that sentiment by shoving my middle finger in their direction. Luckily their lane had begun to move otherwise I might have had to defend that lapse in judgment.

Listening to the radio and old *Gladys Knight & The Pips* tune began. *"It's sad to think, we're not going to make it. And it's gotten to the point, where we can't fake it…"* The tune had taken me by surprise, reflecting on the words I began to cry. "Damn this traffic!" As the music continued in the background the traffic slowly moved forward with the turn lamp signaling my lane. "I really screwed up this time." The caution light quickly illuminated with one car in front of me. "Shit!" Looking across from me both lanes had a trail of cars going by so I knew it would be tough to make the light. After the car in front of me was able to pass, I counted the cars I would have to yield to before turning.

"Alright…alright…now, now…here we go!" My attention was so fixed on the cars ahead that I neglected to look in the direction I was heading or listen for ambient noise. As the car made the turn bright red lights flashed before my eyes. A fire engine was coming full speed headed to an emergency. Neither the driver nor I ever considered the next emergency was about to happen. Reacting as quickly as I could to push the brake, Tyler's face passed through my mind as Gladys sang. *"Farewell my love, goodbye. Goodbye…"*

Clarissa

Awakened by the chirping of birds, I moved his arm from around my waist then got up from the sofa. It had been quite some time since I last slept on the couch but resting in his arms made it all the more special. Tamara came to the kitchen with Tia trailing behind. "Good morning." "Good morning." "What are we having for breakfast?" Pressing the button on the coffee machine, I turned towards Tia holding my index finger over my lips. "You don't have to be so loud young lady." "Oops, I'm sorry mommy."

"I'm making some waffles this morning." Neither had noticed Franklin in the den so I asked Tamara to turn on the morning news…After hearing the joy in her voice, I knew she found him. "Tia dad's here." Tia sprinted towards the den then stooped in the walkway looking back at me. "Mommy that's not fair. You didn't tell us daddy was here." I just shook my head laughing as she turned around heading for the den.

Mixing the batter for the waffles, I started thinking of Tyler wondering if she came home last night or this morning. After plugging in the griddle, I took a peak at the clock calculating the time I had before work. "Franklin dear, would you mind taking the girls to summer camp this morning?" "Sure that's not a problem is there anything else I can help with?" I looked around to find him standing in the kitchen. "Thanks but I've got breakfast under control." I said while pouring the batter into the griddle. "Everything will be ready in about fifteen minutes. "Well that gives me time to take a shower. You wouldn't happen to have another change of clothes for a brother?" Licking the blueberry batter from my finger, I turned to face him and replied. "No but I can promise we'll work on it together."

While the waffles baked, I opened a pack of sausage placing 10 links on a microwave tray. "Tamara sweetie, would you come and set the table for me please?" "Yes mam." I poured myself a cup of coffee then realized something was missing. "Tamara, keep an eye on the food while I go outside for the newspaper. "Okay, do you want everyone to have orange juice or milk?" "Just put both on the table baby."

When I returned to the kitchen Franklin was serving the food and the girls were seated waiting for me. "Oh mommy can I have the funnies please?" Opening the paper, I handed Tia the funnies then took my seat across from Franklin. He extended his hands toward the girls to begin prayer. Listening to his words of praise and thanks made me feel warm inside…

"Franklin, do you think we should share the plans we discussed last night about us?" Chewing quickly to swallow and respond he held up a finger signaling me to give him a moment. "Well, I thought we could make it a surprise during the move. What do you think?" The girls were staring at each other trying to interpret what we were saying. "Mom what are you and dad talking about?" "Oh it's nothing you should be concerned with right now. Come on now finish your breakfast so you can leave on time."

After breakfast, the girls went to their rooms to dress while Franklin and I cleared the table and washed the dishes. "You know that's a neat idea…surprising the girls with the move." Embracing me around the waste he kissed my ear. "I love you Clarissa." My heart skipped a beat not because I didn't know rather because he hadn't told me in a year. I turned to face him extending my hand to cup his cheek. "Dido."

Our mood was disrupted when Tia came running into the kitchen. "Tia what have I told you about running inside?" She looked at me dejected and muffled a response. "Don't do it." "Please don't make me have to remind you again alright?" "Yes mam. Daddy is it time to go yet?" "Sure as soon as your sister is ready we'll leave."

I walked them to the door after Tamara announced that she was ready. I hugged the girls and for the first time in months I kissed my husband to wish him a good day. Looking at the clock again, I recited the things that needed my attention. "Get dressed and call Tyler but not necessarily in that order." I picked up the cordless phone on my way to the bedroom closet…

"Hey girl, how are you?" Listening to sniffles and heavy breathing, I begin to sense some strange vibes. "You know me, I'm okay just straightening up the house" Sitting on the bed, I held the phone with my shoulder while slipping a pair of stockings over my feet. "Well you don't sound that way. What time did you get back?" "I arrived this morning." There was a pause while I stepped into my skirt. "Tyler you seem distant, did something happen on the trip?" "Oh God Clarissa!" She burst into tears speaking incoherently. "Wait a minute Tye;

I can't understand what you're saying." "He fucked her Clarissa! The bastard fucked her."

I inhaled raising my head to the ceiling to gain strength and compose myself. Again, I looked at the clock making a mental note of how the morning was cruising by so quickly. I had just over an hour cushion before having to arrive at work. "Where's Miles right now?" "I asked him to leave." "I'll be there directly." After hanging up the phone, I finished dressing and was out the door. Along the drive over, I called the office to inform them that I was in route to work but had to make a stop. Amber answered the telephone so I told her that I might be a half hour late but wasn't yet certain. "Okay, I'll phone if I'm definitely going to be late…"

Broken glass, plates and books were scattered everywhere. It seemed like I had just walked into the aftermath of a storm. "Come here girl." I extended my arms pulling Tyler close to me. "I'm so sorry for what you're going through." Her body shook uncontrollably as she buried her face in my bosom crying. The tears flowed so heavy that I could feel the moisture through my blouse.

Holding her tightly as though she were one of the girls, I slowly escorted her to the sofa. When we sat down she moved away from me covering her eyes. "I hate him Clarissa!" "Tyler don't…you're just hurting right now." In my heart I knew she didn't hate Miles which certainly was the reason for her present state. Because if she didn't love him with all her being there would be no way she could feel the hurt she's experiencing. "I don't want him anymore! I just wish he would go someplace and die!" "Tyler you don't mean that girl." From experience I knew that people often say hurtful things in the midst of anger and as sure as my name is Clarissa Green, Tyler had reached that level of anger.

As her friend, I could not sit idle while she fell into that destructive pit. Sure she needed to be angry and arguably she needed to vent her frustration but I would not allow her to wallow in pity. I cupped her face looking directly into her eyes. "Tyler you know that I love you…" I observed her eyes for some clue that she understood. "I know you're hurting right now but you can't make wishes like that in anger or any other time for that matter." Shifting her head side to side she softly uttered a response. "I do Clarissa because if he was gone I wouldn't have to put up with his shit. And nobody…especially those heifers would have him." Pushing away my hand she stood and walked to the window.

"Tyler I know you're hurting. I've been there too." I knew shifting emphasis to my own personal story seemed insensitive but given her attitude it felt like the best course of action. "That's why Franklin and I were apart. Because of some other person I pushed him away only to find out that it was a mistake. In anger my objectivity was clouded and we've had to endure this separation as a result. Tyler I never stopped loving him and if that is your situation you have to be patient with yourself. Not for his sake but for yourself and your inner peace." She turned staring at their wedding photo on the wall. "Clarissa I do love him that's why I'm still here but it bothers me to consider that he's not satisfied with just us."

Sensing the calm in her voice, I got up and walked over to join her next to the picture. "I know how you feel Tyler but please...don't allow anger to control your tongue." She threw her arms around my neck hugging tenderly. "Thanks for being here for me. You don't know how much your friendship means especially in a time like this." "Tyler you know I've always thought of you as family and that's what a family does...support each other."

Stepping away she began straightening and picking up debris. "I don't know if I can ever forgive him." "If you expect to heal as a woman that will have to happen...don't misunderstand that doesn't mean forget. He has to earn whatever's been lost and that part takes time."

(Doorbell)

"Girl I look a mess do you mind answering the door for me?" Looking at my watch I said, "No problem but I have to get to the office. Some of us are working today." When I opened the door a tall slender gentleman was standing wearing a blue uniform and badge. "Good morning Mrs. Stewart?" I held up my finger. "No, I'm not Mrs. Stewart. I'm a friend of the family." His serious and deliberate tone made me uncomfortable. Realizing that the house was in shambles and Tyler would never forgive me for inviting a stranger under these conditions I asked him to wait outside. "Excuse me while I go and get her."

In the kitchen she was dumping broken glass into the garbage as I entered. "Clarissa why do you look so, I don't know. It's like you've got the world on your shoulders or something. Who was it at the door?" "Tyler there's a police officer at the door. He wants to see you." "A police officer..."

"Mrs. Stewart?" "Yes is there a problem officer?" "Mrs. Tyler Stewart the spouse of a Mr. Miles Stewart?" "Yes! Now please tell me! Is there a problem?" "I'm sorry. Please...may I speak with you inside?" Looking at his uniform I could see that he was a Jacksonville police officer so whatever the news it was local. I stepped behind Tyler to offer my hand in support as she motioned for him to enter. "Mam there was an accident this morning involving your husband." Releasing my hand, she covered her face in disbelief bracing for the remaining news. "Oh my God...is he okay?" "Mam he was taken to Memorial

Hospital. I don't know anything more." Tyler turned walking slowly towards the kitchen. "Thank you officer I'll take it from here." "Yes mam, I'm sorry."

After closing the door, I turned to discover Tyler with keys in hand headed for the door. "Tyler you shouldn't be driving right now I'll take you." She nodded her head in disagreement. "You have to go to work I'll get there myself." "I'll call the office along the way..."

At the hospital the doctor spoke calmly but direct. "Mrs. Stewart your husband's suffered severe trauma. He's in critical condition but I can assure you we're doing all that's medically possible." Tyler stood motionless and obviously devastated by the news. "Mrs. Stewart is there someone here with you?" Stepping forward, I told the doctor that I would be with her. "Okay, please excuse me I must return to the OR. We'll keep you informed. As he walked away Tyler muffled, "Can someone please tell me how this happened?" The doctor stopped in his tracks acknowledging Tyler's request. "Certainly, I'll make sure someone comes to discuss that with you right away." Wrapping my arms around her shoulder, I escorted her to the waiting room. "Come on Tyler let's sit down."

Once we seated I asked if she wanted something to drink. "I'll have some water and an aspirin please." "Okay I'll return shortly." Rummaging my purse, I couldn't find aspirin so I asked one of the nurses. She offered to take Tyler the water and aspirin so I agreed taking the opportunity to call the office and Franklin.

When I returned to the waiting area a police officer later followed. He sat next to Tyler to explain what happened. "Mam from what I've gathered from witness accounts your husband made a turn hitting a fire engine head on. Apparently the fire engine, while responding to an emergency was driving in the lane your husband turned into. Witnesses say it appeared he never saw or heard the fire engine. We're still investigating the matter so that's all that I can tell you for now."

"Clarissa I hope that..." I knew exactly what she was thinking but wanted to assure her that she wasn't at fault. Placing my hand over her mouth to prevent the words from escaping, I held my friend to offer support. "Should I phone his parents for you?" "I think it should come from me. God I can only imagine how they'll feel. Lamar has been gone less than a month and now this." "Wow, I hadn't considered that fact." "I'm going down the hall to use the telephone. Make sure you come for me if there's any news?"

Moments after Tyler had gone to the phone Franklin arrived. I felt so relieved to see him that I rushed into his chest wrapping my arms around his shoulders. "Clarissa, I came as fast as I could. How's Tyler?" "I'm so glad to see you." "Has there been any change?" I exhaled then lead him to a seat in the waiting room. "Tyler went to phone his parents. The only thing we know so far is that he's in critical condition." "What happened?" I proceeded to tell him about the collision with the fire truck. "Did the officer indicate who was at fault?" "No but at the time that wasn't a concern. Besides recalling his description it sounded like an accident." "All right we can deal with that later. In the meantime Tyler needs you right now."

Tyler

I stood resting my head in the corner of the wall while explaining to Mr. and Mrs. Stewart what happened. There was nothing I could say to comfort or soothe their worry. After all they had just lost a son and now in a tragic twist the uncertainty of their only living son's fate weighed heavy. Mr. Stewart said they would be on the next flight. I told them to take their time and that I would be okay.

When I hung up the phone, I felt what seemed like the weight of the world on my shoulders. For the life of me I couldn't escape the feeling that my words caused this event and guilt was on my hands. Squeezing myself so tightly that my shoulders rose touching the lobes of my ears, I closed my eyes exhaling deeply to temper my stress. When I opened them the entire passageway looked different. In my haste to find the telephone, I had walked through these halls oblivious to all the signs. Now at this moment one sign in particular caught my attention.

Holding my shoulders tightly, I paced slowly feeling unworthy to enter. "GOD...I don't know how to pray so I'm just going to talk to you." After entering the sacred place I knelt down at the altar with my head raised. "GOD if you can hear me right now...my whole world is crashing around me. And quite frankly I deserve to be punished for the things I've said...I ask you...No, I beg you to forgive my anger and my poor choice of words. Please GOD...Please spare him, not for me but for his parents. They've just buried a son and I don't want my vengeful tongue to cause them more pain. I know that you don't hear from me often and my voice is a stranger but I have no place to turn...No place to turn at all...I know what I said earlier today but I don't want you to take him. But if you must...please give me the strength to accept it, as I will ultimately have to bear the burden of my harsh words. And if this is the way it has to be...please strengthen his parents. I beg you GOD...spare him and punish me. Spare his parents and deal with me. He hurt me so badly that anger controlled my tongue...I do love him-I just hate what he did to me. I wanted him to feel my pain and the words seemed to be my only recourse. Please...intervene as only you can...Thank you...Amen"

Wiping the tears from my eyes, I stood and turned to exit the chapel. When I looked up Clarissa was standing at the door. My heart began racing in anticipation of some news. "Has there been a change?" "Nothing yet, I just came here to light a candle for you two." "I won't stop you." "Well...let's light one together?" She took my hand and together we walked back to the altar. "Franklin's in the waiting room so if there's news he knows where I am." After lighting a candle, we both kneeled down in silence.

Following a few minutes of silence, we adjourned to the waiting room. As we approached the doctor came to the nurse's station. I raced towards him to ask if there was any news. "Mrs. Stewart your husband is stable but there was head trauma which caused some swelling of the brain." "What does that mean? Is he going to be all right?" "Well he's weathered the immediate storm. I've given him some medication to reduce the swelling." "Can I see him?" "Yes, but please be aware he won't respond verbally because we're keeping him sedated to minimize brain activity...just until the swelling reduces."

I squeezed Clarissa's hand then exhaled. "Here goes." Mustering every ounce of my remaining strength, I made my way to the recovery room. Inside a nurse was standing over him. She raised her head and smiled acknowledging my presence then continued checking his vital signs as I stood still observing her actions. After completing his vitals, she approached me. "You can visit with him now. I'll just be outside if you need anything." "Thank you."

Miles

It had been a week since the accident. Although my body was returning to normal things between Tyler and I had been everything except normal. She had been very attentive to the medical regiment prescribed by the doctor which I have to admit was comforting. But the subject of Desiree hadn't come up and I believed that it was still occupying her thoughts. She would visit every morning, then after work however, most evening visits were shortened to spend time studying with Clarissa. Feeling somewhat short changed, I broached my concern on this day.

"Tyler you seem to be spending a great deal of time with Clarissa. I realize that I'm in no medical danger but you're giving me so little time." "Miles I've been dealing with some issues the last few days and it's been a challenge. This situation with Desiree followed by your accident has turned my world upside down. And Clarissa...she's introduced me to a place I can take my fears, doubts and frustrations. Quite frankly, without her support and the study I'm not sure what would happen." She said a great deal but all that remained in my mind was Desiree and how that mistake had brought us to this point.

"Can you and I discuss any of this? I mean, what is Clarissa doing that's so great?" She just shook her head as if to suggest I needed to get a clue. I wanted to press the issue more but her demeanor gave every indication that now wasn't the time. "Miles, I prayed that nothing would happen to you when you were lying in that operating room. I asked to be forgiven for saying those horrible things to you before the accident. And right now, I need help to forgive you." "So does that mean we still have a chance?" "Miles the only thing I'm saying is that I have to forgive you for my own benefit. Beyond that I can't say because it's too early. You hurt and betrayed me Miles. I may forgive you but it will take a great deal on your part to give me the courage to stay. Equally as important, I need to work on me...inside." She cupped her right hand pointing to her chest for effect. "I also need strength of acceptance if love still exists." She spoke somberly and walked towards the window looking out into the gray sky.

"You know the sky typifies how I'm feeling and the news I need to share with you." I sat up in the bed studying her demeanor. I wasn't certain where she was going in the conversation and prudence dictated that I remain silent and cautious. "I don't' think you should return home. I need time to heal and you need time to figure out if you want this marriage." "Tyler isn't that a bit rash? Do you want a divorce or something?" "We just need some time to heal." I adjusted in the bed reaching out for her hand only to withdraw it in disappointment. "Baby I don't want to lose you. It was a mistake, a terrible mistake that I can't reverse…

For years after it happened, I pondered the idea of letting you go. My betrayal made me feel worthless and unworthy of your commitment to me…all the while constantly asking myself how I could have possibly allowed this to happen. The honorable thing it seemed would have been to let you go and save you from this despair but I was afraid." Waving my hands above my head in submission tears began to form in my eyes.

"I was supposed to be the perfect gentleman but now it seems I'm nothing more than the knuckleheads we both despised" The nurse returned to the room as Tyler continued looking out the window. I put on a 3 cent smile conjuring some fake courtesy. "Is it time for my medication already?" The nurse nodded, sensing the tension she quickly performed the task then left the room. "Miles I'll visit with you tomorrow, Clarissa is waiting for me. We are attending a mid-week service tonight."

After Tyler had gone, I took the unwelcomed time alone to reflect on what had happened. Before the accident, I wanted Tyler to understand that I truly loved and never intended to hurt her. I had tried so desperately to erase that part of my life. Now here I sit about to lose the best and most important person to enter my life.

Thinking of losses reminded me of Lamar. He was now gone but our last conversation echoed in my mind. Selfish, egotistical, covered in self-pity and doubt regarding my purpose or place in this world, that's the person who began to appear in my mental mirror. The thought saddened me to shame. I had been privileged to have her in my life and now through my own fault, I was on the verge of losing her.

I wanted Tyler but the thought of feeling unworthy couldn't be escaped. How could I possibly be worthy of her after such a betrayal? I'm not this perfect man she fell in love with and so earnestly deserves. "God, how can I ever make it right with her after such a betrayal?"

Clarissa

The atmosphere was electric as peopled sang praises joining in with the choir. I couldn't imagine a better time and place. Franklin and I had reconciled our marriage and the last few weeks had given reassurance that our being together was most important. There were still therapy sessions to attend but he had made a huge breakthrough. Within that last week he had forgiven Sheila. That was a difficult experience but we made it through and I even let go of some baggage myself. Don't get me wrong we're not having Sheila over for dinner but we're no longer imperiled...just trusting and loving more each day.

The girls were excited having Franklin home. He had surprised them with the news and they even helped him pack. I have to admit, I was happy too and that was proven to me just a few nights ago. GOD forgive my thoughts for straying in your house of worship, but I just give you all the glory for what's happening...

"Do you accept Jesus Christ as your personal Lord and Savior?" Wiping the tears from her eyes Tyler uttered the most important response ever. "Yes sir, I do." The last few weeks Tyler and I had been studying together. The sessions ministered to both our hearts. Tyler and I were very close and because of that we shared deep feelings unconditionally. We were supporting each other in one of the most difficult times and following tonight's altar call she touched my hand asking me to be at her side.

"Is there anything you want to share with us?" Tyler took the microphone in her hand and began to speak. "I'm new at this...I wanted you all to know how wonderful my heart feels right now. I thank GOD for my friend, Sister Green. I've been going through some things and she has encouraged me and shared with me a special gift that was missing in my life." She looked into my eyes and all I could do is whisper, "God Bless You." "I just want to thank you Clarissa and say to this church I'm ready for that gift." The entire assembly clapped speaking in unison. "Praise GOD, Praise Him!"

After we had taken our seats, I reflected on my blessings. Not too long ago this man in my life had strengthened me during a time of challenge. I wanted to crucify Sheila but he refused. Here I am the Christian women succumbing to temptation but thanks to my deliverer, Franklin happened to be in my life offering strength and encouragement...

On the way home, Tyler asked if she was too hard on Miles. "Tye your new journey has to be about you and strengthening your relationship with GOD." Touching her hand in assurance I said, "He'll take care of the rest. Just let his spirit guide you." I must admit that in my mind I felt as though something more should have been said but for now I brushed the thought aside to focus on my heart. "I asked him not to return home and that has inherent uncertainties. There's a possibility that I could lose him you know...strangely my heart won't allow me to react to that fear. If he wants me and our marriage is meant to be he'll come back right?" I remained silent uncertain if she wanted an answer or if the question was rhetorical. "In the meantime, I need to focus on my heart and forgiveness regardless of the outcome."

As I listened to her speak it was clear the question was rhetorical. Joy circulated my body as I observed a light burning within that gave her peace. I reached across the seat to take her hand. Squeezing gently, I didn't say a word but only smiled feeling certain she knew my joy...

Once the car stopped in the driveway, I gathered my things and asked if she wanted to stay for a while. "No, I should be getting home." Opening the door, I stepped out of the car walking towards the front door. "Clarissa! Thanks for being such a wonderful friend." I turned without saying a word. Then I just smiled and waved goodbye as I unlocked the door. When I entered, I thanked GOD for my family then my friend. "Give her courage to do what she must, strength to accept your will and wisdom to know the difference."

Miles

Three months had gone by since the accident and I was up and back to normal. Tyler and I were still apart but we saw each other daily. On the day I was discharged from the hospital we drove home to pick up some things for my new residence. We talked for a little while then I cleaned and made repairs around the house. I didn't leave until it was time for bed.

The next morning, I went to work and afterwards visited with her again. The same thing happened and continued for another five days when there was nothing more to do in terms of cleaning and repairs.

I entered the house on this particular day and sat down for a long discussion where we both opened our hearts. The talk was both powerful and therapeutic. Sitting in the kitchen we held hands pouring out our fears, our insecurities. "Tyler I know that you've been hurt by my infidelity but please realize it had nothing to do with you. I mean, you're not less of a woman or lacking in anything for that matter. It is me that is less of a man and seriously lacking in knowledge of manhood."

She just listened to my words. "It was my selfishness, self-pity and arrogance that caused all this to happen. If I never gain your confidence then it's justified. But know this; I will never cease trying to make retribution for hurting you this way. "Miles, you don't have to make any promises or declarations. The fact that you're here and I'm here suggests something but you need to search yourself regarding us. No declarations just soul searching."

The room was silent and still until I arose from the chair. It was nearly bedtime and we both needed some rest. "Tyler I'm going to leave so that you can get some rest." Slowly and hesitantly, I walked towards the door. "I'll see you tomorrow." "Okay." Pondering a moment, I turned to observe her still seated. "I love you Tyler." She placed her head in the palms of her hands then exhaled. "Good night Miles."

After exiting, I got into the car and drove off. Inside the car my heart was full of emotion just begging to escape. "How stupid can I be to say that to her." In my heart I felt like she should know but that wasn't the point. I hadn't given Tyler reason to believe she wasn't loved. I had betrayed the love and although a woman wants to hear the words, after a betrayal words have little meaning. With that thought, I whipped the car around making a u-turn. "Damit! Home is where I should be."

After arriving, I rang the doorbell. Tyler cracked the door open but did not remove the chain. "Miles it's late. Why are you here?" "Please Tyler, I know that I don't deserve you or your consideration but I'm begging you right now. Don't send me away. You don't have to talk to me and I can even stay in the guest room. Please, just allow me to be with you." Her face gave no clue to her intentions nor had she commented. She just stood there behind the little gold chain resting her face against the door.

Then to my surprise the door closed. My heart sank to the ground just as quickly as her face had vanished behind the door. I hesitantly turned walking away just as the sound of the door caught my attention. When I turned the door was opened and the gold chain was no longer visible. I walked cautiously towards the door entering then called out for Tyler. "Make sure you lock the door." After that she went into the bedroom and closed the door.

I have been in the guest room since that night and although six months have passed, I feel privileged. It would have been easy to maintain a separate residence but that's not what I wanted. The logical thing to do was take my punishment making sure that every opportunity that permitted, I earned her confidence.

Tyler had been spending a considerable amount of time with Clarissa and the church. Initially I feared that my indiscretion had triggered an extreme impulse but the more we talked I discovered otherwise. Tyler was growing in a way that I couldn't yet understand. She hadn't shown overt affection but her demeanor offered a unique assurance that something special existed between us.

I'm not certain how long we'll have this arrangement but I hold on to the belief that we were meant to be. The tragedy is that my revelation had to come at such a great expense.